CAPE COD CREAMERY · 1

the

SWEET LIFE

SUZANNE WOODS FISHER

Revell

a division of Baker Publishing Group
Grand Rapids, Michigan

Published by Revell
a division of Baker Publishing Group
PO Box 6287, Grand Rapids, MI 49516-6287
www.revellbooks.com

Library of Congress Cataloging-in-Publication Data
Names: Fisher, Suzanne Woods, author.
Title: The sweet life / Suzanne Woods Fisher.
Description: Grand Rapids, MI : Revell, a division of Baker Publishing Group, [2022] | Series: Cape Cod creamery ; 1
Identifiers: LCCN 2021035599 | ISBN 9780800741525 (casebound) | ISBN 9780800739478 (paperback) | ISBN 9781493436286 (ebook)
Subjects: LCSH: Ice cream parlors—Massachusetts—Cape Cod—Fiction. | Ice cream, ices, etc.—Fiction. | Mothers and daughters—Fiction. | LCGFT: Domestic fiction.
Classification: LCC PS3606.I78 S94 2022 | DDC 813/.6—dc23
LC record available at https://lccn.loc.gov/2021035599

Some Scripture used in this book, whether quoted or paraphrased by the characters, is taken from THE HOLY BIBLE, NEW INTERNATIONAL VERSION®, NIV® Copyright © 1973, 1978, 1984, 2011 by Biblica, Inc.® Used by permission. All rights reserved worldwide.

Some Scripture used in this book, whether quoted or paraphrased by the characters, is taken from THE MESSAGE, copyright © 1993, 2002, 2018 by Eugene H. Peterson. Used by permission of NavPress. All rights reserved. Represented by Tyndale House Publishers, Inc.

This book is a work of fiction. Names, characters, places, and incidents are the product of the author's imagination or are used fictitiously. Any resemblance to actual events, locales, or persons, living or dead, is coincidental.

Published in association with Joyce Hart of the Hartline Literary Agency, LLC.

Baker Publishing Group publications use paper produced from sustainable forestry practices and post-consumer waste whenever possible.

22   23   24   25   26   27   28   7   6   5   4   3   2   1

"Suzanne Woods Fisher has written another winner! Filled with her signature heart, *The Sweet Life* is an uplifting reminder of the joy of restored relationships, the importance of bravery, and the hope of second chances. Grab a scoop of your favorite ice cream and dive into this inspiring treat."

Liz Johnson, bestselling author of *The Red Door Inn* and *Beyond the Tides*

"An oft-used meme states, 'I followed my heart and it led to ice cream.' Now Suzanne Woods Fisher has gifted us with an inspiring, irresistible story in which following the ice cream leads to a whole bunch of heart. Fisher is a winsome storyteller who never disappoints, and that's certainly true here as she celebrates variety as the spice of life, love, and ice cream flavors. *The Sweet Life* is an effortless charmer!"

Bethany Turner, award-winning author of *The Do-Over*

Praise for *At Lighthouse Point*

"*At Lighthouse Point* rounds out Fisher's charming modern-day Three Sisters Island trilogy. . . . Christian faith and prayer are central to the book's message, and themes of trusting God's steadfast plan and empathy toward others are grounding beacons amidst the tumult of the unexpected."

Booklist

"*At Lighthouse Point* is a charming read, with gentle truths and great characters. I'm glad I got to revisit their little island."

Interviews and Reviews

"All three books of this series were fun reads where each sister learns something about themselves."

Write-Read-Life

Praise for *On a Coastal Breeze*

"Christy Award–winner Fisher delivers a delightful second installment to her Three Sisters Island trilogy. . . . This winsome tale will hit the spot for fans of contemporary inspirationals."

Publishers Weekly

"A lively, witty, and charmingly entertaining read from cover to cover."

Midwest Book Review

"This book was such a delightful read, and so is the author who wrote it. I love anything she writes!"

Interviews & Reviews

"Everything I wanted in a book. . . . I cried, I laughed, and I fell head over heels in love."

Urban Lit Magazine

Praise for *On a Summer Tide*

"Fans of Suzanne Woods Fisher will love this story of three sisters coming together on a rugged Maine island to refurbish a camp. *On a Summer Tide* is an enduring tale of love and restoration."

Denise Hunter, bestselling author of *On Magnolia Lane*

"*On a Summer Tide* is filled with memorable characters, gorgeous Maine scenery, and plenty of family drama. I can't wait to visit Three Sisters Island again!"

Irene Hannon, bestselling author of the beloved Hope Harbor series

"Fisher creates a vibrant cast of charming, plucky characters set on redefining themselves."

Publishers Weekly

"Suzanne Woods Fisher offers a contemporary novel of a family rebuilding their connection, adding a touch of suspense and just enough spirituality to make this a heartwarming read."

New York Journal of Books

the

SWEET LIFE

Novels by Suzanne Woods Fisher

People have an emotional response to ice cream; it's more than just food. So I think when you combine caring and eating wonderful food, it's a very powerful combination.

—Jerry Greenfield of Ben & Jerry's Ice Cream

Cast of Characters

Dawn Dixon (age 27), CPA at a Boston firm, known for being an exceptional planner. Her favorite quote: "I adore spontaneity, providing it is carefully planned."

Marnie Dixon (age 58), mother of Dawn, recently widowed, breast cancer survivor, known for being spontaneous, creative . . . and maybe a skosh too impulsive.

Kevin Collins (age 27), architect at a Boston firm, former fiancé to Dawn. Broke her heart into a million pieces.

Lincoln Hayes (age sixtysomething), Chatham resident, permanent volunteer to charitable causes, lover of ice cream, friend to all.

Brynn (age 27), childhood friend of Dawn's. Has a tendency to worry.

Mrs. Nickerson-Eldredge (age seventysomething), Chatham resident born and bred, chairman of the Historical Commission. Considers herself to be the guardian of Chatham.

Nanette (age seventysomething), Chatham resident, runs a T-shirt shop, known for being on the nosy side of nosy.

Leo the Cowboy (age 5), lover of any and all ice cream, smitten with Dawn.

Glossary
of Ice Cream Making

add-ins—premade food products that are mixed into ice cream base

artisanal—produced by a skilled worker in a trade that involves making things by hand

base—the egg-dairy-sugar mixture that is the main ingredient in all ice cream products

curing—usually a twenty-four-hour period to allow the flavors in the ice cream base to blend and mature

custard—the base for ice cream products if it includes eggs

dasher—churning tool of the ice cream machine, also known as beater

frozen custard—has more egg and less air than regular ice cream, making it both rich and dense. Popular on the East Coast and in the Midwest.

frozen yogurt or Froyo—contains less fat than regular ice cream. Popular on the West Coast. Perceived as a healthier option, though sugary toppings are usually piled on it

gelato—Italian style ice cream

overrun—air pumped into each batch of ice cream (varies dramatically)

pasteurization—the process of involving heat to sterilize a product, destroying microorganisms, to make it safe for consumption

prepackaged base—ice cream base from a dairy that is pre-made and prepasteurized

Chapter
ONE

Never ask a woman who is eating ice cream straight from the carton how she's doing.

—Anonymous

Needham, Massachusetts
Thursday, February 6

Dawn parked in front of her childhood home in Needham but couldn't make herself get out of the car. For this brief moment, the terrible news belonged only to her. As soon as she told someone, especially her mom, it would make it somehow more real. More true.

Maybe it wasn't real. She reviewed the conversation she'd had with Kevin last night. Was it possible that he'd suffered from premarital jitters? Just a case of cold feet. Cold, cold feet.

Tears flooded Dawn's eyes again. It wasn't just cold feet. Kevin said he wasn't sure he was in love with Dawn, not the way he thought he should be. Or the way he used to be. She looked around the car for a clean tissue, but all she could find were scrunched-up soggy ones. How in the world did she end up in a mess like this? Dawn Dixon was known as a level-headed, objective, logical woman. Her nickname was Teflon Dawn. She could handle anything. Prepared for any crisis. Yet she'd missed Kevin's growing vacillation about getting married.

The front door opened and Mom stood at the threshold, the obvious question on her face. Why had Dawn come home, to Needham, on a weekday when she should've been at work in Boston? Dawn dreaded this conversation. Calling off the wedding, after all her mom had done to make it unique and one-of-a-kind, would devastate her too. Dawn thought of the hours her mother had spent making origami doves that would hang from the enormous and expensive rented tent.

Another image of Kevin popped into her head—one from just a few weeks ago. They were at the wedding venue to finalize some details. Dawn and her mom were talking to the wedding event planner. Like always, her mom had some new ideas, and the wedding event planner was listening with rapt, wide-eyed interest—Marnie Dixon had that effect on creative types. It was like opening a shaken can of soda pop and the fizz spilled every-where. Dawn turned to ask Kevin a question, but he had slipped away. She found him close to the bay, facing the water. As she approached, he turned to her, his sunglasses hiding his eyes.

Something was off, she thought. "Are you feeling okay?"

"I'm fine. Just thinking about things."

Things. Like canceling their wedding. Their marriage. Their happily ever after. Those kinds of things.

Gag. Dawn felt queasy, thinking of what a cliché she'd be-come. Jilted. Just two months before the wedding. Maybe not left at the altar, but pretty darn close.

Mom stood on the threshold, arms folded against her chest. Dawn slowly got out of the car and closed the door. Steeling herself, she walked up the brick-lined path. "Mom," she said, her voice breaking. "There's something we have to talk about."

"She told you, didn't she?"

Dawn jerked her head up.

"I told her not to tell anyone. Blabbermouth. That's what she is. That's what I'm going to call her from now on. Maeve the Blabbermouth."

"Aunt Maeve?" Dawn scrunched up her face. "Maeve told me—"

"I didn't want anyone to know. At least not until after the wedding. I just wanted to get this surgery taken care of. I don't want you to worry, honey. It was caught early. I promise. That's the thing about breast cancer. Catch it quick and take care of it. So I did. And I have plenty of time before the wedding for treatment. The doctor promised. Come April twelfth, I'll be just fine. I hope Maeve didn't get it wrong and make it sound like something worse than it was. I'm sure she meant well, but she's in big trouble."

"You have . . . breast cancer?" Dawn's voice shook and broke and then stopped.

"Had. It's gone. I'm fine, honey. I promise."

For one dreadful, disorienting second, Dawn's mind emptied, stilled. Then denial roared in—loud and large. *No! No way. Not my mom.*

"Caught early. Taken care of. Gone." She snapped her fingers, like it was no big deal.

But it *was* a big deal. "When did you find out?"

"A month or so ago, I had a routine mammogram—and you know how much I hate going to doctors—but I went. And they called me back in." She shrugged. "That happens. I wasn't concerned. Not until they wanted the ultrasound. Then the biopsy."

"Biopsy?"

"Yes. On the day you were getting your makeup done for the wedding. You didn't want me there, remember? You said I would get in the way."

"I said you would turn me into someone I didn't recognize."

"Well, it all worked out, because that was the day of the

biopsy. And then things happened fast, honey. Surgeon, oncologist, boom. Surgery. They move fast when they find cancer."

"When?"

"A week ago."

"Mom . . ."

"I know, I know. Maybe I should have told you, but I just want this wedding to be perfect. I was going to tell you after you got back from the honeymoon. I promise. I'm not trying to hide anything from you."

"You had surgery and didn't tell me?"

"I left a letter for you that Maeve was supposed to give you . . . just in case something went wrong."

"But . . . how are you feeling?"

"Not bad. A little sore. Like I don't want anyone to accidentally bump into me kind of sore. But relieved. And grateful. I had good doctors who helped me make decisions."

"All alone? You didn't talk to anyone else?"

"I told Maeve about the surgery. And she took me to and from the hospital. She's brought me food and checked on me. I suppose I will forgive her, eventually. But I really didn't want you to know about any of this yet. I was so clear with her about that. What is the point of having a best friend if they go behind your back and tell your daughter that kind of news . . . right before her wedding?"

"Mom. Stop talking and listen to me. Kevin doesn't want to marry me. There isn't going to be a wedding."

Mom finally stopped talking.

There wasn't going to be a wedding. And her mom had cancer. Dawn and her mom stared at each other in a mixture of shock and disbelief.

● ● ●

There wasn't much in life that could knock Marnie Dixon down, but seeing her daughter sit at the kitchen table, head in hands, weeping, did the job. Her friend Maeve always said that mothers felt whatever pain their child felt, only magnified. Marnie jumped up, got a box of tissues to set on the table between them, and pulled out one for Dawn and another for her.

Dawn rarely cried, even as a little girl. When she was learning to walk, she would fall, pick herself up, and try again. That was Dawn. Philip used to say that their daughter was born accepting the fact that life would require grit and determination.

Dazed, Marnie dabbed her eyes, rose again, and went to get two cups of coffee. She filled them, then remembered they'd run out of coffee creamer. A brilliant idea struck. She opened the freezer and rummaged for a container of vanilla ice cream. She dropped a big spoonful of it into each mug and handed one to Dawn, who peered vaguely at the melting lumps.

"Everything's better with ice cream," Marnie said. She slipped into the chair next to her. "Start at the beginning. Tell me what happened." The timer on her phone went off and she jumped up to take her pain pills. Dawn sat at the kitchen table, watching her with worried eyes. "I'm fine, honey. I really am. This is just a little blip on the radar."

"Mom, please sit down."

Right. Marnie needed to settle. She sat in the chair opposite Dawn and put both hands around the warm coffee mug. "Let's talk about your wedding."

"I keep trying to tell you. There is no wedding."

"But . . . what are the chances that Kevin just has a bad case of pre-wedding jitters?" Dawn's eyes filled with tears again. That should have told Marnie, right there, all she needed to know. Those beautiful blue eyes of Dawn's, they were bottomless pools of sadness.

"Last night, Kevin came over to help me address wedding invitations. I was showing him how to put the stamp on just so." Dawn took a shaky breath, closing her eyes for a minute.

Marnie sighed. "Gorgeous stamps," she muttered. She'd

designed them herself—two Eastern Bluebirds, building a nest—to complement the avian-themed wedding. Marnie loved birds.

"When I handed him the stamps, he held them in his hand and said he just couldn't do it. I didn't know what he was talking about, so I just showed him how to do it again. Then he said that he knew how to put a stamp on. What he couldn't do—" Her voice choked up. She reached for another tissue and dabbed at her eyes. "He said he couldn't marry me."

"Why? What reason did he give?"

"He said he didn't think he loved me. Not the way he thought he should."

"That's not possible! Kevin's loved you since the first time he laid eyes on you." Could there be another woman? Marnie didn't want to ask, didn't want to think it. After all, this was Kevin—nearly a son to her. He even spoke at Philip's memorial service—he was that much a part of their family tapestry. There was hardly a picture in the family albums that he wasn't in.

They'd known Kevin since he was fourteen years old, when his father accepted the call to be the senior pastor at their local church and moved his family to Needham. Kevin and Dawn met in youth group and shared a common circle of church friends. They started to date in their junior year of high school, went to the same college, dating steadily throughout all four years. They were the perfect couple, both immensely sensible and well suited. No drama, not ever. As Dawn and Kevin graduated from college, everyone expected they'd get engaged. Ever reasonable, they decided to wait a few years, to get work experience, live with friends in Boston, and not miss out on any young adult experience. That's exactly what they did. Two years passed, three, then five. Getting engaged was always the plan . . . someday.

But then Philip died, suddenly and unexpectedly, and every-

thing changed. Everything. Kevin proposed, Dawn acc
and elaborate wedding plans got underway.

Dawn picked up her mug and crossed the kitchen to th
coffee-maker. She refilled her coffee and spooned more ice
cream into the mug, then took a spoonful straight from the
carton and ate it. Marnie noticed how Dawn's shoulders
slumped in that way they had after Philip died, and her heart
ached for her daughter. Dawn brooded, internalized every
blessed thing, whereas Marnie shared every thought and feeling. Even now, Marnie had a dozen questions she wanted
to ask but prudence kept her quiet. She needed to let Dawn
reveal what she wanted to, and when. A lifetime of experience
had taught her that if she asked too much, Dawn shut down.

"Looking back, I can see now that there were signs." Dawn
returned to sit at the table, hands gripped tightly around the
mug. "He never had any opinions about the wedding. I tried
to get him interested, but he just kept deferring. He would
say, 'You and your mom can make that call.'" She took a sip
of coffee. "I thought he was just accommodating us, but now
I realize he didn't want to be a part of it."

"So you think it was the choices of the wedding that caused
this?" And if that were true, Marnie felt furious with him. He
was a grown man, after all. He could have spoken up at any
time.

On the heels of anger came guilt. The wedding, she admitted, was teetering toward over-the-top. Perhaps a tiny bit more
than Dawn had asked for, definitely more than Kevin wanted.
When they first got engaged, he said he'd always wanted a
wedding on the beach with only family attending. Ridiculous! Imagine Dawn's wedding dress train dragged along the
sand. For goodness' sakes, Dawn was an only child who had
recently lost her father. Why shouldn't she have the wedding
of her dreams?

Dawn stared into her mug. "I don't know. I just know that

pted,

e

easy between us, not like they used to be,

ed up. "That's what I don't know." She
it's so humiliating. We have all the same
will forever be known as the girl who was left at the
altar."

"True friends aren't like that."

Dawn ran a hand through her hair. On a typical workday, her long red hair would be tightly pulled back and pinned, out of the way. She tried to look older than her years. Marnie thought that was silly. Dawn oozed such confidence and self-assurance that people had always thought she was a decade older than she was.

Today, though, wasn't a typical day. Dawn's thick tangled hair looked like it hadn't been combed recently. Dark circles rimmed her eyes. "This morning he sent a text asking to talk again tonight."

"Maybe—"

"No, Mom. No maybes. The wedding is off. That much, I'm sure of. I gave him the ring back."

Marnie's eyes slipped to Dawn's left hand. The ring—one that had belonged to Kevin's grandmother—was gone.

"We're only going to talk about how to divide up the cancelations. In his text, he said he would help call vendors. He'd make as many calls as needed."

Marnie sat back in her chair. "So he's really serious about this."

Dawn nodded. Another tear escaped and she wiped it off her cheek. "Dead serious."

Okay. Okay, then. Marnie jumped up and grabbed the wedding notebook. "I can handle everything, Dawn. You don't have to do a thing. Maeve can help. We'll take care of everything, sweetheart."

Dawn looked a little bewildered. "Hold it. Slow down. I know you can pivot on a dime, but I can't move quite that fast. Besides, Kevin is the one who is calling this wedding off. He offered to make the cancelations and I think we should let him." She leaned on her elbows. "Mom, you have cancer. We haven't even talked about that yet."

"Had cancer. It's gone." Marnie turned to a new page in the wedding binder. "I think you're right about letting Kevin make as many cancelation calls as possible. He shouldn't get off scot-free here."

"You're not going to talk about it?"

Marnie looked up. "It?"

"Cancer."

"No." She looked back down at the binder. "I'm not giving it any more space in my life."

Dawn sighed. "I'd better get to work." She rose.

Marnie's mouth went as round as an O. "Work? After such a traumatic event?"

"I'm in the middle of a big project. Don't worry. It's a good distraction." She paused. "Mom, are you really, really okay?"

"Well, I'm furious with Kevin."

"Not that. I meant . . . having cancer."

"*Had* cancer," Marnie said. "It's gone."

"Well, we're going to talk more about it. I'm glad you're recovering well from the surgery. Not so glad that you didn't tell me." She bent down and kissed Marnie on the top of her head. "Get some rest. I'll call you later."

"Promise?" There was a pleading note in her voice.

Dawn gave her a thumbs-up as she headed to the door. Marnie went and watched her leave. She felt as if her heart was breaking for Dawn. She wished she could take the pain away for her daughter, or take it on herself. But she couldn't. No mother could.

She knew she drove Dawn crazy some of the time. Most of

the time. To be honest, Dawn drove Marnie a little crazy too. In a nutshell, Dawn thought Marnie was too dramatic, and Marnie thought Dawn wasn't dramatic enough.

She supposed her uncharacteristically calm reaction to a diagnosis of cancer could be a shock in itself to Dawn. Frankly, Marnie was still in shock over it. She was careful about food. She exercised every single day. She did yoga. She had a deep and abiding faith in God that helped her cope with stress, with the tragedy of losing her husband. How in the world did Marnie Dixon have cancer? Scratch that. Had.

Having cancer was like having an unexpected and unwanted houseguest. Literally. Marnie didn't invite it, she didn't want it to stay, and she wanted it out as soon as she could evict it. It wasn't that she ignored the diagnosis—she faced it head on, underwent all the pre-op tests required before surgery (so many machines and needles! her poor little breast). She begged her surgeon for the earliest date for surgery that she could possibly give to her. *Get it out of me!* That's all Marnie could think about. *I have a wedding to put on! I have a life to live!* She could hardly wait to get on the other side of surgery, to wake up in the morning and soak in the awareness that the cancer was gone.

But like a clueless houseguest, cancer didn't get the hint. It left its mark, like a lingering odor. Whenever Marnie used to fry fish, the house would stink of it for days. That's what cancer did. It just stunk.

She knew that Dawn was upset she hadn't been told, but Marnie was still glad she'd listened to her gut instinct. They were so different that way. Dawn's guide in life was her black-and-white principles and Marnie respected that quality about her daughter. There was no one she'd rather trust with money, and she could see why Dawn had excelled in her chosen field of public accounting—which sounded astonishingly dull to Marnie. Dawn's work was all about reacting to what others had done. Looking for problems, checking for errors, bringing mistakes to light.

Marnie was led by intuition, by prayer. Things that were invisible, while principles were made of concrete. Philip was like Dawn in that way. Philip and Marnie's marriage had been a good one, but it wasn't without its bumps now and then. And whenever they had those inevitable rocky patches, those strong disagreements, it always boiled down to how they viewed the world. Philip's principles vs. Marnie's intuition. After thirty-two years of marriage, they had never quite solved that quagmire. And then he was gone.

She felt badly Dawn was upset that she hadn't told her about the surgery, but she kept quiet so the wedding could proceed without a hitch. And she had to admit that she did it for her own benefit. Getting a diagnosis of cancer thrust her into a world that she had always preferred to ignore. She had so much to learn about, so many decisions to make quickly, and then came the healing part. She needed the quiet. Even Maeve, dear Maeve, kept telling her stories of friends with cancer, and frankly, she just didn't want to hear them. Every single person was a distinct being and their medical situation was as unique as their fingerprints. That's why she stayed away from cancer stories. *No thank you.*

Marnie had thought once this health glitch was behind her, it would be smooth sailing. She plopped into Philip's favorite armchair with a sigh. No wedding? No Kevin in their lives?

Marnie's thoughts bounced to wondering how difficult it would be to cancel everything as quickly as possible. The wedding venue, the caterer, the florist. Could a wedding dress get returned? Doubtful. It would seem like a bad luck dress.

She closed her eyes, breathed in and out, a deep cleansing breath. In and out, in and out. *Everything will be okay. The Lord is sovereign. All things work together for good for those who love God.* Her mind clutched on every comforting Bible verse she could think of. *Breathe in and out, in and out. It will all turn out okay.*

She opened her eyes.

She wanted to kill Kevin.

Chapter
TWO

Why does ice cream go with a broken heart? Because if you eat enough of it, it freezes the heart and numbs the pain for a bit.

—CC Hunter, author

Boston, Massachusetts
Thursday, February 6

Kevin wasn't dead, but it felt to Dawn like someone had died. The sickening feeling settled over her, the knowing that the path ahead was going to be a long, hard, bumpy road. Knowing she would survive this loss, but life would never be the same.

Dawn survived the workday by reminding herself of how she had gotten through those early weeks after her dad had died. She didn't need to figure out how to navigate the rest of her life without her dad, just that one day. She could make it one day at a time.

Around five o'clock, she received a text from Kevin asking when he could stop by her apartment to talk.

She paused before responding. Seeing him in person . . . she just couldn't handle it. Too high a risk of a hysterical breakdown.

Dawn
Let's just talk on the phone. Call after 8.

Kevin
Oh. OK.

She waited to see if he had anything to add, then turned her phone on silent and put it in her purse. She finished the project she'd been working on, tidied up her office, and went home to shower, tried to eat something even though she had zero appetite, and prepared herself for Kevin's call. She couldn't even let herself think about Mom's breast cancer. She couldn't even go there, not with all the what-ifs and what might've happened.

The one bright spot in this horrible day was that her roommate was away for a few days. Brynn was her best friend, as close to a sister as a friend could be, but Dawn wouldn't be able to hide anything from her, and she just couldn't handle trying to explain anything right now. She had no words to describe how her entire life had turned upside down in just twenty-four hours.

At eight o'clock sharp, Dawn's cell phone rang. Kevin's punctuality was something she'd always appreciated about him, but tonight it annoyed her. She let it ring a few times before she picked up. "Hello."

"Dawn, how are you? How did your day go?" He sounded genuinely concerned for her.

As her brain circled back to Kevin's "We're just not working" statement from last night, she wondered again what the part was that hadn't been working, because so much of their relationship *did* work. "It was a busy day. Super busy. In fact, I still have something I have to finish. So, what exactly did you want to discuss?"

He saw beyond her smokescreen. "This is important too, Dawn. If you can sit down for a moment and listen, I'll make it quick."

She plopped down on the sofa, holding the phone with one hand, rubbing her forehead with the other. "Shoot."

"I made some calls today and started the process. There are some vendors who are charging a fee. I'll cover all those costs, of course."

You bet you will, buddy.

"I'll send you an email with all the details about, well, specifics."

She noticed how carefully he avoided the words: canceling their wedding.

"Dawn, there's one thing I discovered today. To get the honeymoon package on the hotel, I had to pay it all up front. Nonrefundable. So, it's either forfeit the money or . . ."

If Kevin said he was going with someone else, Dawn would release a bloodcurdling scream. He knew how much the Cape meant to her. Her dad had once told her that the closest he'd been to Heaven was a spring day on Cape Cod. Dawn had never forgotten those words, and even planned for her wedding in April, just so she would have that chance for a heavenly honeymoon on the Cape.

". . . I thought that maybe . . . you could go. You know . . . take a friend. Take anyone you want to. I'd like you to go to Cape Cod, Dawn, and have a vacation. Take the package. It's already paid for. Please go. Go and enjoy yourself."

The first person who popped into Dawn's mind was her mother.

* * *

Needham, Massachusetts
Tuesday, April 8

Two months had passed and Marnie was still in shock that Dawn had invited her along on the groomless honeymoon. Three times she asked her if she was absolutely sure she wanted her to go, and three times Dawn said yes . . . and to please stop asking or she might change her mind.

Then Dawn surprised Marnie with a hug. "I think this would've made Dad happy. You know, the two of us, going together to a place he loved. His girls, together."

That's what Philip always called them. Marnie and Dawn were his girls.

Frankly, despite the bleak circumstances, Marnie couldn't remember ever feeling so excited about a vacation. She had just finished six weeks of radiation and was eager to forget the daily treatments. Eager to move on! And Cape Cod was a place she loved. When Dawn was little, they would spend a summer week camping on the Cape. That was before Philip started booking Dawn's summers at camps for gifted children, which weren't really camps at all. Science Camp, Engineering Camp, NASA Space Camp (Philip's favorite). Marnie thought those camps squelched Dawn's creative spark and what she really needed was an unscheduled summer of "sacred idleness."

Rubbish, Philip would say. She remembered one conversation in particular when Dawn was turning twelve years old. They were sitting at the breakfast table, drinking coffee, listening to a classical music station. "Do you hear, Philip? Do you hear those pauses in between the notes? They're necessary, to allow the ear to rest before the music starts up again and takes you to another place entirely. That's what Dawn needs this summer. A pause."

Philip scoffed that off. "You mean boredom. Marnie, you romanticize boredom. I was bored as a child. We had no money for anything. Not swim lessons, not tennis lessons, not anything. I would never let my own child face a summer of boredom." He was the eldest of five children, raised by a single mother. Too many to care for, he believed. That's why he was satisfied with only one child.

Marnie found another empty suitcase and heaved it onto her bed. Better too much of everything than not enough, she thought. She had high hopes for the week together with her daughter, whose heart and soul needed serious mending.

Early Sunday morning, the two women planned to drive down Route 6 to stay at the very ritzy Chatham Bars Inn. Marnie had never stayed in such a fancy hotel. Saturday, April twelfth, was the official (canceled) wedding day, and Marnie had wanted to do something special for Dawn, something to make her feel cherished. So she booked a spa day for her—the works!—and paid for Brynn, her longtime friend and apartment mate, to go too. They'd met at one of those camps Philip had found. Chess camp, she thought. Or coding. It was hard to remember.

She folded her new one-piece spandex bathing suit—called a Miraclesuit and Marnie hoped it would live up to its name. She was a big believer in miracles. Big ones, small ones, everyday ones. You just had to keep your eyes on the lookout for them. Not miss them. That was her theory on the topic, anyway. As she tucked it into her suitcase, she wondered again if Dawn regretted not bringing Brynn with her. Brynn would've been the logical choice of a traveling companion for Dawn. They could've played chess together on the beach.

But Marnie wasn't going to ask Dawn a fourth time.

She was over-the-moon excited for this trip, for her own sake as well as Dawn's. Marnie felt out of balance in her soul after that dreadful bout of cancer and desperately needed to restore harmony in her life, to find that settled center that had gone missing. She needed to step out of her own life and see it with fresh eyes. A pause from the music's frenetic pace, before it started up again and took her to an entirely new place.

Something wonderful was going to happen during this week on Cape Cod. She could just feel it, bone-deep.

* * *

Chatham, Massachusetts
Sunday, April 13

Nothing about Dawn's honeymoon had gone according to plan. First and foremost, there was no groom. Second, she was on her husbandless honeymoon with her *mother*. And while Mom could be quite amusing, and even good company, she wasn't Kevin, the missing groom.

It was April, and the weather was spectacular, soft and sunny and springlike, but Dawn wouldn't say this was her idea of Heaven. After all, she was spending her honeymoon with her mother. Marnie Dixon wasn't Dawn's first choice to come on the honeymoon, but she was the right choice. No doubt.

Dawn reminded herself that she and her mom had a strange relationship. Nothing like her friends', whose mothers were predictable, reliable. Logical. Not Dawn's mom. A little bit of Marnie went a long way. She was just too much. Too exuberant, too dramatic, and way too distractable.

Mom said and did things all the time that made Dawn cringe. For example, her clothes made her look like a hippie earth mama, she collected quotes in countless journals, and she thought God was constantly talking but people didn't tune in to the right frequency. Like people were all human radios. There were signs and wonders all around us, Mom often enthused, and Dawn would only roll her eyes.

Dad had always gotten a kick out of Mom's kookiness. He considered her eccentricities to be amusing. Like when she brought home a pig and wanted to keep it as a pet. The church had been planning a big luau-themed auction to raise money for mission work, and when Mom found out they'd been given a pig to roast, she couldn't bear the thought of something so dastardly happening to an animal in the name of mission work, so she talked the church into accepting a sizable donation in exchange for the pig. (Later, Dad and Dawn took the pig to a farm.) Mom's intentions were always good, but someone always had to clean up her mess. She needed a "minder." And that minder was Dad. Had been.

Dawn would be the first to admit that everybody loved Marnie Dixon. She was fun to be around and always up for something exciting and new. Great traits in a friend. Not such great ones in a mom. Physically, Dawn resembled her mom more than her dad. She and her mom were both medium-sized height and weight, both had long red hair (Mom's had faded to strawberry blond in her old age), both had pale white skin that burned easily. But in every other way, Dawn was her father's child, the polar opposite to her mother. Marnie was spontaneous, spur-of-the-moment, up for anything. Dawn was deliberate, prepared for everything. Her favorite word: plan.

Despite the grim reality of being on a groomless honeymoon with her mother, Dawn had to admit that everything else was perfect. It was a beautiful Sunday afternoon on Cape Cod—sunny and unseasonably warm with a gentle sea breeze. The kind of day you dreamed about in the depths of January. And then . . . the Chatham Bars Inn! Dawn had no idea such a paradise existed, especially here on Cape Cod. Her vague memories of the Cape were camping with her parents—sand and sunburn and horrible bugs called no-see-ums. She had no regrets when the camping trips ended, and she had even surprised herself when she suggested honeymooning on Cape Cod to Kevin. It probably had something to do with her dad.

As Dawn and her mom settled into the hotel room—ocean view! With its own balcony! Kevin must have spent a fortune—

they were both quiet. Their eyes did the talking for them. Dawn had stayed in some nice hotels on business travels, but nothing compared to the Chatham Bars Inn. Built in 1914 as a semi-private hunting lodge, it was now a luxury beachfront hotel, open to the public—if they could afford it.

As Dawn observed her mom's delight, she felt pleased she'd brought her. Mom and Dad had never treated themselves to anything fancy like this. They had scrimped and saved for Dawn's college education and then for her wedding. She knew all they had sacrificed for her, and she appreciated it oh so much. Yes, it was the right decision to bring Mom.

"Let's go check out the hotel," Mom said, after oohing and aahing over the antiques in the room, the wood paneling, the fancy soaps in the bathroom, the sheer luxury of it all. "Let's walk all over the hotel grounds, then head into town. I want to get thoroughly familiar with Chatham. I want to memorize every inch." She stood on the hotel deck as she said it, over-looking the ocean, breathing in the ocean air. "This week is going to go by way too fast."

But all Dawn could think about was getting down to the beach and the need—as real as hunger—to be there, alone, if for no other reason than to try and shrug off the dark cloud that had followed her here. Getting through yesterday was painful, even harder than she had expected it to be, especially as the clock neared 4:00 p.m., the time the wedding would've started. "I hope you don't mind, but I'd like to spend some time on the beach . . . alone."

Mom hesitated, then smiled and said she didn't mind at all. So they parted ways and agreed to meet back up in their hotel room at sunset for a glass of wine on their balcony.

Crossing the road, she went past the pool and down toward the stretch of beach. Wandering along the water, she wondered if the surf was going in or out. She didn't know how to read telltale signs of the tide's coming and going, but Mom would know. She took off her sneakers and dipped her toes into the water—so cold!

Two shiny huge dark gray seals swam alongside her, popping their heads up now and then as they followed her path, either keeping her company or planning to eat her if she walked too close to the surf. She kept her distance.

After a while, Dawn stopped and pivoted on her heels to soak in the Chatham Bars Inn from this vantage point. Despite the sad circumstances that brought her here, she couldn't deny that Kevin had chosen well. The grand hotel was stunning, the town of Chatham was quaint and charming, and the beach—it was perfect. Noisy gulls circled overhead, their cries blending in with the sounds of the waves. The scent of the ocean was heavy in the air. Everything was exactly as she had imagined it to be.

All that was missing was Kevin.

She fought back sudden tears.

Dawn felt crushed, truly devastated. Kevin had been her first love, her first everything, and she'd assumed they'd always be together. It came as a complete shock when he said that he didn't think their relationship was working.

As she resumed her walk along the beach, her mind circled back to that initial conversation, when she felt the foundation of her world shift from under her. They were seated at the table in her apartment. She'd made an assembly line of wedding invitations. "Not working?" she had asked Kevin, her voice small. Not working? Since when?

He held a sheet of postage stamps in his hand. "We haven't been working for a while."

The air rushed out of her lungs—as if she'd been kicked in the gut. "You didn't think to tell me?" she said, unable to fully grasp what was happening.

"I tried. A couple of times. You shut me down."

"When? When did you try?"

He set the stamps down. "Just before you put the deposit down on the wedding reception venue, I took you to that really pretty farm. I brought up the idea of having the reception there and you burst out laughing."

"Kevin! You can't be serious! It would've meant picnic tables on grass and dirt. The last time I'd been to a wedding in the country, I ended up with chigger bites up and down my legs. I was in agony for a week." But she did remember how eager he'd been to show her the farm. He loved it, Mom loved it, but Dawn had felt it held too many unpredictable elements. Like horses neighing and pigs snorting and flies buzzing during the ceremony. She cocked her head. "So you think we're not working because of the venue for the wedding reception?"

"No, it's not just that," he said, rubbing his hands on his thighs self-consciously. "Though I did feel like the entire wedding became a bus that left the station without waiting for me to jump on."

So not fair! "You kept relinquishing decisions to Mom and me."

Tilting his head, he scraped his beard with one hand. "Why do you think I did?"

"Because . . . you didn't care about the details."

"No. Because no one cared what I thought."

Dawn put her fingers against her temples. "So you're saying that if I had agreed to have a wedding in a barnyard, then you'd be just fine with everything. And you're just telling me now."

"That's not what I meant. The wedding seemed such a symptom to this . . . feeling."

"What feeling?"

"Like . . . the feeling of being tied to a train track"—he avoided her eyes— "and the only way I can loosen the ropes and free myself is to . . ."

She finished his sentence. "Pull out."

A long silence followed. "Dawn, the wedding was only part of the problem. Actually, it's not even the wedding. It's us. We're the problem. A few weeks ago, I brought up premarital counseling, but you said we didn't need it."

"That's because it would've been with your father! I'm not about to go tell my deepest thoughts and feelings and secrets to your dad."

"Then who, Dawn? Who would you tell your deepest thoughts and feelings to? Because it's not to me. You're just . . . so sealed off."

She dropped her chin, staring at her feet. Kevin had always wanted more from her, and as much as she wanted to give it to him, she couldn't.

"There's a reason your nickname is Teflon Dawn."

That smarted. She gave him a sharp look. Some boy called her that once in junior high and it had stuck. She took in a deep breath. "Why did you ask me to marry you?"

"It had always been our plan to get married when the time was right. And after your dad died, I thought . . ."

"You thought what? That then I wouldn't be so sad? So you asked me to marry you because you felt sorry for me."

"No, Dawn. Nothing like that. Don't keep putting words in my mouth. It's just . . . I think we rushed things because of your dad's death. He had wanted us to marry years ago. Every time I came to your house, he asked me when I was going to propose. Every single time. Getting engaged seemed like a way of honoring his memory, and to help you move forward. But now, I think what you've really needed was time to heal."

"I need time?" She coughed a laugh. "Yet you're the one who wants to break off our engagement." There. She said it out loud. Hoping he would back things up, correct her, take her into his arms and apologize, and say it was all just nerves. Just a misunderstanding.

But he didn't do any of those things.

In his eyes, she saw a combination of sadness and determination. "Kevin, do you not love me anymore?"

He looked away, and she had her answer. "I've loved you from the first day I met you. I'll always love you. But I'm not sure it's the right kind of love. I just don't know if we're right for each other anymore. I'm not sure we can make each other happy."

That moment hit her like a sucker punch, forcing a sharp intake of breath. Panic seized her, a sense of having her heart ripped into pieces. She wanted to tell him not to give up on her, on them. She wanted to tell him that he was wrong—that they were right for each other. They'd always been meant for each other.

But she could tell he had already made up his mind.

Do not cry, she told herself. *Do not cry. Not in front of him.*

She slipped off the engagement ring he had given to her, a family heirloom, and held it out to him. Slowly, sadly, he picked it up off her palm. Then she went to the door and opened it.

He took the cue. At the door, he stopped. "Whenever we talked about getting married, you kept telling me you weren't ready yet. So why, after your dad died, did you say finally say yes?"

"Because," she said softly, "I love you."

"Sometimes, I'm not so sure." Then he left her.

He was wrong about that. She loved him deeply.

The loss she felt over losing Kevin hurt in a way she didn't know if she could ever fully recover from. Her grief was immense. It fused with the grief she felt about her dad and the feeling that her life was out of her own control.

A couple of kids raced past her, splashing her as they went, snapping her back to the present. She needed her dad. She missed him every single day. At times, the need to connect with him felt almost overwhelming. That's probably the real reason why she had asked Kevin if they could honeymoon on Cape Cod. What she wanted, she supposed, was some sign from the Great Beyond that the connection with her father wasn't entirely broken. The thought of that made her almost smile, because it sounded like something her hippie-joujou mom might say. But it was true that Dawn was here because she needed some kind of help to get on with her life. One tear rolled down her cheek, then another, and another, and when she came across a big log of driftwood, she plopped down beside it, leaned her back against it, and let the tears flow.

A thick gray cloud covered the sun, and suddenly cold, she wrapped her arms around her torso. Through the cloud, a single ray of sunshine appeared, beaming down on her. She could actually feel the sun's warmth, as small and tiny a ray as it was. It felt like a little message from her dad, reminding her that she wasn't alone, that everything was going to be okay. She breathed in the scent of the salt and sea, listened to the slap of the waves against the shore, and peace began to steal over her.

More clouds were gathering, and the wind was picking up, whipping her hair around her face. She'd pulled it back in a braid, but a few strands had worked loose. Her stomach cramped. When had she eaten last? She glanced at her cell phone, startled to see how long she'd been down on the beach. As she rose to her feet and brushed sand off her backside, she wondered what her dad might have to say to her right now, if he were here. Probably . . . that she still had a choice in this situation. It was the only choice that remained to her. Acceptance.

She would have to accept the fact that she and Kevin were history. She needed to put their relationship behind her. That little beam of sunlight through the cloud had given her the tiny ray of hope she'd so desperately needed—that she could find her way through the darkness and into the light. She just wasn't sure how.

Chapter
THREE

You can't buy happiness. But you can buy ice cream and that is pretty much the same thing.

—Anonymous

Sunday, April 13

Marnie walked the entire town of Chatham for the second time, almost giddy, waving to people as if she knew them. She couldn't believe she was really here. As bittersweet as it was that this week should have been Dawn and Kevin's honeymoon, nothing could deflate her happiness at being here. Something about this little beach town just spoke to her heart. Like she belonged here.

Chatham was a walkable town. Quaint, tree-lined, utterly charming. She combed through every open shop, not so much to purchase anything—though she did buy seashell earrings for Maeve. She was Marnie's best friend and had been a rock to lean on over the years. What she was really trying to do, she supposed, by wandering the streets and going through the stores, was to create an entrenched map on her brain of this little piece of real estate on the elbow of the Cape. It was the only way to really know a place—to walk it.

Meandering along Main Street, she saw a sidewalk chalkboard that pointed up the road to ice cream. That made her smile, as if Philip were right here with her. He was a ridiculously self-disciplined man whose sole vice in life was ice cream. He loved ice cream the way most men loved sports, the way Italians loved food and French loved wine. Ice cream was Philip's lifelong passion.

Philip and Dawn made excellent ice cream together. It was the kind of process that required absolute precision—exactly their style. Marnie would provide suggestions for unique flavor combinations, and the two of them would ponder, discuss at length, and more often than not reject her ideas, shooting them down with reasons as to why they wouldn't work. Mostly, they remained stuck on one or two flavors, trying to get them just-so-perfect.

Closing her eyes, Marnie heard the echo of their fun as a smile came to her lips. Philip and Dawn had made fifty-nine batches of vanilla before they were satisfied. Fifty-nine! Marnie thought they were starting to show signs of obsessive-compulsive disorder, but they insisted that vanilla was the most difficult flavor to get right because it was so pure. Nothing could be hidden with vanilla, they said. Chocolate, peppermint, strawberry—those strong flavors could mask inferior ice cream. So could add-ins, like swirls of fudge or ribbons of berry compote or chunks of brownies. But not vanilla. Marnie smiled. She hadn't thought about those endless attempts to make perfect vanilla ice cream since Philip died. Dawn hadn't made ice cream since.

Her eyes popped open.

As a teenager, Philip had spent his summers with a friend whose family had a cottage in nearby Harwich, and the two boys had worked at an ice cream shop. It was where Philip's love of ice cream was sparked, and his love of Cape Cod. She couldn't remember the name of the shop, only that it was housed in an old building—but that described most of Chatham. She remembered how Philip said the ice cream shop was known for giving unreasonably huge scoops. Absolutely enormous. He had spoken so fondly about those summers, about fishing off piers, and swimming at beaches with his friend. She would give anything to hear him describe those summers again.

She continued along Main Street, looking for the ice cream shop that the sidewalk chalkboard pointed to. She went up one block, then another, turned back and searched again, puzzled, unable to figure out where that shop could be. She kept passing a shabby three-quarter Cape Cod with an off-center front door, two windows to the left of the door, one window to the right. It bore signs of historical architecture—weathered cedar shingle siding, double-hung windows, twelve over twelve, even a few panes of bullseye glass. But the paint was peeling, cedar shingles were missing on the siding, shingles were missing on the roof. On the front that faced the street, hanging crooked, hidden behind a bush, she noticed a ship's big black quarter board engraved with *Main Street Creamery*.

Marnie's heart stopped. It literally stopped, then started again.

No. This couldn't be it. Could it? The same shop where Philip had once worked?

She walked closer, curious about this old building. She peered in the grimy windows. It was dark inside, so dark. She shuddered. She didn't like darkness. As her eyes adjusted, she could make out a long freezer counter in the dim interior.

Slowly, she walked around the entire building and kept getting a whiff of smoke in the air. A small slanted-roof addition jutted off the back of the house like an afterthought. She backed up a few yards to look at the addition from a distance and discovered a tarp covering a blackened hole, evidence of a fire. She walked around the entire building again, then another time. She wondered about the history of this shop. About the owner. She couldn't tell if the disrepair and neglect were entirely due to the fire, or if the fire was due to the disrepair and neglect.

On a whim, she tried the door to the addition. It was unlocked. Marnie glanced around, then slipped inside. "Hello? Is anyone here?"

No answer.

The scent of smoke was everywhere. As Marnie's eyes adjusted to the dim light, she could see the addition was a small galley kitchen—it had stainless steel counters, a sink, a dishwasher, a refrigerator, a chest freezer that jutted out, a stove, and on the far end counter . . . an ice cream maker. It drew her in.

Clearly, she thought, tiptoeing around the small kitchen, the fire had started at the stovetop. All around the stove was blackened wood, straight up the walls to the small opening in the roof. Most likely, the firefighters had created the hole to allow heat to escape. Turning around, she bumped her hip on an old chest freezer and barely stifled a yelp.

Rubbing her hip, she left the kitchen to explore the front room, the customer service area. No actual fire damage was in here, but smoke residue was on the windows, which explained the grime. It wasn't dirt, it was soot. Standing in the middle of the room, she gazed around. This room was actually well suited for serving a lot of customers—large, with windows on three sides to let in plenty of natural light. A folding table was pushed up against a large display counter for ice cream. She tiptoed toward the counter and put a hand on the glass. It was cold . . . but the entire case was empty. Not a single container held ice cream. Everything about this shop seemed defeated, like it had given up.

Slowly, she turned in a circle. "What do you think?" she said to Philip, because sometimes she did that. It wasn't like she expected an answer; it just felt good to keep talking to him. He would've enjoyed brainstorming improvements with her, something they did when they visited ice cream shops. They always sounded like they knew what it would take to make each shop a success, though neither had any experience with a commercial food service business. Still, they had fun dreaming.

Back in the kitchen, she examined the ice cream machine. It was large and cylindrical, taking up a ridiculous amount of square footage in the small kitchen. Because of Philip's thorough study of ice cream machines, she was familiar with this brand. She flipped the on switch and, to her shock, it rumbled to life, not unlike a vibrating rocket ship trying to blast off. It got louder, louder, louder, until she panicked, flipped the switch to off, and the machine reversed its wheezing until it sputtered to a stop. She stared at it for a long while. It wasn't an ice cream machine; it was an old, outdated, nearly dead Buick.

How could anyone hear themselves think with that machine on? How could a customer shout his order over the sound? Philip would be outraged. "The first thing to go!" he would declare.

Outside, a dog barked. Marnie glanced at her cell phone with a gasp. Dawn would be expecting her at the hotel by now. She slipped out the back door and made sure the door was shut tight. As she turned to take a step down, a dog barked again. Startled, she lifted her head to see a man and his dog across the street, watching her. "Just making sure the door was shut tight," she called out, knowing it sounded utterly lame. She raised both hands in the air as if to say, "Can you believe someone left it unlocked?" but she was actually trying to convey that her hands were empty. *I didn't steal anything, if that's what you're thinking.*

He was too far away for her to see his features. What she did notice was the way he intently stared at her, his head cocked at an angle, trying to figure out who she was and where she belonged. He must have decided she didn't look like a thief, because he finally lifted a hand in a wave and turned to leave.

Marnie decided not to tell Dawn about her venture into the Main Street Creamery. Her daughter would accuse her of breaking and entering. While Marnie hadn't broken anything—after all, the door was unlocked—she did enter. Dawn was a strict rule follower and would've read her the riot act. She didn't suffer from acute curiosity combined with fearlessness, as Marnie did. A dangerous combination, Philip had often said.

She started to leave but stopped at the sidewalk and looked back. It was hard to believe that a piece of prime commercial property on Main Street in Chatham, Massachusetts, could be so neglected, so overlooked.

The drab old building looked run-down, tired. Its better days were behind it.

Like Marnie's life. It, too, had seen better days.

A shaft of excitement sizzled through her. Her mind's eye started cleaning and scrubbing, rearranging and updating, sanding and painting. What would it take? she wondered. How hard would it be to whip that place into shape? How much money would be needed to turn it into someplace special?

There was just something about this building, something that called to her. Like it was longing for another chance, a fresh start. It wasn't done with living yet . . . there was more it had to offer this world. So much more.

It was just like Marnie.

* * *

Tuesday, April 15

It took two full days for Dawn to unwind and actually start to feel relaxed. And once she did relax, she felt downright lazy.

She slept late, had a luscious breakfast downstairs, came back to the room to gather a few things, then strolled through the hotel lobby, admiring the carpets, the woodwork, the antiques, the grandeur of this place. Outside, she practically skipped down the steps, crossed the road, passed the pool, and went straight to the wide strip of beach that framed the Atlantic Ocean.

Sitting on the beach, listening to the waves, half reading a novel, dozing off and on—it was just what Dawn needed. Being here was a complete escape from her reality. Best of all, it held no memories of Kevin.

Actually, there were. On her phone. Hundreds of pictures of the two of them together. The screensaver was her favorite. It was the first time Kevin had taken her sailing on a lake in New Hampshire, where he'd spent his summers as a boy. The wind had kicked up powerfully in the late afternoon and made her uncomfortable. But he had obviously known what he was doing and handled the boat so skillfully, so carefully. It had ended up being a wonderful experience, she thought wistfully.

In the picture, he wore jeans and a windbreaker, and his confident posture emphasized his strength. Solid, she thought. The kind of guy who took care of his girlfriend. Even as a teenager, she'd been mature enough to appreciate those qualities. While most of her friends had been drawn to the bad boys, she'd wanted to feel safe. Loved. Kevin had never driven drunk or partied too hard. He'd always gotten her home on time, he'd always called when he said he was going to. That was Kevin's style. Comfortable and dependable. She thought she'd been so lucky. She had found the perfect guy, a man just like her father.

Fierce longing swept through her. She wondered if Kevin missed her like she missed him. Did guys have an innate ability to just move on? Most could, but Kevin had seemed different. She'd thought he was, anyway. Maybe she didn't know him the way she thought she had. Maybe no one really knew another person.

Best not to go there, she told herself. The past was just that—in the past. She took a deep breath and pressed the button to remove the picture. She replaced it with a photo she'd taken moments ago of the beach. A new horizon.

She wondered where Mom had gone today. Each morning, she rose earlier than Dawn and took off to explore Cape Cod. Yesterday Mom drove all the way to Provincetown and came home with a stricken look on her face. "Interesting" was all she had to say.

To her credit, Mom would ask Dawn only one time, each morning, if she wanted to come sightseeing and didn't persist when she said no. She seemed comfortable spending the days independently. To Dawn's relief, Mom was giving her plenty of space. She didn't press her, didn't try to encourage her to talk about Kevin.

Aunt Maeve's work, Dawn thought. She suspected Aunt Maeve had given Mom a long lecture to hold back, because it wasn't typical of Mom to not try to air out feelings. Mom's parenting style was based on an iconic quote of Fred Rogers: "Everything human is mentionable. And if it's mentionable, then it's manageable." True, but for some reason, whenever Dawn was pressed to talk, she would clam up. Just like her dad.

She wished they had another week to spend here, though staying at the Chatham Bars Inn was pricey, even off-season. Just thinking of going back home on Saturday filled her with dread. Back to her demanding job, back to her awesome city apartment with her best friend Brynn, back to her enviable life—but one without Kevin in it.

* * *

Chatham folk were Marnie's kind of people—early risers. As she strolled through town, she saw all kinds of people out

45

and about, their day already started. Some bikers in bright yellow spandex outfits whizzed by her, a dad pushing a stroller at breakneck pace passed her, two women heading in the opposite direction were walking at a spritely clip and returned her cheery wave with a nod, a wordless hello. *Like Maeve and me*, she thought with a smile. *Walking as fast as we can while still being able to carry on a conversation.*

She stopped for a cup of coffee to go at Monomoy Coffee Company, her new favorite coffee spot, and decided to head down to the lighthouse. She walked around it, sipping her coffee. Lighthouses had always intrigued her, and the history of this one was particularly interesting. Originally, it was built of wood, as there was no stone to be found on the Cape. Later, the wood was replaced by stone. It had been two towers, not one, and called the Twin Towers, until one of the lighthouses was moved to Eastham. "Sma-ht," she could imagine Philip saying in his thick Boston accent. "No need for two lights when one will do."

Lighthouses served such a quiet, relentless purpose which, she felt, provided a wonderful spiritual parallel: to shine a light and save lives. In a bookstore yesterday, she'd read that the Cape Cod coastline, full of shoals and currents, was responsible for over 3,500 known shipwrecks. And the coastline was continually changing, with shifting sandbars. She'd been here only a few days and had already heard locals, worried about their houses, lamenting over the ever-changing coastline. As pertinent to them as weather to a farmer.

After circling the lighthouse and the keeper's cottage twice, she walked down to the beach. It was considered one of the best beaches around—fairly long and walkable, by Cape Cod standards, anyway, unlike so many of the beaches that were merely thin ribbons of sand. She went down to the water and stopped a few feet away from the surf, watching the waves of low tide gently lap the sand. Low tide had a certain smell to it, earthy and musty. Philip had laughed when she told him as much. He used to say her senses were stuck on overdrive. Maybe so, but he was as drawn to the ocean as she was. He could spend long stretches just watching the water—rare for him to be still for so long. She always thought that because the ocean moved, he didn't have to.

Two seagulls went soaring past, chased by a large golden retriever. The dog saw Marnie and veered away from the water's edge to race straight toward her. Marnie bent down on one knee, and the dog skidded to a stop right in front of her, sat on its haunches, panting heavily, waiting expectantly. She petted his head and he looked up at her with big brown eyes, making her grin. She picked up a stick of driftwood. "By any chance would you like me to throw this stick for you?" The dog's tail thumped on the sand, as if he'd been waiting for her to ask.

Marnie's smile broadened. She rose, preparing to toss the stick, when she noticed a man standing off in the distance. Assuming the dog belonged to him, she threw the stick as far as she could in his direction. The dog chased after it, tearing down the beach, kicking up sand behind him. If you didn't know what unbridled joy was, she thought, go to the beach and watch a dog with a stick.

The man lifted his hand in thanks. Something seemed familiar in that motion, and she realized this was the same man she'd seen yesterday, the same dog, right as she slipped out of the ice cream shop. He wasn't hard to remember—he bore an uncanny resemblance to a middle-aged Clark Kent. Mid to late fifties, she gathered, though perhaps in his sixties. Not older than early sixties, not with the way he held himself as he walked. She wondered who he was and why he kept crossing her path, though it might be simply because he had a dog that required a lot of walks. And she liked to walk a lot too.

Across the expanse of beach, they stared at each other for several moments until Marnie grew uncomfortable. She spun around and walked back toward the lighthouse to head up Shore Road to the Chatham Bars Inn.

* * *

Dawn spent way too long moseying through the hotel gift shop in the afternoon, but when had she last moseyed? She was looking for something Brynn might like. She picked up an expensive soap, sniffed it, loved it, but put it down. Too risky. Brynn had allergic reactions to all kinds of things.

She felt her phone vibrate in her purse and dug for it, thinking Mom was looking for her. They were going to meet down by the pool around three o'clock. She pulled out her phone and her breath caught in her throat when she saw the text was from Kevin.

Everything okay?

She stared at the screen, knowing he was waiting for a response. They'd always responded immediately to each other's texts. She knew he was waiting to see the bubble signs that she was texting back. How should she answer? Something like this?

Sure, Kevin. I'm having a wonderful time on my honeymoon. Mom sends her love.

No. Way too sarcastic. She startled herself with how sharp those words sounded. Besides, she knew that his question was genuine, that he wanted to make sure everything had been paid for, that there were no hidden charges. He knew how careful she was with her money.

The familiar feelings of sadness and loss returned. She pushed them away, telling herself that she could just ignore his text. Just because someone texted you, it didn't mean you had to respond.

But this wasn't just someone, this was Kevin.

The Kevin who broke her heart in a million pieces. That Kevin.

Right. She tossed her phone back in her purse.

●　●　●

Wednesday, April 16

For the first time since Philip had died, the very first time in the last year, Marnie slept straight through until morning and woke up feeling rested. On Wednesday morning, moving quietly so she wouldn't wake Dawn, she changed into her yoga pants, sweatshirt, and sneakers, and scribbled a note for Dawn to text when she was awake and ready to have breakfast. Marnie wanted to come back and eat with her, with hopes that she could persuade her to do something more today than sit on a beach. As cooperative as the weather had been this week, there was more to do on Cape Cod than sit. Maeve had warned Marnie to give Dawn time. Three days seemed enough.

Marnie went out the lobby's grand entrance and stopped on the top step. The sun was still below the horizon, but its light was filling the sky. "Let there be light," she said aloud. God's first spoken words in the Bible.

The power of light was fascinating. Even while undergoing radiation treatments for breast cancer, she felt a grudging admiration for the ability of light rays to penetrate and kill any remaining cancer cells. Light was mysterious, powerful, and holy.

Closing her eyes, she exhaled all thoughts of cancer. Slowly, she inhaled tranquility, held on to it as if to gain strength, listening to the steady pounding of the surf. Slowly, she let out her breath, opened her eyes, and set off. She walked all the way down Shore Road to the lighthouse and turned around, then decided to head into town before she went back to the hotel. She stopped for coffee at an open shop and the chatty waitress told her to enjoy how quiet the town was now. Come Memorial Day, she warned Marnie, tourists would swarm the Cape. "You'll nevah find a spot to pahk the cah," she said with an air of concern, her eyebrows pulled together. "Not til aftah La-bah Day."

Sadly, the coffee was insipid. Marnie walked a block away from the shop, looked around, and tossed the full paper cup in the garbage can. She kept heading up Main Street, drawn like a magnet to the Creamery. She had gone past it each day as she went exploring, hoping to see a sign of the owner, but it always looked closed. Why was it neglected? Who owned it? What was the story here? Today, she was going to find out. When she reached it, she stopped on the sidewalk to gaze at it.

"So, we meet again."

Marnie swiveled. Crossing the street to come toward her was that man who had caught her snooping through this very building. The man on the beach. The Clark Kent double. As he approached, she was able to get a closer look at him. She guessed that they were about the same age; he might be a few years older. His hair, from what she could see of it under a navy-blue Chatham Anglers' baseball cap, was salt and pepper, with more salt than pepper. His eyes were a deep shade of brown. He was taller than her by several inches, with a lean, lanky body. As far as looks went, he wasn't especially handsome, but there was a boyish youthfulness to him—the way he walked, held himself, moved. Jaunty. That's it. He was jaunty. His was a kind face, his eyes sharp and bright, like they could see through things and they liked what they saw. She felt a little nervous around him, but that might have something to do with the fact that he saw her breaking into and entering the Creamery. "Oh, hello."

At his side was that big golden retriever dog, the kind that bounced when it walked. "Are you looking for ice cream at seven thirty in the morning?"

Marnie smiled. "Ice cream is always a good idea. Any time of the day."

"Now that's the kind of thinking the world needs more of." He came closer, or more accurately, his dog pulled him toward Marnie, his big feathery tail wagging like a metronome.

She bent down to pat the dog, and its whole body wagged, not just its tail. "What's his name?"

"Mayor. He thinks he's running the chamber of commerce. Knows everyone in town. Even the summer tourists."

Marnie laughed, patting the exuberant dog. "I'd never fault anyone for being friendly." She held out her hand. "Marnie Dixon."

"Lincoln Hayes."

"Let me guess. Your parents were history buffs."

"Coin collectors. My dad is still looking for a very rare 1969 Lincoln penny in which he sported a mustache. Let me know if you happen to see one."

She grinned. He was funny. "I'll keep a look out." She glanced at the ice cream shop. "Do you happen to know if the owner ever comes to the building? I've come by each day this week, during different times, and it always seemed to be closed up."

"Well, there was a fire a few weeks ago."

Which she already knew.

"But even before the fire, it was rarely open. The owner is rather . . . sporadic . . . with her ice cream making. Which is not such a bad thing."

"Why is that?"

He looked around, leaned in, and whispered, "The ice cream is terrible."

"Oh no! That's so wrong. A crime."

He grinned, and she noticed that he had quite a nice smile. "If I were to take a guess, I would say you are rather fond of ice cream."

"I am. My family is passionate about ice cream. Some have

51

used the term *obsessive*. On every vacation, we would stop along the way to sample local ice cream. Each shop. Each town. Each city. My husband and daughter even went to Penn State's Ice Cream School."

"Ice cream school? There really is such a thing?"

"Yes. During the month of January, Penn State holds Ice Cream School for hobbyists and professionals. All the greats have gone. Ben and Jerry, Baskin and Robbins. And"—she waved her hand with a flourish—"my husband and daughter."

"They must be quite a team."

"They were. Ice cream was the focus of their lives."

"Past tense?" His dark gaze locked with hers.

She looked away. "My husband . . . he passed away. My daughter hasn't made ice cream since." Why was she telling her family story to him? A complete stranger? There was something about Lincoln Hayes that was open and sympathetic, nonjudgmental, caring. She wondered what he did for a living, if he was a counselor or minister or something like that. He seemed to have a skill for listening . . . deeply. A rare quality, especially in a man.

He glanced at the ice cream shop. "I can't get you ice cream at this hour, but I can buy you a cup of coffee." He pointed down the road. "Monomoy Coffee Company just opened for the season. Unlike Bonnie's ice cream, they make very good coffee."

She stiffened. "Oh, no. Thank you. I was going to head back to the hotel. My daughter sleeps later than I do, but she'll be waking soon." She knew she sounded flustered, but she couldn't help it. She wasn't accustomed to a man asking her to have coffee with him. She even glanced at her cell phone, acting as if she might have missed a call from Dawn, which was thoroughly ridiculous. Knowing Dawn, she was conked out cold.

"Another time, then," he said kindly. "The Mayor likes me to extend an invitation to newcomers. Nice to meet you, Marnie."

He gave her a nod and went around her, looking back to give her a friendly wave as he headed down Main Street.

Good grief, Marnie. The man just offered you a cup of coffee. He wasn't proposing. It's just that he offered to buy her coffee after he found out she was a widow, not before, and that made her uneasy. She wasn't at all ready for a man in her life. Frankly, she didn't think she ever would be. Besides, she was heading back to Needham on Saturday morning.

Only four days left.

Whenever she thought about returning home at week's end, she could feel her heart grow heavy. She didn't want to go back to her old life, to the gaping emptiness of Philip's absence. She didn't want to slip right back into the sadness. She needed a change. A radical, enormous, shocking change.

She waited until Lincoln Hayes and his dog were no longer in sight, then started down the street, planning to head back to the Chatham Bars Inn to meet Dawn, but stopped and turned. Her gaze swept over the Main Street Creamery, and in her mind's eye, she saw it well maintained, cared for. Thriving.

That was when she figured it out. It wasn't her imagination. It started to make perfect sense: Cape Cod was more than a place to visit; this was where she needed to be. And Chatham, this beautiful little beach town on Cape Cod, was exactly where she wanted to be.

A knock on the window caught Marnie's attention. Inside, a woman with a bright red kerchief covering her hair held a large sign against the windowpane and Marnie gasped aloud. It was a FOR SALE sign. This couldn't be a coincidence. It had God's fingerprints all over it, as much a message as a burning bush, or a cloud by day and a fire by night. She had prayed for guidance and here it came. It felt like this was meant to be.

The woman beckoned her over with a welcoming wave.

Yes, yes, yes, yes, yes . . .

Marnie crossed the street and went inside.

Chapter
FOUR

Ice cream solves everything.

—Anonymous

Wednesday, April 16

It was obvious that Bonnie Snow, the owner of the Main Street Creamery, seemed extremely eager to have Marnie agree to buy the shop. "I've got a good feeling about you," she told Marnie as they sat at a wobbly table in the front room that was pushed up against an enormous ice cream display counter—a counter that was empty of ice cream—and talked through the sale of the building. "I can sense these things."

"Me too!" Marnie loved meeting like-minded people, the type who listened to their hunches, their intuitive nudges. She thought of it as the Holy Spirit's whispers, and it took practice to recognize those whispers, to gain a familiarity with them. They were subtle, so very easy to overlook in a noisy world.

And yet, as keen as she was to sell, Bonnie was fair. She tried to give Marnie a full picture of the Creamery. "You understand that the economy here is mostly tourist driven," she said. "In the winter, Chatham clears out. Snowbirds head to Florida. It can be something of a ghost town."

"I understand." Marnie tipped her head. "Is that why you're selling?"

"No. I don't mind the winters. Not at all."

The front door opened and Bonnie groaned at the sight of an imposing older woman standing in the threshold.

"Bonnie Snow, as soon as the trash collection empties the garbage containers, they must be taken off the street and hidden from street view. I've told you repeatedly. Everyone else in this district seems to comply. Yet here it is Wednesday and your containers have been on the street since Monday."

"I'll get right on it, Mrs. Nickerson-Eldredge," Bonnie said in a voice dripping with honey.

Distaste ripe on her face, the older woman turned and left.

"Don't mind her." Bonnie rolled her eyes. "She's a Nickerson." As if that explained everything.

Marnie looked at her blankly.

"Descendant of the original settlers," Bonnie said. "She considers herself to be Chatham's guardian angel. If you can't prove your lineage, you don't belong here." She shrugged. "I was a transplant. Came from Bourne, which wasn't good enough for her." Loosely, she waved a hand in the direction of the door. "It's right across the Cape Cod Canal. As far as she was concerned, I could have been from Timbuktu."

Through the sooty window, Marnie saw Mrs. Nickerson-Eldredge come out of a shop across the street and stare at the Creamery, radiating disapproval. She turned to Bonnie. "Can I help you move those garbage cans?"

Bonnie dismissed her offer. "Don't pay any mind to Mrs. Nickerson-Eldredge. She's wound a little too tight." She glanced up at the ceiling as if she'd left something there. "Now, where were we. Oh yeah. I'm selling because I'm moving to Alaska. I met Al online and we fell in love and I'm not going to let this chance slip out of my hands." She grinned. "At our age, sweetheart, we need to grab every moment of happiness we can get."

Marnie bristled at being lumped in that "at our age, sweetheart" category—fifty-eight was not old, people!—but she didn't disagree about grabbing every moment of happiness. Still, it did worry her that Bonnie might get to Alaska and regret it. "Have you actually met Al? Face-to-face?"

"Oh yes. Don't you worry! You sound like my sister. She thinks I'm loco, but I know what I'm doing. Al's come here, and I've gone there, and it's all good. Better than good. Love is even sweeter at our age." She sighed. "I suppose it comes from knowing time is growing short."

Another reference to age. Did Marnie look like she was ready for a wheelchair and an oxygen tank?

"You think I'm crazy? For following my heart?"

Marnie considered Bonnie's question for a moment. "I believe the heart acts as our compass. It tells us if we're headed in the right direction. And the heart will tell you if you've made a wrong turn." She almost said Bonnie would know when it was time for a U-turn, but she wasn't sure she wanted to add that part.

"I like that. The heart acts as the compass. I'm going to use it on my sister the very next time she tells me I'm making a terrible mistake." Bonnie slapped her palms on the table. "Say, have I told you there's an apartment upstairs? Fully furnished. Turnkey." She rocked her hand in the air. "Pretty much."

Oh wow. The upstairs apartment was an answer to an unvoiced prayer. Marnie hadn't even considered where she might live if she bought the Creamery.

"Can I see it? My daughter . . . she's a little bit fussy. You know how millennials can be." Marnie was a little concerned for herself too. The condition of the Creamery was alarming—even more than she had realized when she had slipped inside a couple days ago. This place wasn't just messy, it was filthy. The grunge was thick on the windows. The gray carpet in the front room was stained and sticky. The linoleum in the kitchen was streaked with dirt and debris. The entire kitchen was a petri dish of growing bacteria. Dawn, a bit of a clean freak, would immediately go buy a hazmat suit.

"Turn left before you reach the kitchen." Bonnie thumbed toward the stairs. "Go on up and look around. Don't mind my office. It's my catchall room. There's a twin bed somewhere in there. Say, did I tell you I had all the cast-iron plumbing replaced? Cost me a pretty penny, I can tell you that." She beamed, as if she had installed them herself. "All these old dinosaurs had cast-iron pipes that rust out and create all sorts of horrible troubles for the homeowner. H-o-r-r-i-b-l-e troubles."

"Rusty water?"

"That was the least of it. Made a big difference to get those new PVC pipes in. They hardly shake anymore when someone takes a shower. You should've heard it with those cast-iron pipes." She wiggled her whole body like she was walking on hot coals. "I worried the whole place might just rattle apart." She stilled with a smile. "Go on up and check it out."

"I'll be back in a few minutes."

Marnie went upstairs, opened the door, and peeked inside. Her first thought was that it was a DIY project gone bad. She could see through the entire apartment, from one side to the other. There were two-by-fours where walls should be.

Her second thought was that Bonnie Snow was a serious hoarder.

Every horizontal surface was covered with . . . stuff. Bonnie appeared to have dabbled in every craft imaginable. In a single glance, Marnie saw a half-done quilt top, a bag of yarn with both knitting needles and crochet hooks sticking out of it, a spinning wheel, oil paints and canvas, watercolors and paper, a soldering tool next to stained glass, and stamps for card making. Each project showed evidence of Bonnie's dabbling. Projects started, then stopped, her attention caught by something new.

Marnie's hand tightened around the doorknob. *This could be me.* This chaos was not far off from the spare bedroom in the Needham house. Not with crafts, but with party-planning paraphernalia. She kept her chaos hidden, but so did Bonnie. The downstairs part of the Creamery looked nothing like this. The downstairs of the Needham house looked nothing like the spare bedroom. She had more in common with Bonnie Snow than she would've thought. It was a disturbing insight.

A memory came to mind: She'd asked Philip to change a burned-out lightbulb in the ceiling fixture of the spare bedroom. Such a simple task, but he kept putting it off. When he did finally get around to it, he made a big show of it. He tied a long rope around his abdomen and handed the other end to her to hold. The room was so messy, he told her, that he might never find his way out again.

Taking a few tentative steps inside, tiptoeing along a narrow pathway bordered by boxes, she inspected the entire upstairs. Calling it an apartment was a euphemism. It was really just two small bedrooms with dormer windows and a bathroom. An unmade bed was the only clue to which one was Bonnie's bedroom and which was the catchall room. Calling this an office was laughable. There was no room to work! The bathroom was like the kitchen—mold growing in corners, a thick ring of dirt around the tub, the sink clogged with hair and gunk. Marnie turned on the tub faucet to observe the hot water flow and felt the handle practically shudder, heard the pipes groan, before water blasted through. But . . . it was hot. And flowed clean. Not rusty.

She turned off the water and left the bathroom, pausing to give the apartment one more look. Really, all it needed was a thorough purging, a few finished walls, a deep, deep clean, and some fresh paint. With a little hard work, she could soon have it livable.

Marnie came back downstairs and found Bonnie outside, moving the trash containers. She helped her wheel the last one around the corner, near the kitchen.

Bonnie brushed off her hands, looking pleased. "What do you say? Do we have a deal?" Marnie hesitated, just long enough for Bonnie to thrust her hand out. "Honey, I can tell you are ready for a new chapter in life. You gotta seize the day. Grab what the universe is offering to you. That's how I feel about my Al. If not now, then when?"

Not so fast, Marnie thought. There were still a few things to work out. "Bonnie, what plans do you have for your . . . belongings?"

Bonnie's forehead wrinkled in confusion. "Oh, you mean my crafts? Don't you worry. They're coming with me to Alaska. After all, you need something to do during those long cold winters." She wiggled her still outstretched hand. "So . . . do we have a deal?"

Grab what the universe is offering to you. Marnie knew what Bonnie meant, but she would edit it. Accept what the Lord was offering to her. A new chapter in life. If not now, then when? *Well?* a voice within her asked. *What's stopping you?*

An icy chill tingled down Marnie's spine, followed by goose bumps spreading all over her. An idea clicked into place, fitting perfectly, like a key in a door lock. She could see, suddenly, her path forward, as vividly as if it were playing out in front of her. While everything at the Creamery obviously needed TLC, Marnie didn't care. She didn't care about the condition of the building. This was where she wanted to work, and be, and live and retreat at the end of each day.

She had a strange sense that Philip wasn't far away. Not in a weird way, not like he was literally present. But he wasn't *absent*, the way she'd felt ever since the day he had died. So terribly absent. Dawn would roll her eyes at this kind of thinking, but to Marnie, it was almost as if Philip had sent her here, knowing that this was the one place where she would fully heal.

She asked a one-word silent prayer to the Lord. *Yes?*

Yes, came the answer.

Yes, yes, yes, yes, yes . . .

Marnie reached out and shook her hand. "If we can come to an agreement on the purchase price, then yes, we have a deal."

"Wonderful!" Bonnie nodded enthusiastically, with what seemed to be great relief. "Is Saturday too soon to sign the papers?"

"Um, Bonnie, I haven't actually made an offer yet."

Bonnie pointed to the sign. "That's my bargain basement price."

Marnie took out a piece of paper and scribbled down a figure. "It's all I can offer you. I know it's lower than you listed on the sign, but I could give you all cash. Talk it over with someone you trust. Your sister, maybe. Then get back to me."

Bonnie read the slip of paper. Her face crumbled.

Chapter

FIVE

Ice cream is cheaper than therapy.

—Anonymous

Wednesday, April 16

When Mom came back from a long walk into downtown Chatham with an announcement that would change their lives, Dawn held up her hand to stop her. "No thanks." The last time Mom said that, she had bought an alpaca with plans to sell its wool. The alpaca slipped out of the backyard, ate leaves from a neighbor's oleander bush, and died.

Dawn grabbed a can of soda and went out on the hotel room deck, settled into a glider rocker, looked out at the vast Atlantic Ocean, and watched the seagulls soar across the surf. She closed her eyes, enjoying the gentle sea breeze. Cape Cod was as idyllic a paradise as any honeymooner could want.

"Dawn, this is a wonderful surprise." Mom plopped down in the other gliding rocker on the deck. "It's something your dad and I had talked about for years."

One eye opened. "Dad?"

"I have sampled every ice cream shop up and down the streets of Chatham. Guess what I've discovered? Nothing compares to your vanilla ice cream. There's not a single shop here that holds a candle to your ice cream."

Ice cream making was a hobby Dawn shared with her dad. It was their special thing. During Dawn's senior year of high school, Mom had given her and Dad a gift to attend a weekend certification program at Penn State's Ice Cream School. It was an intensive workshop for hobbyists, though there were a few people who planned to open their own ice cream shops. To Dawn's surprise, she liked making ice cream. A lot. And she was good at it. Really good. "So that's your life-changing surprise?"

"That's not my surprise. That was my reconnaissance. My information gathering."

Dawn thought Mom's voice had a funny little lift to it, like she was saying one thing and thinking another. She opened her soda can, sensing a change in the air. Like that weird stillness right before thunder and lightning struck.

"I was walking around Chatham and saw the owner of an ice cream shop put a For Sale sign in her window." Mom cupped her knees with her hands like she did whenever she was excited about something. "Well, Dawn, honey, brace yourself. Today, I put in an offer to buy that very ice cream shop. Right here. In Chatham!"

Dawn stared at her mother, open-mouthed. "You did WHAT?" She set the soda can down on the table with a *thunk* that sent a spray of liquid all over the tabletop. "Please tell me you're joking."

Mom looked a little taken aback. "No, I'm not joking." She started mopping the spilled soda with a tissue. "When I saw the Main Street Creamery, I just knew. It was meant to be."

Dawn clenched her fists. On Main Street, of all streets. Of all towns. Chatham, Massachusetts—one of the most expensive beach towns in the entire country. "I never would have brought you with me this week if I thought you were going to do something crazy like this."

Silence fell, strained, before Mom broke it. "I can't explain it, Dawn, but this is my destiny."

"And where do you think the money is coming from to buy it?"

"From your father's life insurance policy," Mom answered smoothly.

"Dad bought that life insurance policy to keep you secure. He didn't buy it so that you could blow it all on a whim." Dawn stared at her mother—the long hair pulled back in a loose bun, the hoop earrings and maxi dress that made her seem like an ageless hippie—and saw instead the signs of age. Strands of white sprinkled through her reddish hair, crows' feet fanned out from her blue eyes. And she thought she'd noticed a varicose vein or two running down the back of her knees. In a gentler voice, Dawn said, "Mom, you don't even know how to make ice cream."

"I've spent hours watching you and your dad make dozens and dozens—hundreds—of batches. You both just never let me join in."

"I've seen the way you cook. You throw things together and voilà, it comes out. Ice cream isn't like that. It's an exacting science. To even consider being in the food industry business, you have to make a repeatable product."

Mom gave her a curious look. "A repeatable product?"

"Every batch of ice cream has to taste the same as the one before. It's the only way to gain customer loyalty."

"See?" Mom lifted her palms in the air, like a problem had just gotten solved. "You're a whiz at this. A natural."

Dawn squeezed her eyes shut. Too much was happening too quickly and she was going to need a minute to process everything. She pressed her hands on her knees, grateful she was sitting so she didn't have to worry about freaking out and fainting. She gathered her thoughts, trying to find a way to break through her mom's tangled thinking and bring her to reason. "A week like this can make it seem that all of life should be—maybe even could be—like a vacation. But it can't be like that."

"Why not?"

Dawn ignored her question and asked one of her own. "What would Dad have to say about this? He hasn't even been gone a year. Everybody knows that you're not supposed to make any big decisions that first year. Stay the course, that's what everyone told us. No major changes."

"I think . . . no, I *know* he'd be thrilled."

Dawn scoffed. "Dad would never, ever support this idea of moving to Chatham. Of buying a business. He would say that this time, you've gone too far."

A shadow of irritation crossed Mom's face. "That's not true. We talked a lot about ideas for retirement. Downsizing, simplifying, moving to the coast—"

"Cape Cod is not just the coast. It's a destination spot for everyone up and down the I-95 corridor." Dawn folded her arms against her chest. "What about winters?"

"What about them?"

"People don't eat ice cream in the winter. That's why Penn State's Ice Cream School is held in January."

"It is a grave error to think that ice cream consumption requires hot weather." Mom waved that worry away. "I can't remember who said that, but I agree with them. However, I am aware there's a substantial drop in tourism during the winter. So . . . that's when the Main Street Creamery becomes a coffee shop for the locals. A gathering place. The heart of the town. Like the Brewster General Store."

Okay. Switch tactics. "Where will you live? In case you hadn't noticed, Chatham isn't cheap."

A Cheshire cat smile covered Mom's face, like she'd been waiting for that question. "Would you believe that there's an apartment in the upstairs of the Creamery?" She rocked her hand back and forth. "Sort of an apartment. Two bedrooms and a bathroom."

Dawn leaned forward in the rocker. "Mom, what about the cancer?"

Shifting in the rocker, Mom set her gaze on the ocean in the distance, beyond the bar. A few puffy white clouds moved lazily along the horizon. "What about it?"

"You've got cancer."

"Had cancer. It's gone."

"But maybe it's causing you to act even crazier than you normally do."

"All a brush with cancer did was to make me realize I'm not bulletproof. I won't be here forever, so I might as well get rolling on those big plans your dad and I used to have."

Dad never had any big plans. Mom was the one with the big plans. Dawn's father was thoroughly content living his life in a suburb of Boston, a respected electrician, a faithful deacon at his church, a man who played tennis on a public court every Saturday morning with the three same friends. But then, nearly a year ago, Dad died. There'd been no warning. Losing him, so suddenly and unexpectedly, changed everything. Dawn and her mom were still working through the aftermath of losing that wonderful, thoroughly predictable man.

But this?

"Mom, Florida makes sense. Not Cape Cod. It's completely illogical to uproot and move here. You can't risk the money you have. Not at your age."

"My age?" She coughed a laugh, giving her a *look*. "Fifty-eight? You think that's old? I know a woman who started medical school at sixty. Another friend started law school in her fifties. And then—"

"Call the shop owner and tell him or her you've changed your mind. Tell them you've got buyer's remorse."

Mom's eyebrows lifted in surprise. "But I don't have any remorse."

"Mother. You have to be sensible."

"I am being sensible." Mom's chin came up a notch, as if preparing to defend herself. "I didn't realize how much I needed this until the idea presented itself to me, and now I feel I'd just perish without it. We need this, both of us. We both need some fresh air in our lives. A new vocation. New people. New horizons. Dawn, this will be such a thrill for us."

"Me? NO way. I am not leaving Boston to make ice cream." She pinched her finger and thumb together. "I am *this close* to becoming a partner in the firm. I am on the brink of complete financial security for the rest of my life."

"But at what cost? You've never been passionate about your work, not the way you are about making ice cream. Making it, experimenting with it, sharing it. You're happiest when you're making ice cream."

"I'm happy with my work." Dawn hoped she sounded genuine. "Happy enough."

"Oh, honey. Isn't life supposed to be more than just 'happy enough'?"

How to answer that? Dawn didn't like to let herself consider what a happy life might look like. If she'd learned anything this last year, it's that there wasn't really much stability in life. You could try as hard as you could to create the life you wanted and the rug could still be pulled out from under you at any moment.

"Dawn," her mom said in a tone so tender it almost hurt, "what are you so afraid of? Why is change so difficult for you?"

Dawn looked away. What was she afraid of? She couldn't articulate it, couldn't even frame it. She still couldn't talk about what had happened with Kevin. She didn't want to have to acknowledge that Kevin had fallen out of love with her. That was a horrible discovery to hear from the man whom she loved dearly, the man she planned to marry and spend the rest of her life with. She fought back sudden tears as her mind flitted through snapshots of the past: meeting Kevin at fourteen, dating at seventeen, going to the same college, living near each other in Boston. She could hardly remember a time without Kevin in her life. Nearly every memory, every picture on her phone, included him.

How do you get over something like that? How do you trust someone again? Love someone again? She wasn't sure she ever could.

Dawn glanced over at her mom, wondering if she was still waiting for an answer. But her mom was staring out at the ocean, a pensive expression on her face. A thought occurred to her. "Mom, did you sign anything?"

"No. But I shook hands with the owner. Bonnie is her name. Bonnie Snow."

Oh, thank heavens. Nothing in writing. Nothing could be proved. It was simply a conversation between a shop owner and a nutty tourist. This was just another one of Mom's big ideas, something they would laugh about later.

"I have a bone-deep feeling about this, Dawn. It's meant to be. Something wonderful is going to happen. I just have to be brave enough to take this chance."

Calmer now, Dawn allowed a smile to tug at the corners of her mouth. Mom and her weird bone-deep feelings. "I've heard that same phrase from you for twenty-seven years, Mom. You start something with lots of enthusiasm, then when it gets difficult, you lose interest and move on to something else."

A cloud passed over Mom's face. Her shoulders slumped slightly. "Well, don't worry. I made a lowball offer. Chances are, Bonnie will refuse it."

"Think so? Oh, that would be great!"

And just like that, Mom's happy mood had fizzled to nothing. Dawn felt like a joy thief. She wondered if this might be one of the reasons Kevin didn't want to marry her. Once he had told her that she had a knack for popping people's balloons with reality checks. Was that true? Probably. She preferred to think of it as remembering the facts. She was a CPA, for Pete's sake. Her work was a study of detail and fact, finding and fixing clients' mistakes. And *this* was a massive mistake. It was a ridiculous notion to buy a tired old ice cream shop in an expensive beach town . . . while on vacation! She remembered something her dad used to say: Never invest with your heart, only with your stomach.

A cell phone chirped from inside the room and Mom rose to answer it. A minute or two later, she returned to the deck with a funny look on her face, like a child waking up on Christmas morning. "Bonnie accepted my offer for the ice cream shop. No conditions. As is. She's already made some phone calls to set things into motion." She covered her mouth with her hands, bowed her head, and when she lifted it again, she was beaming. "This is *wonderful.* Dawn, we're in the ice cream business!"

Dawn pressed her fingers to her cheeks. This was her fault. She should never have brought her mother on her botched honeymoon. After a long pause, she dropped her hands to her lap. "I'll fix this. I'll get you out of it."

Slowly, firmly, Mom shook her head. "I don't want to get out of it. I want to stay right here. I want to wake up that weary ice cream shop and give it a new lease on life. This is my fresh start. My new beginning. I'd hoped it might be yours, too, but that's up to you." She looked out at the ocean, took in a few deep breaths—she called those her cleansing breaths—released them and smiled. "Wow, wow, wow. I am now officially a small business owner on Cape Cod."

One who had never ever made ice cream. Not once.

Chapter
SIX

What you take out is as important as what you put in.
What you don't say is as important as what you do.

—Jeni Britton Bauer, founder of
Jeni's Splendid Ice Creams

Wednesday, April 16

It had come as no surprise to Marnie that she hadn't had long to wait for an answer from Bonnie, but she'd thought surely her lowball offer would be countered. Surely, Bonnie's sister would talk her out of accepting it. Surely, there'd be a little more time to think this through. But no. Bonnie accepted her lowball offer and had already put a call in to someone— her title company? Her real estate agent? This was all new for Marnie and she wasn't sure what the process was to start the paperwork. To close the sale in rapid time. It was happening, and fast. Saturday morning, eleven o'clock, Bonnie said. Don't be late, she added.

Slowly, Marnie had gone back to the deck where she'd left Dawn and sat back down in the gliding rocker. She had taken in a deep cleansing breath, let it out, braced herself . . . and given her the news.

Dawn's reaction to Bonnie's *acceptance* of Marnie's offer had been similar to her horror at discovering her mother had *made* an offer to buy a run-down ice cream shop. Dawn pointed out every single reason why this ice cream shop was a ridiculous idea—and nothing she said could be disputed. It was an outlandish, impulsive thing to do. Still, Marnie was determined to see it through, a feeling she hadn't had for a very long time.

"Dawn, I'm not expecting you to stay here and help me with this venture. Not if you don't want to. But you're not going to talk me out of it either. I want to do this. I need to do this."

"You *need* to open an ice cream shop?" Dawn said in a flat voice. "How is that a need? From my perspective, you're risking your entire future on a pipe dream."

"Let's start with the simple facts: everybody loves ice cream."

"Sure, but it isn't all hot fudge sundaes and gummy bear toppings. There's a lot more to running an ice cream shop than just picking flavors, perfecting the scoop, and sprinkling on toppings. Not to mention how seasonal it is."

"That's why I'm adding coffee and tea and baked goods. It'll help the shop stay profitable through the shoulder seasons and the winter." Those were Bonnie's suggestions and they sounded like good ones to Marnie.

Rubbing her temples, Dawn said, "I keep thinking this is all because of the cancer."

Marnie hadn't expected that tactic from Dawn. It sent an icy shiver down her spine. "No. Not at all. It's time for a change, that's all. I suppose . . . if anything, that brief bout of cancer reminded me that life is passing quickly. I can't live in the past any longer. You must understand. Isn't that what Kevin complained about? Feeling trapped in a life he wasn't sure he wanted to live?" She didn't mean to say that, not at all—it had just popped out.

The look on Dawn's face.

Marnie had stepped in it, for sure. She let the air clear. "I just feel like I've been stuck. Stuck is wrong. Your dad wouldn't have wanted me to remain stuck." *Or you, either*, but she swallowed that down.

Dawn gave her an ironic look. "But aren't you doing this *for* Dad? He was the one who was crazy about ice cream. Not you."

"I was crazy about it. I am crazy about it. Eating it."

"You may be the greatest indulger of ice cream in the northeast, but that doesn't mean you're going to like making and selling ice cream. Every single day. For years and years and years."

"I know I'll enjoy selling it. I like meeting people."

"A lot of people! Do you realize how many people have to come through a shop, buying one little cone of ice cream, just to break even?"

No, Marnie hadn't considered these points.

"Mom, you said yourself that the owner was eager to sell. Clearly, she hasn't had much success in Chatham."

"Apparently, Bonnie's ice cream was terrible. I'm going to start with the best ice cream in the world."

Dawn rolled her eyes. "You've never made a single batch of ice cream."

Marnie cast a sideways glance at her daughter. "You could teach me."

Dawn lifted a hand like a stop sign. "Before we launch into the actual mechanics of making ice cream, I really want to hear your answer to this question, Mom. Are you doing this *for* Dad? He was the ice cream aficionado in the family. You say you want to move forward, but to me, it sounds like you are sailing into the past, determined to stay there."

Marnie paused, taking a moment to gather her thoughts. She knew she needed to express this carefully. "Not *for* your dad, but because of him. His passion for ice cream was such a delight, Dawn. When I first met him, he had big plans to have his own ice cream store."

"What happened?"

"Life got in the way."

"Me, you mean."

Marnie pressed her hands against the table. "Life . . . as in, family responsibilities. All ones that your dad was so grateful for. As you know, he was a very responsible guy. But there was a little side to him that he kept hidden. A creative flair."

"The ice cream side."

"Yes. Exactly! About the time you were getting ready to leave for college, I could see that his spark was flickering. He seemed, well, to be perfectly honest, he was getting depressed. That was the year I sent you both to ice cream school. And it worked. Suddenly, he was making ice cream each night and on weekends, and even when you went to college, the two of you would talk about his latest efforts. It wasn't just about ice cream. It was about keeping that spark of creativity that gives so much joy to life, keeping it alive and well in your dad." These last few months, Marnie realized her own spark of creativity was in danger of flickering out. Life was just getting too hard. She'd never admit that to Dawn, though. Not to anyone.

Dawn rose from the rocker and went to the deck's railing, resting her forearms on the edge, staring at the ocean. She stayed there so long that Marnie thought their conversation had ended and not in a good way. After a painfully long time, Dawn let out a deep exhale and turned around.

"I'll stay through Labor Day."

Marnie's eyebrows lifted in surprise. "You'll stay?"

"Only until Labor Day. I'll take some time off of work and help you get the business started."

"What if your company won't let you?"

"They'll let me. I'm sure of it. I didn't take any time off when Dad died. And I only took a week for my . . . um . . . my

72

honeymoon. I have six weeks of accrued vacation. After that, I'll ask for a leave of absence."

"But—"

Dawn held two fingers in the air. "I'll stay on two conditions. One, there's a cancer support group that meets on Saturday mornings at the local community center. You have to attend it. At least once."

Marnie's mouth dropped. "Why would I want to do that?"

"Because you're living in denial."

Not true! So not true. She had just chosen to not think about it. As far as she was concerned, her brush with cancer was over and done with. "What's the second condition?"

"If by Labor Day, we haven't turned a profit, then we sell it. As in, to the first buyer that makes an offer."

Marnie bit her lower lip. "What exactly do you mean by a profit?"

"Exactly what it sounds like. I'm not going to let you hemorrhage Dad's life insurance policy on a melting ice cream cone."

Marnie was floored. She had prepared herself for battle. The most she had hoped for was to talk Dawn into staying in Chatham an extra day or so to help her wade through the paperwork of the sale. But she never dreamed Dawn would stay long enough to get the store opened, up and running. She rose from the rocking chair, folded her arms around Dawn and pulled her close. "It's a deal." She thought she'd better agree before Dawn saw the actual condition of the shop.

●　●　●

On the drive over to see this Main Street Creamery building that Mom had bought, Dawn remained silent. As did Mom. She knew that her mom was tense—could see it in the way her hands kept gripping and releasing the steering wheel.

No doubt Mom was wondering what had been running through Dawn's mind when she suddenly agreed to stay in

Chatham through the summer. Oh, the look on Mom's face! Shock, followed by astonished delight.

What had been running through Dawn's mind? It was an imagined conversation with her father. She could practically hear him say, *Give her this chance, Dawn.* Dad had always gotten a kick out of Mom's wacky plans, most of which fell apart. But he never discouraged her or made fun of her. Not like Dawn did.

Sometimes it was difficult to have such an open-minded woman for a mother. Dawn was in second grade when she first realized her mom was different than other moms. Marnie had volunteered to lead Dawn's Brownie Girl Scout troop. One afternoon, they had an art project with paint. Mom always planned for masterpieces but never planned for cleanup. There were no smocks, no paper towels, no soap and water. One little girl, Elisa, started to paint her arms and all the other Brownies followed along. And then Mom joined in! By the time the mothers came to pick up their Brownies, paint was everywhere. On the Brownies' arms, legs, faces, hair, uniforms. You couldn't even tell the dresses were once brown.

Things got worse. Elisa's psoriasis condition was aggravated by the paint on her body and she ended up in the ER that evening. Mom felt it was all a gross overreaction, that Elisa could be a bit of a hypochondriac, that kids will be kids and it was just an afternoon of artistic expression, of freedom. The other mothers felt differently. They had a secret meeting and voted to replace Marnie with Elisa's mom as Brownie leader. Marnie took the coup in stride, but Dawn felt humiliated.

Marnie Dixon always meant well, but things often went so terribly wrong. Dad was more forgiving than Dawn about cleaning up Mom's messes.

And that's why Dawn would stay here through Labor Day. She would help clean up this current mess her mom had gotten herself into, for her dad's sake. Maybe . . . for her own sake too.

She could put all the blame on her mom, but the truth was, this ridiculous business venture gave her a solid-gold excuse to stay away from Boston. From Kevin.

That's what she'd been thinking on the short drive from the Chatham Bars Inn to the downtown area. And then Mom parked the car and Dawn got her first look at the Main Street Creamery and her heart dropped to her stomach. It was worse than she thought. So run-down, so neglected. Drab and dreary.

Mom read her mind. "Now, Dawn, remember, I bought it as is and I got a great deal on this building. Almost miraculous!"

"Oh yeah. Behold the miracle," Dawn said, her words dripping with sarcasm. She got out of the car and walked around the entire building, then returned to the car, furious. "A fire? There was a fire in this building? What were you thinking?"

"Dawn . . . please try to see it not as it is, but what it could be. Just think for a moment. We own a piece of property on Main Street in Chatham, Massachusetts, one of the best main streets in the entire country."

Dawn shook her head vigorously. She pointed to her mom. "You own it. Not me. I'm just your consultant." But she couldn't deny that the location was pretty incredible. Her spirits lifted with a possibility: if they knocked down the building, maybe they could sell the property more easily—

"Try to see everything through my eyes," Mom said, interrupting Dawn's train of thought. "The roof can be fixed. So can everything else inside."

Dawn let out a heavy sigh. "Let's go inside."

They got out of the car and went to the front door. Mom lifted the brass knocker of an ice cream cone on the door once, twice, three times. "Bummer. Bonnie must have gone out. We'll just have to wait for the full tour."

She didn't seem at all disappointed. Suspiciously so. How bad could it be inside? Pretty bad, if the interior was anything like the exterior. Dawn tried peering in each window, but the sun was setting and it was getting too dark to see much of anything.

The drive back to the Chatham Bars Inn was a silent one. Mom seemed relaxed, a smile kept tugging at her lips, as if she was thinking of all kinds of ideas for the Main Street Creamery. This time, Dawn did the driving, hands clenched around the steering wheel, fingernails digging into her palms. Two thoughts kept circling in her mind: *Do I know any good lawyers who can untangle my mother's mess?*

And the other was, *Where did I put that recipe for vanilla ice cream?*

Chapter
SEVEN

Ice cream brings people together.
—Doug Ducey, politician

Wednesday, April 16

That evening, a rainstorm blew through the Cape. A good night to stay inside and read. Marnie had brought a novel Maeve had given her and sat down with it, but her mind was too full to concentrate. She kept thinking of calls she needed to make, details she needed to iron out before Saturday's closing on the Creamery. She had to keep pinching herself that she was going to live in Chatham for good, that she was going to run an ice cream shop—she could hardly believe what was happening!

She gave up on reading and jumped up to look for her phone. It was on the nightstand by her bed. As she reached for it, she noticed a leaflet placed on her pillow.

Cancer Support Group. We meet every Saturday morning at the community center.

"You promised that you'd go."

She whirled around to face Dawn as she came out of the bathroom, toweling dry her hair. "It's just not necessary."

"Mom, you're ignoring something really big in your life."

"I'm not ignoring it at all. I've done everything my doctors had wanted me to do."

"Except deal with it. On the inside." Dawn plopped down on the bed opposite her. "I want you to go to this support group."

"I don't want to hear everyone's cancer stories."

"Just try it." When Marnie didn't respond, Dawn said, "Look. I have uprooted my life for you for the next few months. I'm asking you to go to this one little meeting. It's the least you can do for me." She wrapped her hair in the towel and twisted it, tucking in the end. "I think you're in for a surprise. There's just nothing like talking to people who've walked the walk. Pretty sure it's all women too."

Marnie frowned.

"It's this Saturday morning at nine o'clock. Our escrow appointment is at eleven. There's nothing you can do to the shop until you're handed the keys. Mom, just try it one time. I'll go with you if you like."

"Just one time?"

Dawn nodded.

After a taut moment, Marnie let out an exasperated sigh. "Fine. I'll go. But I'll go alone."

Dawn's cell phone rang and she pulled it out of her pocket. "It's Brynn. I should probably take this. She's called a couple of times. I think she's worried about me."

"Go ahead. In fact, that reminds me that I wanted to call Maeve. I think I'll go down to the lobby and make the call."

Marnie closed the door behind her and smiled when she heard Dawn laugh at something Brynn must have said. It felt good, really good, to hear Dawn laugh.

●　●　●

"Hey there. You're impossible to get hold of!"

"I'm sorry," Dawn said, pleased to hear her best friend's voice. "It's been surprisingly . . . busy here."

"What have you been up to? Are you having fun? I picture you sitting on the beach each day, drinking one iced tea after another."

"Pretty close." That described the first few days . . . quiet and tranquil . . . up until this afternoon. Now Dawn felt as if her blood pressure had permanently spiked.

"Tell me everything. Don't leave anything out."

Oh boy. This was it. Saying it out loud. Making it real. Dawn took in a deep breath. "Mom bought a dumpy old building and wants to turn it into an ice cream store. And I'm going to stay through the summer to help her get it up and going."

Silence. Followed by more silence.

Dawn could just imagine Brynn, a trained engineer, with her pretty face scrunched up in confusion as she tried to make sense of what she'd just heard.

"Did I misdial? I was calling my friend Dawn Dixon, who fills out her daily planner weeks in advance. Who plans out her day in fifteen-minute increments."

"Very funny. This is another side of me. The spontaneous Dawn, who's flexible and easygoing and can pivot on a dime."

Brynn burst out with a laugh. "That's why you have a sign on your desk that says 'I adore spontaneity, providing it is carefully planned.'"

Dawn cringed. She loved that sign. "I'm coming back after Labor Day. Don't worry. I'll cover the rent."

"I'm not worried about the rent. I'm worried about you."

"I'm fine." Dawn started walking around the room, a little anxiously. "There's nothing to worry about. Really. Consider it an adventure with my mother. You know, *Travels with Marnie*."

"That's exactly what worries me. You always complain your mom drives you crazy."

"She did. And does." Dawn let out a deep sigh. Surprisingly, it was filled with relief. "But she's also right about something. I need a change." She just couldn't face going back to her Boston life right now.

"Go on a safari to Africa! Go on a cruise to Antarctica. But don't go into the ice cream shop business with your mother."

"Why don't you come and visit us this summer?"

Brynn wouldn't let up. "Dawn, you know the grim statistics of small businesses. The failure rate for start-ups is 90 percent. And you know why—lack of financing, ineffective marketing, not having expertise in the industry, poor partnerships. That's you and your mom, right there."

Dawn stopped pacing. Brynn had a demanding job as a civic engineer for the city of Boston and had learned how to work with tough construction types, most of whom were chauvinistic. They would take one look at Brynn—small and slender, dark-haired and doe-eyed—and try to intimidate her. They would try, and they would fail. They underestimated Brynn. She might be tiny, but she never backed down.

"And of all things . . . ice cream!"

"What's wrong with ice cream?" Dawn stiffened. "Ice cream has always been a big deal to my family. It's our . . . thing."

"Right . . . but it was always about you and your dad. This is you and your *mom*. I mean, I love your mom . . . I've always loved her. She's the best! Unlike my mom, she never forgets my birthday. But the two of you working together sounds like a disaster in the making."

Dawn felt herself bristle. Had she asked Brynn for advice? No.

"What's your role in this?"

"I'll be making ice cream."

Brynn let out a groan. "It's just . . . this is so out of character for you. What if you accidentally poison someone?"

Dawn felt deflated. She had hoped for more support from Brynn. "You know how careful I am. I would never let that happen." She decided not to press Brynn for a date to visit after all.

"Dawn . . . is this what *you* want?"

A few days ago, pre-honeymoon, she might have given Brynn a different answer. She might have said that she felt she had no choice. But somehow, now she knew she did have a choice, and that her choice had been to stay. "I want to help Mom. This is a good change for her. And frankly, if all we do is fix up the ice cream shop and sell it after Labor Day without completely losing our shirt, then it'll be worth it."

"Have you thought about what this will mean to your career? Dawn, what if you miss out on a chance to become partner?"

"I'm not worried. They know me. They know I'll be back in the saddle after Labor Day, raring to go." She was counting on it. "Look, Brynn, I know I should have told you sooner, but Mom didn't want me to. She just finished treatment for breast cancer."

Long pause. "Is she okay?"

"Yes. Really. She's fine. It's just that sometimes things happen that you never expect, and all you can do is to step up to the plate."

Brynn took that in, and then her voice gentled. "So what should I tell Kevin?"

"Kevin?"

"He's texted me twice, asking if I've heard from you this week."

Why? Was it pity? Dawn's throat grew tight as she struggled to hold back the surge of emotion. "There's no need to tell Kevin anything. In fact, please keep everything confidential that I've told you tonight. Everything goes in the cone of silence. Look, I'd better get off. Mom left the room to give me privacy, but she should be back soon. I promise I'll stay in touch."

"You promise? I'm really worried about you."

For Pete's sake! Did she sound so pitiable? Dawn reminded herself that Brynn could always find something to worry about, whether it was a forecast of bad weather or the nuclear arms buildup of North Korea or the rising price of chocolate. "Yes, I promise." She knew Brynn meant well. "I'll call again soon." She pressed the off button and tossed the phone on her pillow, then plopped sideways on the bed, bothered.

Somehow, Brynn had hit the nail on every single anxious thought that had been running through Dawn's mind since Mom had told her she'd bought the Main Street Creamery. The failure rate of small businesses, their lack of expertise, their very different styles, plus how out of character this was for Dawn. But accidentally poisoning a customer? That ratcheted Dawn's worries up to an entirely new level.

Mom didn't return to the room for a long time, and when she did, she looked as preoccupied as Dawn felt. She wondered if Maeve reacted to the ice cream shop the way Brynn did. "Good conversation with Aunt Maeve?"

Mom glanced up, as if she'd forgotten Dawn was in the room. "Better than good. She's . . . in love."

"Maeve O'Shea? At her age?"

Mom gave her a *look*. "Love does not have an expiration date."

Dawn grinned. Maybe not, but it was weird to think of old people falling in love. "So who's she in love with?"

Mom had gone into the bathroom to change into her nightgown and popped her head out the door. "Do you remember the Grayson family? Paul Grayson was a radio sports announcer."

"I do. I remember something about a fire, and his wife died in it, and then he lost his voice."

"That's the condensed version, but yes, that's him. He has three daughters. I don't think you were in school with any of them. They left Needham and moved to Maine to run a summer camp on an island." She turned on the water to brush her teeth.

Dawn waited until Mom had finished brushing. "Aunt Maeve wouldn't consider leaving Needham for island living, would she?"

"She might." She popped her head out of the bathroom again, this time holding a washcloth. Scrubbing her face, she said, "Her son Rick married one of Paul's daughters—Maddie—and now they have a baby."

"Well, I was way off. I could tell you were bothered, but I never dreamed it was because Aunt Maeve had fallen in love."

"I'm thrilled for Maeve." Mom looked at her curiously. "What makes you think I'm bothered?"

"You just seem a little preoccupied. I figured Aunt Maeve might have read you the riot act about buying the ice cream shop." Like Brynn had done, so very effectively.

"No. Maeve loved the whole idea." Thoughtfully, Mom added, "Frankly, she couldn't be more supportive." She climbed into bed and picked up her novel.

Glancing over at her mom now and then, Dawn noticed she stayed on the same page. *Yup. Preoccupied.* Just like Dawn was.

That night, Dawn slept fitfully, tossing and turning with visions of gloppy, soupy ice cream disasters, one right after the other.

She didn't want to poison anyone.

Chapter
EIGHT

If you want to create a beautiful ice cream, you must have
the soul of an artist but think like a scientist.

—Jeni Britton Bauer, founder of
Jeni's Splendid Ice Creams

Thursday, April 17

What worried Dawn most about running an ice cream shop
was whether they could get enough customers in the door just
to break even. On Thursday morning, as the sky was still full
of gray clouds from last night's rainstorm, while Mom was
out doing who knew what, Dawn stayed in the hotel room to
run numbers, check the internet, and make calls to compare
prices for raw materials. Due diligence had always been her
favorite task at work, but she'd never had any skin in the game.
This time she did. This was personal.

And the news was awful.

Her heart sank when she broke everything down and discovered that they would need to sell at least 150 ice cream

cones every single day just to stay afloat. They would have to sell five cones per half hour. All summer long.

No way. It wasn't possible.

What was wrong with her? She was doing everything backward! Due diligence came first and foremost. She was turning into her *mother*. She grabbed her phone and called Mom. "Find out from Bonnie when we go inside the Creamery."

"Why?"

"There are so many unknown pieces to this."

"Dawn, calm down."

"I'm very calm. I've been trying to find out how much money we're going to need just to get the shop in working order. That's why I want to get into the Creamery and see its condition."

She heard a deep sigh. "Dawn, Saturday is only two days away. Bonnie is doing all she can to expedite the sale, plus move to Alaska. She's driving all by herself, did I tell you that?"

No, but Dawn didn't really care.

"Honey, there's plenty of time to figure everything out. It's turning into a beautiful day. The skies are clearing and the afternoon temperature is supposed to get into the seventies. You only have two more days at the Chatham Bars Inn. Why don't you close your computer and go lie on the beach?"

That did sound nice. Dawn went out to the deck and gazed at the ocean. She'd already reviewed the contract Bonnie had sent over. It was clean and simple, a standard contract of sale for an as-is purchase of property, and she was using a bona fide title insurance company. It all seemed legit. Mom had said she would call the bank today to start the process to get money wired to the title insurance company by Saturday morning. Barring any unseen scenario—like Bonnie could have a fight with Alaska Al and want her ice cream shop back—the sale was going to go through. And even Dawn had to admit, Mom had bought the property for a song.

But it was all happening so fast. She knew, from her work experience, that if things went too fast, mistakes were often overlooked. What could she be missing in this transaction? What might be getting overlooked?

Oh no.

She shook her head. She was tumbling down the rabbit hole into Marnie's World! She called her mom back. "I need to get inside the Creamery. Immediately."

Silence.

"Mother, you're not trying to hide anything, are you?"

"No, of course not. I just want to be sensitive to Bonnie."

"This is business, Mom. No sensitivity allowed. If we can't get in today, then tomorrow. I want to see that ice cream machine before we take possession." In a softer tone she said, "If you'll do that for me, that one thing, then I will head to the beach. I promise."

"Fine. Let's plan on a Friday walk-through." On that, she hung up.

Mom was right about one thing. The groomless honeymoon at the Chatham Bars Inn was coming to an end. Dawn spun on her heels, closed her computer, grabbed her bathing suit, and changed into it, longing to get to the beach and listen to the lulling rhythm of the waves. On the way to the lobby, she reviewed how to tell her boss that she needed to take an extended leave of absence. She dreaded that phone call. Before she made it, she wanted to see the ice cream machine in the Creamery, first. She still had plenty of doubts about this venture, and there were only two days left to worm their way out of it.

* * *

The ice cream machine! Marnie had been waiting for Dawn to raise that topic. If Dawn saw the condition of the ice cream machine that Bonnie had been using in the Creamery, she would bring an immediate stop to the sale. Then she would have her mother committed to an insane asylum.

But Marnie had figured a way around that bleak scenario. There was a perfect, top of the line, brand-new—and best of all, extremely meaningful—ice cream machine available, but it was in Needham, out in Philip's workshop.

The ice cream machine had been Marnie's gift to Philip for their thirtieth wedding anniversary. He had been using a stand mixer with a freezable mixing bowl. It worked, but it frustrated him to be making only one batch at a time. It frustrated Marnie because he claimed a large chunk of the kitchen freezer as a permanent home for the mixing bowl. She had scrimped and saved to set aside enough money, and gave him a brochure for an Emery Thompson 2-quart batch freezer, tied with a red ribbon. Philip was delighted but hesitated to pull the trigger and make the order. When Marnie told him that she would order it if he didn't, he sheepishly admitted that if he were to buy an ice cream machine, he wanted to upgrade—not to the 3-quart batch freezer, but to the 6-quart batch freezer. A much larger machine with more capacity, and it would take up valuable kitchen counter space, but it was what he wanted. One step closer to his dream of having his own ice cream shop someday, and she wasn't going to stop him. Shortly before his accident, Philip had put the order in.

In the crisis of Philip's sudden death, Marnie had forgotten all about the ice cream machine until a truck arrived at their house. She remembered the rainy day when two delivery men stood on her porch stoop, asking where she wanted it to go. She thought about refusing delivery, sending it back, explaining to Emery Thompson about Philip's untimely death. They were a family-run business; she was pretty sure they would understand.

The words wouldn't come. Instead, she ended up asking

the delivery men to put it in Philip's workshop behind the garage and keep the packaging on it. She couldn't just refuse the delivery. But then again, she didn't know what to do with it.

Until now.

Last evening, she'd made a few calls down in the lobby. The last one she had made was to ask her friend Maeve for a big favor: to go to the Needham house early Thursday morning and open Philip's workshop. Marnie had scheduled a white-gloved delivery service to come for the machine and deliver it, same day, to the Main Street Creamery in Chatham, Massachusetts.

Bonnie had given her a key, so Marnie was waiting at the Creamery for the shipping company to arrive, to show them exactly where she wanted it to be on the kitchen counter. Still in its wrapping, it looked brand new. She paid the delivery service an additional fee to take away the old machine.

But she hadn't volunteered any of that fast finagling to Dawn. She wouldn't lie. If Dawn asked her about it, she would tell her the truth. The whole truth, despite knowing how Dawn would react to it. Marnie knew she had spent a ridiculous amount of money to get the machine shipped here, practically halfway to buying a new one.

This one, though, was Philip's.

He was a frugal man, some called him cheap, but of this decision she knew he would approve. She thought of the many critiques he would make after visiting an ice cream parlor. "Running a business with someone else's used-up, tired old machine is a terrible business error" or "What is more important to your business investment than the one machine that makes the product you sell?" or "The ice cream machine is the core of the business."

Those were some of the many reasons that led him to purchase a $12,000 Emery Thompson 6-quart batch freezer. He wanted to be the sole owner of that machine, to know it inside and out, to have a commitment to it. It felt like a little part of him was here, with her, rooting for this venture.

After she had taken all the plastic wrapping out to the garbage container, she walked back into the kitchen. Before she left the Creamery, she plugged the machine into the outlet, and a sense that this was all meant to be washed over Marnie. A satisfied smile covered her face. She felt like she was finally back on track now, ready to move forward, to start her life over again in a town—she looked around the small kitchen—not just in a town but also in a home . . . waiting to be filled with happy memories.

* * *

Friday, April 18

On Friday afternoon, Dawn stood outside the Main Street Creamery and knocked on the door. Once, twice, three times. No answer. "I thought you said Bonnie was expecting us."

Mom took a key out and unlocked the door. "She said to go on in if she was out running errands."

"You have a *key*?"

"We've become . . . friendly." Mom walked inside and turned. "Come on in. Isn't there a lovely feeling to this old place?"

"Inanimate objects don't have feelings, Mom," Dawn said, looking around the room. Hard as she tried to find its magic, all she could see was the filth. It covered every surface. Stains all over the institutional gray indoor/outdoor carpet. Soot on the windows. And that ridiculously large ice cream display case! Dawn shuddered. It looked like it needed to be dipped in a vat of Clorox.

"Don't just look at the dirt. That can be fixed. Look at the beams on the ceiling, the large double-hung windows."

Dawn sighed. Maybe there was . . . potential. "Point me to the kitchen." This was the room she'd been most eager to see.

She didn't really care about the upstairs apartment. She knew they wouldn't be spending much time there. But the kitchen—that's where she would be all summer long.

She followed her mom past the stairs and into the galley kitchen, and she had to swallow a horrified gasp. The disgusting, charred kitchen with a bright blue tarp covering the hole in the roof. Bonnie's boxes were everywhere.

"Try to see the positives," Mom said.

Okay, Dawn thought. *Good advice.* She glanced at the countertops under Bonnie's boxes—stainless steel, which was a plus. Stainless steel sink too. Another plus. The stovetop hadn't been cleaned in way too long, but at least it was gas. She opened the chest freezer and checked the temperature. It was old, full of weird-looking frost-covered food that she hoped Bonnie wouldn't leave behind, but at least it was working correctly. Another plus.

And then something on the far end of the kitchen counter caught her eye. She walked toward it, almost in a daze, touching the handle, peering inside. A gleaming 6-quart Emery Thompson ice cream maker. "It's exactly the one Dad had always wanted to buy. The very same brand. The same model. This machine will last forever." She turned to look at her mom. "If I believed in signs, which I don't, but if I did . . . I'd say this was one."

Mom smiled. "Me too."

Chapter

NINE

Ice cream never asks silly questions. Ice cream understands.

—Anonymous

Saturday, April 19

Although Dawn had been awake long before her mother got ready to head to the cancer support group, she pretended to be asleep. She was still surprised that Mom didn't put up a bigger fuss about going to it, but then again, her mom was probably surprised that Dawn hadn't fought her tooth and nail after seeing the interior of the ice cream shop. Maybe they both had reasons for what they were doing that they weren't sharing with each other.

As soon as the room door clicked shut, Dawn grabbed her phone. Kevin had called twice yesterday—she didn't pick up—and she had one missed call from him already this morning. Normally, he would've texted or left a voice mail, but things weren't normal between them. They were broken.

For a brief second, she considered returning his call, but decided against it. The day was going to be full. They'd packed their bags last night, with a plan to meet at the title insurance company's office at eleven o'clock. For now, Dawn had a few hours left to herself before life made a swift left turn and she became a full-time ice cream maker.

She threw off the covers, rose from the bed, and changed into her running clothes. Not that she ran, not even jogged, but walking on the beach each morning had helped to lift her spirits from a looming depression—the oxygen-rich ocean air filled her lungs, the physical exercise boosted her energy. In more ways than one, she'd been in poor condition, out of shape. That was one of the reasons that made her decide to stay put and help her mom for the summer. She was just starting to heal here, and afraid she would lose it all if she returned home right now.

She crossed Shore Road to head to the beach and felt her phone vibrate in her yoga pants pocket. Caller ID showed Kevin's name. Again. She hesitated so long that she missed his call. Again, she debated calling him back, decided not to, and then a voice mail came in. She stopped to listen to it.

"Dawn, it's Kevin. I heard that you're taking a leave of absence from the firm. I just wanted to make sure you're okay. I wondered if . . . well, if it had to do with me. With us. I know you're up for partner soon, and I wouldn't want this . . . us . . . to get in the way of that. You've worked hard for that milestone. Um, if there's anything I can do, anything at all, let me know. Maybe you could . . . you know, give me a quick call. Just let me know everything's okay."

She wished he would stop being so nice. It was hard to hate him when he was nice. She decided to text him.

> Bought an ice cream shop on Cape Cod. Staying put for now.

Not ten seconds later, the bubble writing started and then her cell pinged with a text message:

YOU DID WHAT?

She smiled. It was a nice feeling to shake Kevin up. After all, she wasn't the kind of person who simply walked away without warning. Not like him.

And she was proud of Brynn for not telling Kevin her news. She decided she would invite her to come to the Cape after all. She tucked her phone in her yoga pants and started to walk along the water. She felt her phone vibrate again and stopped, chewing the inside of her cheek as she tried to decide if she should answer Kevin's call or ignore it. She answered. "What's up?"

"What do you think you're doing?"

"What am I doing? Trying to jog along the beach on a beautiful sunny morning, that's what." She planned to start jogging, anyway.

"Dawn, I need to know that you're okay."

"Okay? Of course I'm okay. Better than okay." She started walking. "I'm looking out at the sun over the Atlantic Ocean. How could I not be okay with this view?"

"That's not what I mean."

"What do you mean?"

"You're not seriously moving to Cape Cod to run an ice cream shop! This is a joke, right? You're upset with me and this is the way you're trying to make me feel more terrible than I already feel."

Dawn stopped in her tracks. That was the first time Kevin mentioned how he felt about breaking their engagement. It felt good to hear it, to know she wasn't the only one who was suffering. "It's not a joke. Mom bought the ice cream shop, out of the blue, and I'm going to stay and help her get it started."

"But you can't leave the accounting firm."

"I'm not leaving. I'm only taking a leave of absence." She had made that call yesterday, and her boss had not taken the news well.

"It's committing career suicide. You've said that over and over. That's why you insisted on a short honeymoon."

"I remember. I know I'm taking a risk—"

"More than a risk, Dawn. You told me that anyone who takes a leave of absence can kiss the chance of becoming partner goodbye. One wrong move, you told me, and they'd be out."

She bit her lower lip. She had wondered if taking a leave might postpone her promotion . . . though in the back of her mind she did worry if it might mean she could lose it altogether. Kevin saying it aloud legitimized that fear. She wasn't imagining it. She'd seen it happen, many times. One wrong move . . .

"This isn't like you, Dawn. It's impulsive. It's crazy. It's . . . your mother's style. Not yours."

"Maybe she's rubbing off on me."

"Moving on the spur of the moment like this concerns me. I realize that putting the brakes on the wedding was difficult—"

She couldn't *believe* he was making it sound like it was a small thing he'd done. She'd ached over what he'd done. She'd suffered. She was *still* suffering. Her emotions started to well up, tears started pricking her eyes, and she knew she couldn't handle much more of this. "Putting the brakes on? Wow, that's quite a revision. Kevin, you broke off our engagement. Finis. Over. Done. That was your choice. You don't need to be concerned about me anymore. Not any decision I make. Not where I choose to live. Not what I do for a living. You and I, we are over."

Silence.

"Goodbye, Kevin." She clicked off her phone, pulled her earbuds from her ears, and put the phone on silent. Down by the water's edge, she did a few stretches, then started a slow warm-up jog. Logically, she should feel better now. Obviously, Kevin wasn't indifferent to her, he was keeping tabs on her. She should feel a little bit smug, even. But the call left her feeling physically and mentally drained. Kevin was worried about her, and the thought of him wouldn't leave her alone.

She picked up her pace to a run and went as fast and as far as she could. But she couldn't outrun missing him.

* * *

After stopping at Monomoy Coffee to get her morning fix, Marnie went to the Chatham Community Center and sat in a chair closest to the door of the Cancer Room. That's what she called it. The Cancer Room. She didn't want to be here, didn't want to have to listen to sad stories and private medical details that no one should talk about in public. Plus, Dawn was wrong. There were women *and* men. When a silver-haired man stood up front and introduced himself as Lincoln Hayes, Marnie almost gasped. Him! It was him! The same man who she kept bumping into all over town. The man who asked to buy her a cup of coffee. She wanted to march right home and snap at her sleeping daughter: "I thought you said it was an all-female group. The leader is most definitely a man!"

Lincoln's eyes swept the circle of chairs and landed on Marnie. "Welcome to our support group. Everyone here has had some kind of direct experience with cancer. There's something to discover in this journey. Cancer is a wonderful teacher. If you let it, it'll teach you lessons you never dreamed you needed to learn. We're here together to share those lessons with each other and to help support each other."

Marnie started to boil with indignation. There were no lessons for her from cancer. The disease was diabolical. A silent killer. It wanted to devour her, and it would consume her mind if she let it. No thank you. She felt her body start to flush with heat, knew her face would turn crimson in less than a minute.

She wasn't sure how much longer she could handle being here. She turned to look up at the wall clock, and when she looked back, Lincoln Hayes's eyes were narrowed and focusing on her with laser beam intensity. "It's hard at first," he said, "to learn the lessons of cancer."

Marnie jumped out of her seat and hurried to the exit. Her shoes made a clicking sound on the floor. She could feel the eyes of Lincoln Hayes drill into her back, but she didn't care. She couldn't breathe, couldn't think straight. She had to get out of there.

● ● ●

The signing of the papers went eerily smoothly. Dawn felt an elevated sense of alarm, almost suspicion—there should have been some nitpicking, some conflict of interest. But Bonnie Snow could not have been more accommodating—even to the point of submitting the paperwork to transfer the Creamery's business license to Mom. The two women had grown chummy, known to Dawn as the Marnie Effect. They'd come to the table as the best of friends. Dawn tried to find some loophole, some kind of snag that might delay the sale . . . but there was nothing. It was streamlined. Even the title insurance officer seemed astonished by how seamlessly the transaction occurred. "I'm not accustomed to all cash transactions," she said. "Makes life a lot easier."

For whom, Dawn wondered?

Because in record time, Marnie Dixon became the sole proprietor of the Main Street Creamery. Bonnie Snow blew everyone kisses as she hurried out the door, Mom headed off to the Creamery, and Dawn was left waiting for the title insurance officer to make copies of everything.

While waiting, she texted Brynn:

Done. Mom bought the building.

She added the emoji for a panicked face, then one more line:

> Why is it so easy to buy property and so hard
> to sell it?

Within seconds, she saw the bubbles that meant Brynn was texting back.

> Right? Like . . . why is it so easy to get married
> and so hard to get divorced?

Brynn should know. Her parents had both been divorced, several times. She spent every holiday at the Dixons'. She told Dawn that her parents' divorces had ruined New Year's Eve, Christmas, and everything in between.

After she was handed the file of paperwork, Dawn headed back to the Chatham Bars Inn to check out and pick up their suitcases. Driving along Shore Road, she unrolled her window and said, as loud as she could, "Dad, I did everything I could to stop it. It couldn't be stopped. So now I'll do everything I can to make sure the fruit of your life's work doesn't disappear."

It occurred to her that she wasn't really convinced about an afterlife, not like Mom was, and if she wasn't sure, why was she talking to her dad as if he were upstairs? Mom talked to Dad all the time, convinced that there was still some kind of unbroken connection. Dawn had to admit, it did feel comforting. It wasn't that she didn't believe in God; she assumed there was something huge and intelligent out there, like a cosmic traffic cop. But to take it to the level that Mom did—and even Dad in his last few years—seemed over the top. Simplistic. Unscientific. Unproven.

A little part of her envied their blind faith. This week, especially, when she saw the sun rise each morning over the ocean. It filled her with awe—both a sense of insignificance and a sense of wonder—and Someone deserved that *awe*. But if Someone deserved awe, then that Someone also had some answering to do about the suffering in this world. And that's where Dawn left the conversation. Too tangled.

After checking out of the Chatham Bars Inn, Dawn walked through the big, beautiful lobby and stopped in front of the grand sitting room to take one last look around. An employee was opening a large window and pulling off the screen. A bird must've flown in through a door and found itself trapped in the room. Rather than escape through the open window, it kept whacking into the mirror over the fireplace. Dawn watched for a while, then finally left, hoping the bird would figure out it wasn't trapped, that there was an open path—if it could just figure out the window was open.

She drove past the lighthouse and wove around town for a little while, then realized that going in circles wasn't helping. She needed to face reality. Her mother had just sunk a ton of money into a very risky venture, and Dawn had agreed to help her do it. Why? Why did she say she'd stay through Labor Day? Partly, maybe mostly, to protect her mother from almost guaranteed failure if she were left to her own devices. After all, this was Marnie Dixon, cockeyed optimist. But . . . she also didn't want to miss this albeit slim chance of success for Mom. Her mom had experienced the same losses as she had—maybe even more. She'd lost a husband and a future son-in-law, and had endured treatment for breast cancer. Instead of sinking into despair, she was eager to try something new.

Dawn was the opposite of her mom. Dad's death had caused her spirit to be crushed. Kevin's breakup had caused her heart to be broken. Life was not turning out the way she had planned. Or hoped and dreamed.

She pulled into the small parking lot of the Creamery and gazed at it. There was so much to do. It made her tired just to look at it. The hole in the roof, the chipped paint on the trim, the missing shingles on the siding, the weeds poking up from the brick path. And that was just the outside. Sitting in the car, she felt the weight of responsibility crowd in on her.

The good news was that the Main Street Creamery had potential. Mom wasn't wrong about that. The bad news was that it all had to be managed. The to-do list was endless and kept growing. Get a dumpster. Find some guys who she could pay hourly to help with getting rid of Bonnie's junk. Find someone who could fix the roof and repair interior fire damage. Start shopping for new flooring, tables, and chairs. Check with Mom about interior design ideas. Clean out the freezer. Look into hiring some hourly employees for the summer. Trustworthy, capable ones. Was that possible when you were only paying minimum wage? She picked up her pen and added another to-do. *Add an enormous tip jar at counter.*

Systems. It was all about putting systems into place. Systems made all the difference at work. They could make a difference here. Something simple, that Mom could manage and keep up with. Systems would help them sell the Creamery after Labor Day. Then she could get back to her life in Boston and pick up where she left off. A broken life.

Her thoughts returned to that bird trapped inside the Chatham Bars Inn. She wondered if it had figured out that the window was open yet or if it was still banging its little head against the mirror.

Oh my gosh. That bird is me. "No, it's not me," she said aloud.

At least she didn't want it to be her. But it was. She was the one holding on so tight to the life that had been yanked from her. If she was learning anything from her mother, it was about moving forward in life and not dwelling in the past, in might-have-beens and regrets.

So what was next? She had no idea.

But . . . it was time to find out.

Chapter

TEN

Just taught my kids about taxes by eating 38 percent of their ice cream.

—Conan O'Brien, comedian

Saturday, April 19

After Marnie signed the papers in the title insurance company's office, she walked—almost ran—down Crowell Road over to the Main Street Creamery while Dawn went back to the hotel to settle their account. Marnie had a hunch Dawn didn't want to cut ties with the hotel until she knew escrow would absolutely, positively close.

Marnie was both grateful for her daughter's vigilance and quietly exasperated by it, as was Bonnie, though the former shop owner was not at all quiet about her exasperation with Dawn's nitpickiness. It was an as-is sale, no contingencies, all cash. Marnie had a good feeling about Bonnie, and they had shaken hands on the deal. Was it really that important to nitpick every detail? She didn't think so. But she took care not to show it. Dawn was trying to protect Marnie, and for that she was thankful.

The very second the last signature was notarized, Bonnie jumped up from the table, gave Marnie a bear hug, then excused herself with a "Good luck! I'm off to Fairbanks!"

Just as eagerly, Marnie headed over to her new building. It had rained again last night and she worried about more leaks in the kitchen. She worried about rainwater spoiling that beautiful, brand-new Emery Thompson ice cream machine. She wanted to get a head start on cleaning up before Dawn arrived. She went right upstairs to change in the bathroom and stopped short at the top of the stairs, horrified. Bonnie's junk. It was still here. It was everywhere. The bedrooms looked even messier than they did on Wednesday, when she'd seen them for the first time. *Oh great. Dawn will flip.*

Not now, Marnie told herself. *Don't even think about that now. The downstairs is what matters. That's where the magic is waiting to be uncovered.*

In the bathroom, she changed into jeans and a baggy T-shirt and sneakers, pulled her long hair into a twist and pinned it with bobby pins to the top of her head, to keep her hair out of the way as she worked.

Minutes later, she dragged a ladder she'd found outside and leaned it against the exterior wall of the kitchen, close to the hole. A corner of the tarp that had been covering the hole had folded over in the wind. She claimed a few stones from the parking lot, dropped her supplies into a bucket for easy carrying, then climbed the wet ladder. As she reached the roof, her left foot slipped, and for a second, she nearly lost her balance. She hung on and regained her footing. She pushed the bucket onto the roof, then scrambled up next to it. Close to the actual leak, she smoothed out the folded corner of the tarp and covered the hole. She settled stones into place on the corners and hoped the tarp would hold until . . . until she could figure out how to fix a roof, or find someone who could. Then she turned to make her way back to the ladder.

She was halfway down when she slipped again and barely caught herself. Strange, the thoughts that ran through one's head in a flash. Wondering how she could get the Creamery into shape if she were confined to a wheelchair because of a broken hip. Wondering how quickly Dawn would sell the Creamery, using her mother's nonambulatory status as the excuse.

"Gotcha."

The ladder had stopped trembling. She looked down to see Lincoln Hayes holding the ladder firmly against the building. He smiled up at her with an expression that made no sense. Slightly amused, as if this were funny.

"You!"

"Me."

She made her way down the ladder and jumped off the final slippery rung. She swayed as she found her balance. "What are you doing here?"

"You left the cancer support meeting so abruptly this morning . . . I just wanted to make sure you were okay."

"I'm fine. I just had . . . somewhere I needed to be." Such a lame excuse.

He glanced up at the roof. "Were you trying to fix the roof?"

Marnie brushed off her jeans. "Not fix, exactly. Just stop it from leaking." She pushed back her bangs off her forehead. "I'm the new owner."

"So I heard," Lincoln said. "Word travels fast around town." He climbed up the ladder to peer at the hole in the roof. "I think you're going to need a roofer."

"No kidding."

Marnie spun around to find Dawn approaching from the parking lot. She hadn't noticed her car had pulled in.

As Dawn reached them, she kept her eyes on Lincoln, sizing him up. "Do you know much about roofing?"

"My dad was a construction worker," Lincoln said. "I helped him repair a few roofs in my time. Enough to know what not to do."

Dawn smiled, and Marnie realized she actually seemed relaxed, less tense than she had been during the escrow closing meeting. She wondered what had happened between the end of the meeting and her arrival at the Creamery.

"We need that roof fixed, pronto." Dawn walked toward the kitchen door. "Better come in and see what else needs to be done."

As Dawn disappeared, Lincoln turned to Marnie. "She's right about the roof. It needs to be fixed before you do anything else. I had offered to help Bonnie, but she had stopped caring about the building. Finally, I just put the tarp up without asking her."

Marnie went to the door and held it open for Lincoln. "Follow my daughter. She's usually leading the way."

Dawn stood in the middle of the kitchen with a clipboard. "Okay, team. We're going to make a punch list of everything that needs doing so that we're ready to open as soon as humanly possible." She paused and looked up. "By the way, who are you?"

"Lincoln Hayes."

"First things first," Marnie said. "Lincoln, I need to thank you for that timely rescue." She turned to Dawn. "I was coming down off a ladder and slipped, and Lincoln saved the day before I plunged onto the concrete."

Lincoln grinned. "It was only a couple feet off the ground."

"You saved me from cracking my head open or breaking a hip."

"The ground below was grass," Lincoln said, "and soft from the rain last night."

"Well, maybe I wouldn't have died from the fall, but I could've been seriously injured."

"Maybe so."

Satisfied, Marnie lifted a palm in Dawn's direction. "Lincoln, this is my daughter, Dawn. She's helping me get the Creamery into shape for the summer season."

"Nice to meet you, Lincoln," Dawn said.

"Friends call me Linc."

"Thanks for saving my mom's life and for tolerating her hyperbole."

He laughed. "You're welcome."

Dawn strolled around the kitchen, exploring.

"The fire must have started here," Marnie said.

"It did," Linc said. "Bonnie had left something boiling on the stovetop while she was serving up a customer." He pointed to himself. "Me."

Marnie's eyes went wide. "You were here when it happened?" She clapped her hands together in glee. "Tell us everything. Don't leave anything out."

"I called the fire department for Bonnie. I might have over-reacted, or maybe the fire department did. They sent three fire engines and knocked a hole through the roof. Bonnie was . . . well, she was"—he rocked his hand in the air—"let's just say the whole thing tipped the scales for her. The next day she told Al she was moving to Alaska. Not much later, she put the Creamery up for sale."

Lincoln Hayes was not what Marnie expected, though she really didn't have any expectations. He examined the cupboards near the stovetop. "The cupboards are tinged but not burnt. I think a good coat of paint will take care of them." He gazed up at the hole in the ceiling. "Not too bad from this side. Some plywood, tar paper, shingles, and you'll be as good as new." When no one responded, he lifted his head. "What?"

Dawn was staring at him. "When can you start?"

"Start?" He clapped a hand against his chest. "Me?"

"On the roof repairs. We'll pay a fair wage. All cash. Under the table."

"Dawn!" Marnie was shocked by her daughter's audacity. "Don't you think you should ask Lincoln if he even wants to work for us? After all, I'm sure he has plenty of his own things to do." Like what? she wondered. She didn't have any idea what he did for a living. She didn't know anything about him, other than he walked a dog and he led a cancer support group.

"Fair enough," Dawn said. "I apologize if I sound rather abrupt. We really need the help. You see, we're in a bit of a time crunch."

He looked at Marnie then. "Do you want me to?"

The tone was both questioning and tentative. Something filled his dark brown eyes. Something that looked a lot like sincerity.

"If you have the time to give," Marnie said, "we could use all the help we can get."

"In that case, consider me on the team."

"Great!" Dawn clapped her hands. "Let's get this list finished and figure out how to prioritize it."

Marnie just let Dawn take over and do whatever she wanted. As if anyone could have stopped her! She was a whirling dervish with a thick notepad in one hand and a Sharpie pen in the other.

The three of them spent the next two hours combing through the Creamery, upstairs and down, seeing what was usable, what still worked, and what needed to be replaced. Marnie thought that discovering Bonnie had left all her junk for them would've made Dawn scream, but it almost seemed as if she had expected as much. Topping Dawn's to-do list was drywall to cover the stud framing upstairs. "I love you, Mom, but sometimes I just need my space."

Marnie laughed, not at all offended. She got it. One week in a hotel room had taught her that she and Dawn enjoyed each other more when they had their own breathing room. In fact, she kept a separate to-do list rolling of her own—things she wanted to do to improve the appearance of the shop, ideas to add style and panache to it. Her thoughts spun in several different directions. How costly would it be to add a second bathroom? And she'd love to enlarge the kitchen. There was no way two people could work in there at one time, especially when Dawn was one of those two people. But Marnie kept her mouth closed. She knew she could overwhelm Dawn with creative ideas. She didn't want to do anything to jeopardize her daughter's involvement in the shop.

While Linc went to the hardware store to get supplies for the roof repair, Dawn read through the copious instruction manual for the ice cream machine, and Marnie walked slowly around the large front room. She imagined it on a warm summer day, filled with people of all ages, a long line waiting at the door to get in. She imagined a floor of gleaming hardwoods, a light paint color to replace the drab, mauve-colored walls. (Seriously, what was Bonnie thinking? It looked more like a dentist's waiting room than an ice cream shop.) She visualized different-sized wooden tables and chairs for customers to linger. A refrigerated cooler for drinks and packaged foods. A freezer to hold pints of ice cream to take home. Some kind of coffee bar along the side wall for people to customize their coffee. A community bulletin board where people could post Needs & Blessings.

Was this really happening? She squeezed her eyes shut, then opened them again. It was! It was really, truly happening. And Dawn was part of it, at least for now. Sheer joy filled Marnie, almost a childlike happiness, something she hadn't felt in a very long time.

Yes, yes, yes, yes, yes . . .

● ● ●

As long as Dawn didn't let herself think about how much junk Bonnie Snow had left them to toss out, and how the upstairs "apartment" had only 2x4 framing instead of walls, and how disgustingly dirty the entire Creamery was, she could focus on the one good thing. An Emery Thompson ice cream machine that she was over-the-moon excited to try out. Bonnie must have used it, but it was extraordinarily clean. There were no remnants to clean out from previous ice cream making. Just to be safe, Dawn was sending pitcher after pitcher of hot water through it to sanitize it. Even under normal conditions, you couldn't be too careful when it came to ice cream making . . . and nothing about the Creamery was normal. While filling the pitcher for a fifth time, she heard the familiar chimes of her phone. Caller ID told her it was Brynn. Dawn cringed. She'd called twice today and Dawn had been too busy to pick up. Not hearing back from Dawn would only make Brynn worry.

"Hey there." She tucked the phone under her chin.

"How goes the ice cream making?" Brynn said, sounding upbeat and a little amused. "Made any batches for us lactose-intolerant types?"

"Not yet, but soon. Mom just closed on the building today. In fact, I can't talk long because we're trying to fix the hole . . ." She stopped herself. "Trying to get some repairs done before ice cream making officially commences."

Brynn hesitated, as if there was something more she wanted to say but wasn't sure if she should. Then she blurted it out. "Dawn . . . Kevin seems to be very concerned about you."

"Kevin doesn't need to worry. You don't need to worry. I've got this handled."

"You sound all Teflony again."

Dawn chose to ignore that comment. Why couldn't anyone give her a little encouragement? Was that asking too much?

"I've been thinking," Brynn said, breaking Dawn's silent diatribe, "that maybe this experience will help you figure out the life you really want to live."

I thought I knew. The one with Kevin. But it didn't happen.

And suddenly Dawn was back to feeling all the sorrow, all the regrets, all the pain. They kept finding her, despite her best efforts to try and escape from them. She squeezed her eyes shut and shook the heaviness off, literally made herself shudder. She struggled for the words to explain. "Brynn, this is . . . being here in Chatham has been good for me. It's good for Mom. It's helping us move forward. Out of grief. Out of loss. Out of being . . . stuck." She turned off the faucet before the water overflowed. "I hope you can try and understand."

"Oh, Dawn. I'm sorry. I didn't think about it from that angle. Yes, of course. I understand." She paused. "If Kevin calls again, what should I tell him?"

"Same thing I told him. He no longer has to be concerned about me."

"Right. Got it. Will you send me pictures of this building? I'm curious."

"I will. I'll send before and after." She crossed her fingers that there'd be a lot of good afters. Right now, she wasn't so sure.

They chatted for a few more minutes and hung up on a good note.

Dawn poured the hot water through the ice cream maker. Five times should be enough. She thought she'd take Mom and Lincoln some iced water. She filled the pitcher again, with cold water this time, and added ice, trying not to cringe at the contents in the chest freezer. Everything inside would get tossed out, first thing tomorrow. She was rounding the door of the kitchen when she heard the freezer's motor make an odd coughing sound. The sound stopped, then started up again. Dawn sidled closer to the freezer chest and cocked an ear, listening. The steady hum of the motor was back. She pressed a palm against the top of the freezer chest. "Please don't die on us. Just keep going through Labor Day."

She went outside with the pitcher of iced water and glasses.

"I *think* everything is clean, but no guarantees until I have time to disinfect the kitchen."

Lincoln didn't seem to mind and drained his glass. Mom did the same. Dawn felt a little less thirsty. Brynn's call nettled her, the cough of the freezer motor bothered her . . . and the amount of work needed to repair the Creamery felt overwhelming.

As Lincoln—bless him!—repaired the hole in the Creamery's roof, Dawn and her mom stayed outside to hoist materials up to him as needed and keep the rented nail gun's long extension cord out of his way.

"Stop right there! Stop and desist!"

Dawn turned around to see a stout older woman cross the road, waving her hands in the air like a crossing guard. "You can't do that!"

Mom had been pulling weeds along the foundation of the house. She rose to her feet, holding a handful of weeds. "What can't we do?"

"The roof! You mustn't do any work to it."

"But we must. I'm the new owner. Marnie Dixon. This is my daughter, Dawn."

The woman came to a stop and braced her feet apart, hands on her hips. She looked to be somewhere in her mid-to-late seventies, Dawn guessed, with bifocal glasses perched at the end of her nose, attached to a chain around her neck. She wore a pleated gray skirt, a black collarless sweater, and a patterned scarf that covered her shoulders. She had a stocky build, an angular, unsmiling face, and gray hair that seemed overly sprayed. Not a stray strand dared go rogue, even on a breezy day like today. Had Dawn been casting roles for a movie, this woman would be cast as the Queen of England.

"It doesn't matter who you are or what you own. You haven't had any work approved by the Historical Commission."

Mom's smile slipped. "But it's a hole in the roof. It needs to be repaired."

"Everything must first be approved by the Historical Commission."

"We're using the exact same cedar shingles that cover the rest of the roof." Mom pointed to a stack of shingles. "Lincoln— our roof guy—he even took a sample to make sure it matched."

"It doesn't matter." The woman shook her head. "You must first go through the Historical Commission. Our primary goal is to preserve Chatham's historical integrity."

"But we're not changing anything," Dawn said. "Like my mother said, we're just repairing damage."

The woman pointed to the electric cord running down the side of the building. "If that were true, you wouldn't be using a nail gun."

Mom looked at the cord, attached to Lincoln's nail gun on the roof. "Why not?"

"Because the first colonists, of whom I am directly descended, would shudder in their graves."

"Any chance," Dawn said in a flat tone, "that you're a Nickerson?"

"Indeed I am. William and Anne Nickerson were the first English land proprietors of Chatham. They owned everything, as far as the eye can see."

Mom had talked about the Nickerson legacy. She said the name was everywhere on the Cape. "Mrs. Nickerson, we are—"

"Mrs. Nickerson-Eldredge."

A double dose, Dawn realized. The Eldredge name, Mom had said, ran a close second to the Nickerson name. The name alone should have been a tip-off to the kind of person they were dealing with. Chatham aristocracy.

Mom started again, in her most appeasing voice. "Well, as I was saying, we are the current owners. I bought the shop from Bonnie Snow. The papers were signed this very morning."

"That, in fact, is why I'm here. Nothing happens in Chatham that escapes my notice. I've come as a courtesy call."

Mom smiled. "How nice. Come in and we'll have some tea. Or do you prefer coffee? You seem like a tea person to me."

"I'm not here for *that* kind of courtesy call. If you have any changes in mind for this building, you'll have to petition the Historical Commission."

"What exactly," Dawn said, "do you mean by . . . any changes?"

Mrs. Nickerson-Eldredge's head swerved toward Dawn. "Any and all. Our purpose is to preserve the historical accuracy of our illustrious town, most particularly on Main Street. This property is in the historical commercial district. All eyes are on it." Her words fell like stones.

Unbelievable! "We're not remodeling anything," Dawn said, a little too loudly. "This shop is in disrepair. The paint is peeling, some of the shingles are missing off the side, other shingles are splintered, and the roof is leaking."

Mrs. Nickerson-Eldredge's lips puckered. "All part of its history. This building has been here long before you were here, and it will be here long after you leave."

"Do you mean to tell us," Dawn said, an edge to her voice, "that you'd prefer if we left the shop as it is—a run-down building—than improve it and make it an asset to the town?"

"What I prefer is that you go through proper channels to preserve this historical building." Mrs. Nickerson-Eldredge stiffened her erect shoulders. "Something the previous proprietor refused to do."

Her explanation was met with silence.

Mom gave her a curious look. "So, you're saying that Bonnie tried to make improvements to this shop?"

"Bonnie Snow did not show any regard for the long-held traditions of this town. Nor did she have any experience in the food industry. Enthusiasm alone does not make a successful business." Mrs. Nickerson-Eldredge said it with complete disgust.

Dawn exchanged a look with Mom, thinking the same thought. Their retail expertise matched Bonnie's. All they had to offer was enthusiasm. Imagine if Mrs. Nickerson-Eldredge knew of their own lack of experience. She probably did.

"Mrs. Nickerson-Eldredge," Mom said, "what do you suggest we do?"

"Find an architect who is well schooled in historical preservation"—she peered at Mom over her bifocals—"and have him find a contractor for you who knows what he's doing."

"An architect in historical preservation?" Dawn had never heard of such a specialty.

Mrs. Nickerson-Eldredge sent a withering glance in her direction. "Would you hire an electrician to work on your plumbing?"

Dad would've shot out of his chair at such a question. "Of course not."

"Neither should you hire a retired computer salesman to restore a historical building. Especially not one who suddenly"— she waved her hands in the air—"finds the *light* and tries to convert us all."

At the exact same moment, Dawn and Mom lifted their chins to look up at Lincoln Hayes, hammering away on the roof with the nail gun. They exchanged another look. Lincoln Hayes? A preacher? Dawn would have to keep an eye on him.

"Restoring historical buildings is a careful and intricate process. It's a job best left to the professionals. These old buildings have sacred bones. You just don't always know what's behind the walls." On that note, Mrs. Nickerson-Eldredge spun on her shoes and marched off.

Dawn bent down to unpack another package of cedar shingles.

"There's something both slightly comical and immensely worrisome about that woman." Mom kept her eyes on Mrs. Nickerson-Eldredge, marching down Main Street.

Dawn straightened. "More comical than worrisome."

"You're not taking her warning seriously? You? After all, you're the rule follower in the family."

"What can she do? Turn us in to the Historical Commission police?" Dawn shrugged. "We're doing the town a favor by taking an eyesore and making it beautiful. Even those Puritan founding fathers would approve. They had no patience for government interference." She examined a shingle, sniffing the cedar scent. "Sacred bones. What does that mean?"

"I think it was a warning not to tamper with the original frame of the house."

"Then why didn't she just say that?" Dawn ran a hand along the edge of the shingle. "I know that type of personality from work. If she had her way, she'd make us turn this building into a museum. That lady, she's a button pusher, that's all."

From the edge of the roof, Linc's head peered down at them. "True, but she's also the head of the Historical Commission."

Dawn glanced up at Mom. "Did Bonnie Snow give you any warning about the Historical Commission?"

"'Ignore Mrs. Nickerson-Eldredge,' Bonnie said." Mom's voice sounded vague.

Dawn set the shingle down. "Then again, Bonnie also gave up on the ice cream shop and fled the state."

With that, Mom snapped out of her reverie. "Don't you worry, Dawn." She waved her hands in the air like shooing a fly. "I'll handle Mrs. Nickerson-Eldredge and the Historical Commission."

Dawn hadn't been worried until that very moment.

Chapter
ELEVEN

There were some problems that only coffee and ice cream could fix.

—Amal El-Mohtar, author

Saturday, April 19

The afternoon passed quickly. By the time the sun was setting, Marnie was more than ready to call it a day. A good day, with a lot of progress made on the Main Street Creamery. A great day. She'd even made a friend.

About an hour after Mrs. Nickerson-Eldredge left, a tiny elfish woman popped into the Creamery without even knocking first. "I'm Nanette," she said, clasping both of Marnie's hands in hers. Nanette's cobwebby hair was dyed dark brown—much too dark for her age—and pulled back into an old-fashioned French twist. She wore a white T-shirt with the caption "I ♥ Cape Cod." "My Michael and I, we own a T-shirt shop across the street. The best one in town. Not the only one, just the best." Her eyebrows knitted together in a frown and she squeezed

Marnie's hands until they hurt. "You're not planning to open another T-shirt shop here, are you?"

"Heavens no. It'll remain the Main Street Creamery. My daughter is an artisan ice cream maker."

A bright smile covered the woman's wrinkled elf's face and she released Marnie's hands. "Well, in that case, welcome to Chatham! There's plenty of room for another ice cream shop, especially if your daughter is an artist. Even an artist could do a better job with ice cream than Bonnie."

Marnie wondered if she should correct Nanette's definition of artisan and decided not to. Close enough.

"Don't get me wrong. I loved Bonnie. She was a real sweetheart. But that ice cream of hers . . ." Nanette shuddered. "Now, hon, if you need anything, just ask. I know everything there is to know about this town, and if there's something I don't know, I'll just make it up. My Michael says I am blessed with the gift of conversation."

Marnie was charmed. "Come in. I'll make a fresh pot of coffee."

She didn't need to ask twice. Nanette was in and snooping around, even going upstairs without a look back at Marnie for permission.

In the kitchen, as Marnie filled the coffeepot with water, she could hear Dawn's exclamation of surprise float downstairs as Nanette opened the bathroom door. *Uh-oh.* Marnie cringed.

When Nanette returned downstairs a moment later, she made no mention of barging in on Dawn in the bathroom. "Oh, hon," she said, shaking her head woefully, "Bonnie left all her junk for you."

"Was she a . . ." Marnie knew to tread carefully. She was the newcomer here, and clearly Bonnie and Nanette had been neighborly.

"Hoarder? Big time. Now, she didn't see herself as a hoarder, but I sure did. That girl spent more time at tag sales than she did running the Creamery. She really should've had a craft store, not an ice cream shop. I'm sorry she left it all for you to deal with. Knowing Bonnie, she probably thought she was bequeathing you priceless artifacts."

Marnie poured two cups of coffee as Dawn came downstairs. "Dawn, this is Nanette, our neighbor."

"Yes, we already met," Dawn said, face ablaze, not even stopping. "I need to get outside to help Lincoln." The door closed firmly behind her.

"Cute girl," Nanette said. "Shy."

Not hardly. Easily embarrassed was closer to the truth. Marnie took the two mugs of coffee to the lone table in the front room and sat down. Nanette followed suit, accepted a mug of coffee, laced it heavily with cream and sugar, and gulped it down like she was parched.

"This is good coffee, hon. Really good stuff." Nanette looked longingly into her empty mug.

"Would you like a refill?"

She pushed her mug closer to Marnie. "I thought you'd never ask."

Marnie went to the kitchen to refill the mug and decided to just bring back the coffeepot.

"So, let me in on your secret in capturing the mysterious Lincoln Hayes. Every widow and divorcée in town is after him."

"Capture?" Marnie stopped, midpour. "I didn't capture him. It's not like that. I've only met him a few times. He's helping us out, that's all."

Nanette winked. "I've seen the two of you."

Ignoring that remark, Marnie finished pouring. She didn't know what Nanette could have seen.

"So, what's up with the two of you? Are you sweet on each other? You can tell me, hon. I'm a vault. My lips are sealed."

The warm feelings Marnie first had for Nanette were rapidly cooling. She scooted back her chair. *Change topics, fast.* "Do you have much experience dealing with the Historical Commission?"

Nanette gasped. "Do I ever!"

Nanette talked nonstop for over an hour before she remembered she'd left her T-shirt shop unattended. When she finally trotted back across the street, Marnie let out a sigh of relief. Her ears hurt from so much listening.

The woman could be a little overbearing, and it took a very long time for her to get to a point in a story, if there was a point. But on the plus side, there'd been a lot for Marnie to learn about Chatham in the last hour. Quite a lot.

Regarding how to manage Bonnie's junk, Nanette suggested having a tag sale in the parking lot and sell everything for a dollar.

"Sell it?" Marnie had said. "I'd be happy to give everything away for free."

Nanette had shaken her head quickly, like a dog shaking water. "No, no. Don't do that. You have to make things seem like a bargain. You'd be amazed what people will buy when they think they're getting a deal. Trust me, hon. I've lived here a long time. Folks around here don't part with their eagles without good cause. And a bargain, even if it ain't, is a good cause."

That reminded Marnie of Philip. He could be quite cheap, but he could also be a sucker at a tag sale. Marnie wondered what Dawn would think about a tag sale. Her daughter's solution to dispose of Bonnie's junk was to rent a dumpster. But that wasn't an inexpensive solution, and there actually was stuff that somebody might consider valuable. *National Geographic* magazines, flowerpots, mason jars. "Is there a day in Chatham that's best for tag sales?"

Nanette had slapped her small palm on the table, jiggling the coffee in the mugs. "Saturday. Put word out on Friday afternoon and let the buzz start buzzing." She wagged a finger at Marnie. "As long as there's no rain. That's the killer of all tag sales."

A glimmer of excitement rose in Marnie. Next Saturday, if the weather cooperated, she would host a tag sale. Get rid of everything Bonnie had left behind and maybe even make a little bit of money in the process. Dawn, she knew, would be thrilled as long as she didn't have to participate.

As for Nanette's advice about dealing with the Historical Commission, she had said that most folks in Chatham took the old adage: Do it now, ask forgiveness later. Marnie's heart had warmed up again toward the small spritely woman, because that was exactly the tactic she wanted to take. If the Historical Commission made them tear the roof apart again, at least the kitchen's interior was safe from the elements. Especially . . . the sparkling new Emery Thompson ice cream machine.

What was the big fuss about using a nail gun on the roof shingles? Lincoln had no idea. As he was packing up the rented nail gun to return to the hardware store, he said, "When my father saved up enough to buy himself a nail gun, we all celebrated. It saved him hours of work each day."

For the rest of the afternoon, Marnie considered Mrs. Nickerson-Eldredge's words. She couldn't quite shake off a growing sense of dread and discomfort. As soon as Dawn went upstairs to take a shower and Marnie heard the water pipes shake and moan—evidence that the shower was on—she made a phone call. One ring, and it was picked up. "This is a business call only. No personal questions."

"Got it."

"Why would a Historical Commission object to using a nail gun on a building?"

"This is about the ice cream shop you bought?"

How did Kevin know about the Creamery? "Yes."

"How old is the building?"

She tried to remember what Bonnie had said about it and

realized she'd told her nothing about the history of the building. Worse, she realized she hadn't asked. "Old. Really old."

"So, the Historical Commission has an interest in the building."

"Well, it's in the historical commercial district."

"Is the building registered?"

"I, um, don't know."

Long pause.

"Is it in a prominent part of the town?"

"Main Street."

Another long pause. Really long. Marnie felt a hot flash start. She hated them! They came at the worst time.

"Okay. It's probably safe to assume that the Historical Commission has a vested interest in this property."

"What does that mean?"

"Well, quite basically, it means that there are added layers of restrictions for any remodels or updates."

"So why can't we fix a hole in the roof?"

"That's the nail gun issue? Hmm. Let me do a little digging and get back to you."

The pipes stopped shaking and moaning. Dawn must've finished her shower.

"Marnie, there's one piece of advice I do have."

"Yes?"

"Don't make enemies of the Historical Commission. They can make life very difficult for you. You need to get tight with them and stay tight."

Oh boy. Marnie's hot flash spiked up a few degrees.

"Marnie, how is Dawn—"

"I'm sorry. I can't. No personal questions, Kevin. Thanks for your help." She hung up quickly, just as she heard Dawn's footsteps lightly tread down the stairs. "How was the first shower?"

"Well, it's not the Chatham Bars Inn," she said with a grin, rubbing her hair with a towel. "And I'm going to ask Linc to get a lock on that bathroom door. A Nanette-proof lock. Mom, she walked right in on me and started talking!"

Marnie flashed her an apologetic smile. "Sorry about that." She wondered if the "do it now and ask forgiveness later" might sum up Nanette's entire approach to life.

Dawn picked up her notebook and pen. "I'm going to start tomorrow's to-do list. First thing in the morning, I want to go to the market and get some groceries. I can't wait to try out that ice cream machine."

Marnie clapped her hands. This was the moment she'd been waiting for. "What flavor?"

Dawn looked up, surprised she would ask. "Vanilla."

Oh, of course. She should've expected that. Start with what you know best.

Just as they were debating what to do for supper, Linc surprised them by returning with his dog, Mayor, and a bag full of delicious burritos. Dawn quickly ran a wet Clorox wipe over Bonnie's folding table and chairs before Linc passed out burritos.

"Would you mind," he said, "if I asked a blessing over the meal?"

Pleased, Marnie nodded. "We'd love it. Wouldn't we, Dawn?" She raised an eyebrow at Dawn, poised to take a bite of her burrito. Lincoln's prayer covered not only the meal, but he asked a blessing on the Creamery's future, too, and Marnie was so grateful. Even Dawn seemed appreciative.

They chatted companionably during the meal, and soon all nagging thoughts of Mrs. Nickerson-Eldredge and the Historical Commission slipped away.

Lincoln wasn't one to linger. As soon as the burritos were eaten, he rose to leave. "I've been going to the First Congregational Church on Sunday mornings. Really good preaching. Anyone interested in joining me tomorrow?"

"Count me in," Marnie said.

"Count me out," Dawn said.

Disappointed, Marnie frowned. When Dawn went off to college, she had let her faith go dormant. At the time, Marnie hadn't taken Dawn's spiritual slumber too seriously. It had seemed pretty typical for a young person raised in a Christian home, one who had spent every Sunday morning in church. But the years kept passing. These days, only a shadow of her childhood faith remained. If Philip's death hadn't shaken her out of her slumber, hadn't revealed the need for a deeper resource, and if a broken heart over Kevin hadn't . . . what would it take?

Dawn looked up, as if she realized how abrupt her answer might have sounded. "I just . . . I have something planned for tomorrow morning. I want to find a grocery store and buy ingredients to make ice cream. I'm looking forward to trying out the machine. I'm expecting it to take a lot of trial and error to get the flavors just right. You know . . . Memorial Day looms large."

An image of Mrs. Nickerson-Eldredge's cross face popped into Marnie's mind.

Chapter
TWELVE

Impatience is the enemy of great ice cream.
—Amy Ettinger, author of *Sweet Spot:*
An Ice Cream Binge across America

Saturday, April 19

Marnie lay in bed, her hands folded on her stomach, replaying the day's events, all the up-and-down emotions, when her phone started to vibrate with an incoming call. Fumbling in the dark, she reached for the phone and saw it was nearly midnight and that Kevin was the caller. She sat up in bed and pressed the green *on* button. "Hello?"

"Hope I didn't wake you. I did a little research tonight on historical buildings. A nail gun indents the head of the nail into the wood. If it's important that everything looks authentic—"

"Yes." Marnie spoke in barely more than a whisper, hoping Dawn was sound asleep. Hoping all of Bonnie's piles of junk that surrounded them in each bedroom would muffle her voice. "That's exactly the word that the woman used. Authentic."

"Then every nail has to be hammered by hand. So the nail head is flush to the wood."

"Even shingles on a roof?"

"Even shingles on a roof," he echoed.

Marnie sighed. "Anything else I should be aware of?"

"Yes. Work within the guidelines of the Historical Commission. Study them. Learn them. Their goal is to protect the history of their village. So keep what's there. Everything—especially the exterior—needs to stay the way it had been intended by the original owners. Windows and doors need to remain in their originally framed place. No updating to current high-efficiency items, like vinyl-clad windows. Same with the siding. Is it cedar shingle or clapboards?"

"Cedar shingles."

"Then whatever needs replacing, you'll have to match it exactly."

"Any other advice?"

"Generally, Historical Commissions don't have much jurisdiction inside. They understand that plumbing and electricity and insulation require adaptation and flexibility. Do all you can to make the outside of the building comply to the HC's requirements and the whole project will go a lot smoother for you. Remember, it's all about the exterior. So be sure to talk to them before making any changes to the outside of the building."

Before?

"File the applications well in advance of the work. Wait for approval."

Marnie's head was spinning. What about Nanette's advice to do it now and ask forgiveness later? She preferred that process. Much simpler.

"If there's anything else you need to know, Marnie, any way I can help . . . don't hesitate to ask. I don't mind. In fact, I enjoyed doing the research."

A soft, sad smile tugged at her lips. How she loved this young man. "Thanks, Kevin. Good night." She set the phone on her nightstand and settled back into bed, back to staring at the ceiling. She listened for Dawn's steady breathing in the other room, thankful that the phone call with Kevin hadn't woken her.

Marnie rolled over, facing the grimy window. So much for sleep tonight.

● ● ●

Sunday, April 20

Overnight, spring disappeared and winter returned, bringing cold, hard rain. Mom came home from church on Sunday morning and said the abrupt change in weather was a sign. It was giving them a message—to focus all their energies on the interior of the Creamery. Inside or outside, Dawn didn't care. She just wanted to move things forward.

"The message from the sermon was a little different," Mom said, as if Dawn had asked. "It was a prayer of Moses, more of a rant, really. From Numbers 11, I think. Moses was thoroughly fed up with the Israelites and went on a tirade. You'd almost expect a lightning bolt to strike him down, but the pastor said that God wants to hear those honest prayers. No filter. From the gut, he said."

Honest, unfiltered prayers. Dawn gave Mom a sideways glance. First thing that came to her mind was, *Please, God. Don't let my crazy mother blow Dad's life savings on this.* But she didn't say that out loud.

While Mom and Linc had been at church, Dawn had run down to Chatham Village Market and bought organic whole milk and full cream and eggs, bags of sugar, and as many varieties of real vanilla extract as she could find. There was nothing more frustrating than getting halfway through a recipe and finding that you were missing an ingredient. Preparing in advance, having all the ingredients lined up and ready to go, made all the difference.

On the walk home, church bells filled the air and she stopped to listen. She hadn't noticed them before. Or did they ring only on Sundays? Their sweet, steady call to the village made her feel funny, like she was missing something.

Back at the Creamery, Dawn searched through the cupboards to gather Bonnie's kitchen tools. Double boiler saucepan, measuring cups, spoons, heatproof bowls, whisks, spatulas, a fine-mesh strainer. Examining them, seeing dried food bits on them, she choked back disgust. She filled the sink with hot water, added a few tablespoons of Clorox into it, then dumped every single bowl and utensil in and let them soak. She wasn't taking any chances on Bonnie's germs. After feeling confident all equipment was sparkling clean, rinsed, and dried, she was ready to start mixing the base for the first batch of vanilla ice cream. She decided to start with the last recipe she and her dad had made, the one they had settled on, after fifty-nine batches, for the base.

She heated the milk, and in a separate bowl, whisked together egg yolks. Next came tempering the eggs. She took the milk off the heat and slowly poured it into the bowl of egg yolks to warm them, whisking constantly to avoid creating bits of scrambled eggs. Back into the saucepan and onto the heat, stirring nonstop, keeping it moving, until the creamy, silky custard mixture thickened, then began to steam. *Do not let the custard boil!* Her dad's voice rang in her head. Too much, and it would curdle. Not enough, and it wouldn't be pasteurized.

Satisfied, she turned the burner off and poured the hot mixture through the strainer into a bowl of chilled cream sitting in an ice bath. This would help cool the custard down. Giving the mixture time to cool and cure allowed the flavor to intensify, for the fats to crystalize and the proteins to hydrate. Ideally, the mixture should cool overnight. Dawn was never one to cheat on anything, even ice cream, but today was special. A reasonable time allowed for cooling, yes. For curing, no. After all, an ice cream machine was waiting to be christened.

While she waited, she decided to start cleaning the kitchen. If she hadn't been so eager to try the ice cream machine out, she would've done that job first. Before church, Mom had moved all of Bonnie's boxes in the kitchen out to the front room, so at least the countertops were cleared off. It astounded Dawn that Bonnie left so many of her belongings behind, but maybe the old adage was true: You get what you pay for. Mom might've got the Creamery for a bargain basement price, but with it came the odious task of purging and cleaning someone else's junk.

Dawn wheeled a garbage container inside and set it in the middle of the kitchen. She emptied the contents of the fridge (Bonnie won the prize for keeping every known condiment in the world) and the chest freezer with its unidentifiable frozen products, and soon the garbage container was full. She rolled it back outside, wondering if nosy Nanette might let them borrow space in her container. But then she thought of the ice cream base, still cooling, and all thoughts of purging vanished. All she wanted to do was to try out that ice cream machine.

After church, Mom had been on a mission, bringing Bonnie-boxes from upstairs to the front room to prepare for next Saturday's tag sale. Now and then, she would stick her head into the kitchen to ask, "Is it ready?"

"Not yet," Dawn said, until she finally felt satisfied the mixture was cool enough to pour.

Mom stood at the kitchen doorjamb with a box in her arms as Dawn poured the mixture into the machine.

"Here it goes," she said, looking at Mom over her shoulder, as excited as a kid on her birthday. She closed the gate, turned the switch on, and turned the refrigeration button on. Then she listened to the sloshing sound as the dasher started to whirl—such a hopeful sound!—and set the timer for seven minutes.

"How do you know what speed to use?"

"I'm experimenting. The slower you run the machine, the lower the air content."

"And that's what you want? Low overrun?"

Dawn spun around. "Impressive, Mom!"

"I paid attention while you and Dad made ice cream."

"Apparently so." Dawn wiggled her eyebrows. "I'm not quite sure how much overrun I'm looking for. I'm going to try it a couple of different ways today."

"But how do you know how to use the machine?"

Dawn shrugged. "Studied the manual. And watched some YouTube videos." Last night, she had curled up on top of her lumpy bed, covered herself with a blanket, and watched countless YouTube videos about how to use the Emery Thompson 6-quart ice cream machine. She drifted off to sleep with her phone in her hand.

Mom pushed off from the doorjamb. "Call me when it's ready. I'm determined to clear out space in the upstairs this afternoon. I got up in the night to go to the bathroom and walked smack into a tower of boxes."

Dawn stayed right in front of the ice cream machine, listening to the sloshing of the mix as the dasher churned, eager to grow familiar with what the sounds meant. At the seven-minute mark, she set a bowl underneath the barrel and opened the gate, allowing a small amount to ooze out. Too soft. It looked like frozen yogurt. She closed the gate and set the timer for another minute. While she waited, she sampled its flavor and consistency.

Sweet. Creamy. Cold on the tongue. Melted instantly. Lovely mellow aftertaste of vanilla. Absolutely delicious. Perfect.

But it could be better.

* * *

Tuesday, April 22

As the week progressed, the interior of the Main Street Cream-ery was a hive of activity. While Dawn worked on ice cream, Marnie made endless trips up and down the stairs, hauling Bonnie's stuff to the front room and scooting the boxes against the walls. The front room had become the staging area for Saturday's parking lot tag sale. She worked. And worked and worked. She started in Dawn's room because she knew clean-ing it out would ease the silent tension that radiated from her daughter each time they went upstairs.

Dawn was laser-focused on ice cream making, and that was exactly where Marnie wanted her mind to be. No distrac-tions. No additional problems. No going upstairs except for bathroom breaks.

Because upstairs was a maze. There was little to no room to move with all the boxes and paraphernalia stacked about. Marnie created goat paths leading around tight corners, so she could keep going. Under different circumstances, she might've enjoyed sifting through the boxes to hunt for any treasures, but not with the tight timeline Dawn had created for the Cream-ery. And not with Dawn watching her go back and forth as she crossed the kitchen. Once, Dawn caught her flipping through forty-year-old *Ladies' Home Journal* magazines and shouted, "I knew it!" Marnie dropped the magazine she'd been reading like it was a hot potato. Curiously, she'd been studying a recipe for potato au gratin.

By midday Tuesday, the upstairs was empty of Bonnie's be-longings. Everything looked lighter, brighter, roomier. But it came at a cost to the front room, which was now piled floor to ceiling with boxes, waiting for Saturday's tag sale. When Linc arrived to help for the afternoon, he calmly asked if Marnie knew that heavy rain was due in on Friday night, with off-and-on showers all day Saturday.

"In that case," Dawn said, "we are moving up the tag sale."

Marnie was squatting on the floor, trying to organize contents of boxes. She looked at Dawn. "Moving up?"

"Tomorrow," Dawn said firmly. "Everything goes. One dollar per box. I'm calling a haul-away company to come Saturday. Anything that doesn't sell goes to the dump."

Marnie looked around the front room. It was as crowded as the upstairs had been, with a goat path leading to the front door.

"I'm proud of you, Mom," Dawn said. "I know this hasn't been easy for you. Purging isn't your thing."

So true. Marnie loved stuff, especially quirky old stuff. But she had a sense that the old building wanted everything out. It was necessary for its new beginning, it needed fresh air. So did she. "Done," she said, wiping her hands of dust and dirt. "Tomorrow it is."

That evening, Linc and Dawn helped Marnie move everything out into the parking lot. They set up large poster board signs:

$1 PER BOX. EVERYTHING MUST GO.

Dawn persuaded Marnie to leave an Honor Jar out on the folding table and not even bother attending to the sale. "If people steal the money, so be it. The goal is to get rid of the junk and not have to pay a fortune to have it hauled away."

So that's what they did. The small parking lot of the Creamery was filled with Bonnie's boxes of junk.

When Marnie woke the next morning, she heard voices outside. She looked out the grimy window and saw two people milling around the parking lot. She wiped a spot on the glass to get a better look. She smiled. Nanette and her husband, Michael, were poking through the boxes. Take it, she wanted to shout. Take it all!

As the day wore on, more and more people came through

the parking lot of the Creamery to check out the tag sale. At times, Marnie went outside to tidy up or throw away boxes or move them around or empty the Honor Jar of quarters and dollars. Mostly, she wanted to meet locals and tell them to keep an eye on the Creamery's grand opening on the Friday before Memorial Day, to expect the best ice cream they'd ever tasted. Most seemed skeptical of that claim, but they did take home boxes of Bonnie's junk.

A clerk at Chatham Village Market, a nearby upscale grocery store that Dawn liked, bought three boxes full of cards and rubber stamps for his wife. The florist down the road bought all the flowerpots. Two elderly women asked to purchase every skein of yarn they could find. When Marnie asked what they planned to do with all the wool, they said they crocheted newborn caps for the local hospital. Marnie bundled all the skeins in an empty box and gave them the yarn for free.

The best moment of the day was when Marnie noticed a little boy peering into boxes. He was dressed in cowboy boots and a big hat and leather chaps, and held a wrinkled dollar bill in his hand. "Hi there. Looking for anything in particular?"

He looked up at Marnie. "Yes." He said it with a lisp, and she noticed his two front teeth were missing.

"What's your name? I'm Marnie."

"I'm Leo."

"How old are you, Leo?"

He held up his hand and splayed his little fingers. "Five. My birthday is coming soon."

"Is that right? What do you want for your birthday?"

"Just one thing." Leo gave her a solemn look. "I want to be seven."

Marnie paused, then burst out laughing. "I don't think there's anything in the boxes that can give you that. But if you find something you'd like to have, you can take it. Keep your dollar. Consider it a birthday gift from me."

Cheered, Cowboy Leo kept up his search. She watched him for a long time, hoping he might find something he'd like to have. She'd always wanted to have another child, a little boy like that one—on the husky side, with chubby cheeks. Philip had never been willing to budge—he was adamant that he wanted only one child. Whenever she had broached the topic, he would say, "You have a beautiful, healthy daughter. What more could you want?"

Well, *that*, she thought, watching Leo in his cowboy hat and boots.

By the time the sun was setting, the parking lot had emptied out and so had most of Bonnie Snow's leftover belongings. They didn't make much money because Marnie kept giving things away, but she didn't mind. It was a great start to connecting to the local residents. Dawn, in an expansive mood because the tag sale had been far more successful than she had expected, canceled the haul-away truck. "Nanette said we could use her garbage too," she said. "We can slowly get rid of the rest of Bonnie's junk with the weekly garbage pickup."

Marnie noticed Dawn was wearing a new T-shirt with the logo POINT ME TO THE BEACH. "So you and Nanette have become friends?"

"Not friends, exactly. She's a little too nosy for my taste. But she's a good neighbor to have."

That, Nanette was. Nosy and neighborly.

The Main Street Creamery was now empty of junk and ready for a deep clean. A fresh beginning. Its new lease on life had begun.

All in all, it had been a pretty good day.

※ ※ ※

Saturday, April 26

Once Bonnie's junk was gone, Dawn and her mom scrubbed every surface, every window, every appliance, every wall, ceiling, floor, both upstairs and downstairs. A good deep clean made a noticeable improvement. Now that there was space to move about, Linc was able to add drywall to the open framing upstairs, so the apartment felt far more livable. Dawn had a little room to call her own. The difference was night and day. On the inside, anyway.

Every day but Sunday, Linc arrived in the early afternoon, ready and eager to get to work. Dawn tried to press cash into his hand at the end of each day, but he refused it.

"I enjoy the work," he told her, which was hard to believe because he had painful-looking blisters on his palms. "It brings back a lot of memories from working with my dad. I haven't worked with hand tools since I was a teen." He tapped his forehead. "Only this tired old tool."

Dawn could relate to what he meant. Making ice cream required all of her, not just her brains. Her hands, her senses. While she made ice cream, she thought of nothing else. No one else.

She almost wished that Lincoln would accept money so she could insist that he start coming to work at the Creamery in the mornings, as well as the afternoons. He might not be quick, but he did work hard. He worked smart. He could get a tiny bit preachy at times (or maybe she was just a tiny bit sensitive to preaching), he always said grace before a meal, and he invited them both to church again—Mom said yes, Dawn declined—but he'd also said that getting to sample Dawn's ice cream on a daily basis was better than any salary, which endeared him to her. When it came to his mornings, though, he wouldn't budge. He was only available to help them at the Creamery in the afternoons.

The three of them had just sampled another vanilla ice cream recipe Dawn had made from scraped seeds out of Tahitian vanilla beans and added to vanilla extract. She was pleased. It created a sweet floral note, different from Madagascar vanilla bean's bourbon flavor.

And then Linc asked what they were thinking about a POS system. "Have you decided what you'd like to use?"

Dawn slapped her palm against her forehead. She'd been so absorbed with the making of ice cream, she hadn't given a second thought to how they would actually sell it. Systems! She had forgotten all about her plan to create systems.

Mom gave him a puzzled look. "POS?"

"Point of sale," Linc said. "When someone buys an ice cream cone, that is the moment of a point of sale. Your POS system is both the hardware and software that enables you to make that sale. It's another way of ringing up a customer."

Mom tipped her head. "Same thing as a cash register, you mean. Bonnie had one near the ice cream counter. I moved it into the storage closet under the stairs."

"I put it out in the tag sale," Dawn said. "It was snatched up within minutes."

Mom's eyes widened. "It's gone?"

"A tablet will replace a cash register." But Dawn had forgotten to add the cost of a tablet and software into the budget she'd created on a spreadsheet. A razor-thin budget. A no-room-for-margin budget.

Mom flashed Dawn a look of frustration. "But a cash register could've sufficed."

Lincoln lifted his hand. "Actually, Marnie, a POS system can do a lot more than make a sale. It can keep track of inventory, taxes, menu customization, staff reporting."

She still didn't look convinced. "Dawn and I . . . we're the only staff."

"For now," Dawn said, and felt a prick of guilt when she saw the pleased look flicker through Mom's eyes. She was pretty sure she knew what Mom was thinking: Dawn assumed there would soon be a need for more employees. The unspoken truth was that Dawn meant a good POS system would help boost the sale of the ice cream shop after Labor Day.

"Let me put it a different way, Marnie. It'll make a breeze of taxes." Lincoln rubbed his hands together. "Next time I'm in Hyannis, if it's okay with the two of you, I'll go ahead and get started on purchasing a good POS system."

Mom looked to Dawn to respond. "Yes. That would be a big help, Lincoln," she said, "and of course we will reimburse you." Though the cost of it made her skin itch.

The Creamery couldn't lose money, because there was none to spare. Ever since Dad had died, Dawn held a secret dread of one day having to support her mother in her dotage, of living together in the tiny Boston apartment. A cringeworthy image! The Creamery had to be successful for Mom. It absolutely had to make money or at least break even by Labor Day.

Dawn ran through her internal pep talk: She had made straight A's throughout her entire academic life. She was president of her sorority for three straight years. She was nearly a partner at her firm, the youngest partner ever—male or female—though she did have a niggling concern as days passed without any incoming work emails. She knew her boss was upset with her for taking a leave, but she kept trying to dismiss that worry. In September, when she returned to work, she'd pick up the reins and redouble her efforts. She had never failed at anything in her life. She wouldn't fail now.

Chapter

THIRTEEN

I love revision. Where else can spilled milk be turned into ice cream?

—Katherine Paterson, author of *Bridge to Terabithia*

Monday, April 28

Each evening, Dawn would lie on her lumpy bed and scroll through her phone for information about how to run an ice cream business. Three components seemed to be critical for success: the proper machine (Dawn had one), a good basic mix (she was working on it), and the knowledge of how to freeze ice cream. That last part, the freezing, was a serious concern to her. Quality deteriorated in the freezer. Whenever she and her dad had made ice cream at home, they would sit down and eat it immediately. Quite frankly, most ice cream tasted pretty good right after churning. But keeping it properly stored in the freezer—in airtight containers, safe from even the tiniest chance of melting and starting that dastardly crystalizing—was keeping Dawn up at night.

If freezing wasn't enough to worry about, pasteurization opened up an entirely new area of concern. It wasn't something she and her dad ever considered—but they weren't trying to sell ice cream. It wasn't enough to purchase pasteurized milk, pasteurized cream, even pasteurized eggs. The health and safety people insisted that the entire base had to be pasteurized after mixing. She'd been heating the base and allowing it to cool before it went into the machine, but once the Creamery's doors opened to the public, she'd need a pasteurizer. New, they cost a pretty penny, but she might be able to find a good used one.

She couldn't think about that now. Not pasteurization, not freezing, not work—none of those very substantial worries. For now, the process of ice cream making was sheer bliss. In just a week's time, a rhythm had developed. She spent part of each morning shopping for the freshest milk and cream and eggs she could find. She liked to know where the raw ingredients came from, and quizzed store clerks so relentlessly that they vanished when they saw her coming. Wandering the aisles of the grocery store, she searched for possible products to use as add-ins. After returning to the Creamery with the day's ingredients, she continued to experiment—trying different base recipes (eggs or no eggs? such a big decision), churning the ice cream, transferring it to square-edged containers, freezing it, testing how the flavor and texture changed after time spent in Bonnie's old chest freezer.

Dawn was having a wonderful time. The more focused she was on making ice cream, the less focused she was on everything else. She kind of stopped being Dawn the CPA, the grieving daughter, the jilted fiancée, and became the thing she was doing. Artisan ice cream maker.

She hadn't heard from Kevin since telling him not to call last week, but Brynn said that he had texted her each day, wondering if she'd heard anything from Dawn, and always asking if Dawn was okay. While she wouldn't dare admit it to Brynn, it pleased her that Kevin sounded worried about her.

One morning, Dawn was halfway down Main Street when she realized she'd forgotten her grocery list. She spun around and hurried back, went into the kitchen to retrieve her list on the counter. She froze. For a split second, Dawn didn't understand what was going on. Then it hit her.

Mom stood in front of the ice cream machine, pouring a milky liquid from a big plastic container into the ice cream machine.

"You're supposed to finish painting the front room this morning."

Stopping for a split second, Mom carried on with her pouring, pretending she didn't hear Dawn.

Louder this time, Dawn said, "Mom, just what do you think you're doing?"

Slowly, Mom turned, a guilty look on her face. "I thought you were going to the grocery store."

"I forgot my list. What in the world are you doing with . . . that?"

"I'm . . . uh . . ." Mom finished pouring the liquid and closed the lid, then turned on the machine. She flashed Dawn a nervous smile. "I'm making ice cream."

"With a prepackaged base? No! No no no. We are NOT using a prepackaged base at the Main Street Creamery."

"Oh Dawn." Mom tossed the empty plastic container in the trash. "I've researched all kinds of local dairy sources for the base. This one had the best reviews, so I ordered two to try. The box was delivered late last night. I hid them in the vegetable drawer in the refrigerator. One vanilla. One chocolate."

Seriously? Hidden them in the fridge? How had Dawn missed seeing them? She must be slipping. "Not happening. The stakes are too high for us to succeed."

"We can succeed with a premade base."

Dawn shook her head vigorously. "No. Absolutely not. The

Main Street Creamery needs to stand out in Chatham. A pre-packaged base does not stand out."

"Most every artisanal ice cream maker uses them."

Dawn couldn't argue that point. Mom's information was surprisingly correct. Still. A prepackaged base was not good enough for *this* shop. "Making my own cream base allows for more control, not less. I can tweak the base depending on add-ins, if they're sweet or salty. I can't adjust cream and sugar ratios with a premade mix."

"But we just don't have the time to create perfect recipes right now. Especially if we're going to offer lots of flavors."

"But we're not." Dawn's chin lifted a notch. "We're only offering five flavors each day."

Mom's eyes went wide with surprise. "Five flavors? That's ridiculous! People won't come back on day six and day seven."

"They'll come back if it's the best ice cream they've ever tasted." Dawn put her hands on her hips. "There's nothing wrong with classic flavors. And you have to remember that half the reason people love ice cream is because of nostalgia. They remember turning the old crank with Grandma. Ice and salt, sweet fresh cream . . ."

"Hold it. Hold it right there." Mom's eyes drilled into her. "Are you planning to just make riffs on vanilla and chocolate? You are, aren't you? You're planning to toss in smashed-up Oreo cookies or nuts or cookie dough and give it a name and sell it as a new flavor."

Dawn ran a hand down her long ponytail. "Maybe."

"Ha! And you call *me* the Shortcut Queen!"

"You can take vanilla ice cream and make just about any ice cream flavor you want. Vanilla is the most popular flavor in the entire world, you know."

"How could I not know? You and your dad made fifty-nine versions of it. I've sampled more vanilla ice cream than any other human on earth." Mom shook her head, hard. "No way, Dawn. One vanilla. One chocolate. Maybe one or two variations on the theme. But we have to try to be adventurous and distinctive and give people a reason to return. After all, we want them to skip the grocery store aisle and come here, don't we?" She crossed the kitchen to set her hands on Dawn's shoulders. "You can do so much better."

"Like what?"

Mom inhaled a deep breath. "Like . . . Matcha-Cha-Cha."

"Matcha . . . as in tea?"

"And then there's Pomegranate with Lime."

"Sounds puckery. Is that a sorbet?"

"Maybe." Mom dropped her hands. "I didn't read the recipe. I've been concentrating on attention-grabbing names."

"And yet you're the one who wants to use a prepackaged base! You can't create a pomegranate sorbet out of a cream or custard base."

Mom frowned. "I hadn't thought about that. Okay, for now I'll limit my ideas to a cream or custard base. But I insist we try new flavors. Think of the buzz we could generate by coming up with a new flavor each day. Think of Salt & Straw and the splash they made with their bone marrow ice cream."

Trying to be patient, Dawn inhaled a deep breath. "Mom, you told me you had a vision for a community gathering place. For people to come and enjoy a little bit of happiness. To remember the simple pleasures of their childhood. We cannot try to imitate Salt & Straw with bizarre flavor combinations and think we'll make a profit by Labor Day. This is New England, not Los Angeles. Tradition reigns king here."

"But—"

"There's a time for getting adventurous. Just not now. Right now, we're trying to make this shop ready to open on Memorial Day and be profitable by Labor Day."

"That's the goal *you* put out there. And to achieve that goal, we need to use a packaged base."

"Absolutely not."

Mom sighed. "Dawn, why reinvent the wheel? Why do you have to make things so hard?"

She didn't know. She just did. It was part of her perfectionist nature. It was why she was so good at her job. Attention to detail might not be the answer to everything in life, but it did make the world run a little smoother. Imagine having a neurosurgeon who had a "good enough" philosophy of life. Imagine an airline pilot who cut corners. No, it was not a bad thing to be a perfectionist, not when you were a CPA—or an ice cream maker.

"Look at it this way, Mom. You can be as experimental and creative as you want to be if you're only making five gallons a day. You can make as many weird flavors as you want."

"How weird a flavor can you get when you're only making vanilla and chocolate?"

"Vanilla and chocolate are the blank canvases. Add-ins make them unique."

Mom dropped her chin to her chest, defeated. Then she lifted it up, happiness brightening her face. "I've got an idea. Let's try one batch with the prepackaged base, one batch made from scratch. We'll ask an independent third party to do a blind tasting. Whichever one wins, that's how we will proceed. Deal?" She stuck out her hand.

"Deal," Dawn said, giving Mom's hand a shake.

Lincoln walked in the door carrying a bag. "Hello there, ladies." He held up the bag. "The Main Street Creamery's efficient point of sale system is here."

The two women turned to him and, at the exact same moment, blurted out, "You!"

Lincoln slapped one palm against his chest. "Me?"

"You can be our taste master."

His forehead furrowed. "I have no idea what that means."

"It means you'll be tasting ice cream."

"In that case, I accept."

Dawn clarified. "It means that you're the critical decision maker between us. The tiebreaker. The judge."

Lincoln observed them with alarm. "Alone? It all rests on my taste buds?"

"I like ice cream."

They spun around to find a little cowboy standing at the open door, hands on his hips like he'd just come off a cattle drive.

"Come on in, Leo," Linc said, relief in his voice. "I was just whispering a prayer for reinforcements."

Dawn rolled her eyes. Big mistake, and she had no one to blame but herself. A senior-citizen preacher and a five-year-old cowboy were deciding the fate of the Creamery.

● ● ●

Tuesday, April 29

As Marnie painted window trim in the front room, her thoughts kept returning to the debate over a prepackaged base or a base from scratch. It wasn't that she objected to Dawn's plan to create ice cream from scratch, but it worried her about what would come after Labor Day, when Dawn left. Even though Philip and Dawn assumed she had no knowledge of how to make ice cream, she'd watched them often enough to understand it. Here's what she knew about making ice cream: 99 percent of the ingredients were for the base and everything else was just flavoring or add-ins—nuts, candies, fruit, and so on. If she eliminated the need to *make* the base, all she would have to do was add flavoring and add-ins, put it all in the ice cream maker, and harden it in the freezer.

Marnie felt fairly confident she could make consistently delicious ice cream if she used a prepackaged base. But if she had to make it from scratch, she would be in trouble. It was the process of pasteurization that terrified her. Dawn talked about it all the time, at every meal: You couldn't just use pasteurized products and think you were safe. The entire base had to be pasteurized. Very complicated, very involved, very scientific.

Left to Marnie, she would end up cutting corners and accidentally killing her customers. Spend the rest of her life behind bars. She could see the headline: ICE CREAM SHOP OWNER HEADS TO THE COOLER.

On the other hand, Marnie was secretly delighted to see Dawn's high interest level in the shop. Just as she hadn't expected her to stay through the summer, she hadn't expected her to be so vocal about the quality of the ice cream, to claim full ownership over the machine. To be so thoroughly territorial over the kitchen.

Dawn was almost nonchalant about the actual running of the shop—how the front room would look, or the POS thingy that Linc talked about. She hadn't even brought up the upsetting visit by Mrs. Nickerson-Eldredge and the Historical Commission. But when it came to ice cream, Dawn was in charge.

It worried Marnie to see Dawn falling into a vanilla recipe rut—experimenting over and over and over to get it just so. Honestly, at this point, Marnie couldn't tell a Madagascar vanilla bean from a Tahitian one. Something had to jolt Dawn out of vanilla, to encourage her to stop resisting innovation. There were so many unique variations to try, combinations to experiment with. If she'd only get off the vanilla train.

Still, Dawn's passionate ownership of the ice cream gave Marnie a ray of hope that her daughter might consider staying past Labor Day. Just a thin sliver of hope. So if Lincoln and Leo picked the made-from-scratch base over the prepackaged base as the best one, she wouldn't object. She'd graciously accept defeat and hope it might mean Dawn would stay on.

Dawn had made two batches of vanilla—one from scratch, one from a prepackaged base. This afternoon, after the ice cream had plenty of time to harden, would be the moment of truth. "I've hardly eaten anything all day," Linc said when he arrived, "so that my palate would remain pure."

Marnie laughed. He was taking his taste master role very seriously. Leo, coming straight from kindergarten, seemed less concerned about his palate but twice as eager to sample ice cream.

Dawn set two containers in front of each of them, one marked A, the other marked B. She handed them spoons, papers with questions to fill out, and pencils. Marnie set two glasses of water in front of them.

"I know my letters," Leo said, "but I can't read words."

"Don't worry about that, Leo," Marnie said. "You just have to decide which ice cream you like best."

Lincoln looked over the questions. "Sight. Smell. After tasting . . . does it coat the tongue? Texture . . . is it creamy? Chalky? How does it melt in your mouth? Is it melting quickly? Is it melting slowly?" He dropped his chin. "The pressure I feel. It's overwhelming." Lincoln looked at both of them, at Leo, whose eyes were fixed on the ice cream containers, and back to them. "I feel as if I'm deciding which is my favorite child."

"Yes," Dawn said firmly. "It's that important. The entire success of this shop rests on your decision."

"No, it doesn't." Marnie put a hand on Dawn's elbow—her signal for her to stop jiggling, because she was. Practically jumping out of her skin. "It's only two bowls of ice cream. Lincoln and Leo, you're the ideal customers. You both love good ice cream. You don't have to know everything about it. You just have to pick the one that would make you want to come back for more." She put an arm around Dawn's shoulder. "Maybe we should go to the kitchen and let Lincoln and Leo have a little space."

"Good idea," Dawn said. "We don't want to influence you

in any way. Just pick the very best one. And be quick about it. Don't overthink it."

Marnie steered Dawn toward the kitchen. "Take all the time you need. Call us when you're ready." Just as she rounded the corner, she glanced back at them and had to swallow a laugh. Lincoln seemed a bit befuddled. Slightly terrified. Leo was halfway through the container marked A.

● ● ●

Ten minutes later, Lincoln called them back in. He stood, hands behind his back. All four containers were empty. Licked clean. "It was a photo finish."

Dawn sighed. She turned to Leo. "Let's start with you. Which one was your favorite?"

"That one." He pointed a chubby finger at pint B.

All eyes turned to Lincoln. "Both were excellent. Delicious. Astonishingly so. Really, truly outstanding."

"Lincoln," Dawn said, a warning tone in her voice.

He held up a hand. "I did make a decision. It was painful to choose, but there was one that had a slightly more satisfying aftertaste. And I do mean slightly." He pointed to pint B.

Dawn shouted. "That's the one from scratch!" She high-fived Leo. "I am impressed with your palate, young cowboy." She danced a little jig. "Told ya, Mom. From scratch it is. That's how we are going to differentiate ourselves from every other ice cream shop on the Cape."

Marnie tried to look disappointed, but hearing Dawn let loose with laughter felt too good. Besides, if Dawn chose not to stay past Labor Day—and she hoped she would but just in case she didn't—Marnie would just quietly switch over to a prepackaged base. It was a win-win.

Chapter
FOURTEEN

Life is like an ice cream cone. You have to lick it one day at a time.

—Charles M. Schulz

Wednesday, April 30

The weather cleared up and spring returned. The sun shone brightly through now-sparkling clean windows at the Main Street Creamery, a gentle breeze drifted through the open door, laced with a slight ocean scent. The soft cream color Marnie had chosen for the walls in the front room turned out to be perfect. Light, warm, clean, inviting. Linc painted the ceiling, and the wooden beams popped. Despite the improvements, the room was still lacking. Maybe it was the gray carpet that weighed the room down. Or maybe it was Bonnie's oversized ice cream display counter, especially disappointing if there were only going to be five ice cream flavors. She couldn't quite put her finger on what the large room was lacking, but it needed something.

Marnie had scoured the yard sale ads in the *Cape Cod Times* and found some small wooden tables for sale in Truro. She dropped everything and drove over. She ended up buying only one of the tables, but she also bought four chairs and a box of dishes. She had a specific vision of the front room filled with small wooden tables and chairs, unmatched but complementary. As soon as she found a few more tables and chairs, she would ask Linc to help her sand and stain them, give them a coat or two of polyurethane, and then get glass tops made for each one.

On the drive to Truro, she'd had an idea. Under each table's glass covering, she imagined displayed postcards sent from Chatham's summer residents. Bonnie had warned her that 60 percent of the homes in Chatham were summer residents, and that the town's population dropped, like a stone, come October all the way through May. Marnie thought the postcards might be a way for summer residents to stay connected and feel important to the town during the long winter months. When they returned, they would come to the Creamery and seek out their postcard, while buying ice cream.

Her mind was already moving past Labor Day, past Dawn's five ice cream flavors (honestly! why couldn't that girl be more open-minded?) to expand the Creamery's offerings. Specialty coffees, baked goods. She'd have to keep an eye out for a used espresso machine. The baked goods, she decided, could be purchased from local bakeries.

As she pulled up to the Creamery, she found Lincoln tackling the tangle of overgrown weeds along the foundation of the building. Seeing him hard at work, bent over, yanking and pulling, touched her heart. She hadn't expected his help with the yardwork. He didn't seem to notice she'd returned, so she decided to surprise him with iced tea. Last night, she'd made a fresh jug of it when she saw the weather report for a warming trend.

Marnie paused at the stoop. A large scallop shell in perfect condition lay on the welcome mat. She reached down to pick it up, running her fingers along the ridges. A pectinid, from the Latin word *pecten*, meaning comb-like structure.

Lincoln. It must have been from him. She had started a collection in a glass jar, set on a windowsill, and he must have noticed. Smiling to herself, she picked it up to add to the other shells. She'd seen a wreath made of seashells on Pinterest and thought to make one for the Creamery for the Christmas season.

Inside, she heard the whirring hum of the ice cream maker. Dawn waved when she saw her come into the kitchen, but her attention was focused on her task. Showing her the table and chairs would have to wait. Marnie set her purse down, took two glasses out of a cupboard, and poured cold tea into them. She added ice from the chest freezer, set the glasses on a small tray, then decided to include the pitcher of tea, and carried it outside. Then she waited until Linc was sure to see her. When he did, she held up the tray, a wordless invitation to take a break.

He straightened, stretched, and walked over to where she sat on the stoop. He tossed his leather gloves on the ground and plopped down beside her. Sweat ran down the sides of his face.

"Those weeds must be putting up quite a fight."

"No kidding," he said, and wiped the sweat from his brow with his forearm. "Devil's Tail."

She handed him a glass of iced tea. "Rather an ominous name."

"Yup. It's known as a mile-a-minute weed. Explosive growth. Kills everything in its path. I noticed it when I drove up today and thought I should take care of it right away." He drained the glass. She refilled it. The second glassful disappeared as quickly as the first had. "Hits the spot," he said.

She refilled his glass again, wanting to continue their conversation. Mostly, their conversations had revolved around the punch list—Dawn's term for the Creamery's lengthy to-do list. But Marnie wondered what Linc had done in his career, and why he had left work on the young side of sixty, and what made him move to Chatham. He didn't volunteer much about himself and had a talent for deflecting the conversation right back to the questioner. He asked lots of questions, which struck her as unusual for a man. Lincoln Hayes held his cards close to his chest, which, of course, made him that much more interesting. "So how long have you lived in Chatham?"

"Full time? Two years now."

She watched him drain the third glass and she quickly refilled it again, hoping he might linger for a few more moments. She wondered where he went each morning, because he was never available until after noon. When she'd asked him once, he'd only said, "Commitments." Dawn joked that it sounded like he was doing time for community service, and he didn't correct her.

Marnie had never told Dawn that Lincoln led the cancer support group and didn't intend to. If Linc brought it up, that was one thing. But she had no desire to stir up Dawn's pressure to attend the group. She'd gone, as Dawn insisted, and even though she'd only stayed four minutes, once was enough. More than enough.

Marnie half expected Lincoln to not show up at the Creamery one day, but somewhere between noon and one o'clock, he would arrive and ask to see the daily punch list. Whenever Dawn tried to foist money on him for his time and efforts, he refused it, insisting that her ice cream was payment enough. Clearly, he did love her ice cream. At the end of each day, he never said no to a heaping bowlful of whatever version of vanilla ice cream that Dawn had whipped up. Same with Nanette. She had a knack for popping in the door just as the ice cream was ready to scoop. Dawn said she wondered if Nanette had planted a listening device in the kitchen. Her timing was that eerie.

"And you enjoy living here? Even in the wintertime?"

"Winter is the best time of all. The entire Cape quiets down. The beach is empty. Mayor can go leash-free."

"Does it ever get . . . lonely?"

"Lonely?" From the surprised look on his face, the thought had never occurred to him. "No, not lonely. Never that. There's too much to do." He set his empty glass on the tray and reached for his leather gloves. "A lot has been accomplished at the Creamery in the last ten days. But there's still a lot to do if we're going to open on Memorial Day. I'd better get back to work."

"You're going to spoil us with all the nice things you do for us."

He smiled. "Seems like you both deserve a little spoiling."

"Thank you," she said, and then flopped her hands against her thighs. "See, I've done it again. I'm forever thanking you. What can we ever do to show you how much we appreciate everything you've done for us?" She picked up her glass to finish the last few sips.

He shifted on the stoop, his gaze intently resting on her. "Come to the cancer support group on Saturday morning. We missed you last week."

Mid-sip, she practically choked on her iced tea. She hadn't missed it at all. "Oh, Lincoln," she said between coughs, "it's just not my kind of thing."

"What do you think it's like?"

"Sitting around with a bunch of depressed cancer patients, each with his or her sad story."

He grinned. "The people who attend support groups are the ones who refuse to sit home and be sad and depressed. They choose to be active and take charge—to help themselves, as well as others." He cocked his head. "Will you give it another try?"

Heat began in Marnie's abdomen and coiled upward. Flustered, she felt her face grow warm. *Stupid hot flash!* In an obvious attempt to change the subject, she picked up the tray, stood, and said, "You're right. There's so much to get done around here before Memorial Day." She backed up, using her elbow to push open the door.

"Marnie—"

"I'll leave you to wrestle with the Devil's Tail." She was almost to the kitchen before she realized how strangely cinematic that sounded.

●　●　●

Dawn had to face facts. While the thought of using a prepackaged base made her shudder, she couldn't deny it would eliminate the need for a pasteurization step and guarantee no customer would be accidentally poisoned. Still, she felt it would be a cop-out. Searching Facebook Marketplace each day, she found a used Carpigiani Pasteurizer for sale in Hyannis and contacted the owner—a woman who had opened and closed an ice cream shop within three months and was selling everything off for whatever price she could get.

Dawn cringed. She didn't want to hear the sad tale, but the woman was on a rant: "I had such high hopes, but it was a failure from day one" and "now I'm in debt up to my eyeballs" and "I have to move in with my daughter and she hates my cat." She concluded with a line that struck Dawn like a punch to the gut: "The Cape just doesn't need another ice cream shop."

Dawn tried not to think of how eerily this woman's situation paralleled Marnie Dixon's, and she hoped there'd be a different story ending for the Main Street Creamery. She offered an embarrassingly low price for the Carpigiani and the woman didn't blink. She sent her a deposit for the pasteurizer via Venmo, with the understanding that she'd send the remainder of what she owed her when she picked it up. Or when Linc picked it up. He was heading to Hyannis tomorrow and she hoped he wouldn't mind a quick side trip to get the pasteurizer for her.

If she didn't get that machine into the Creamery quickly, and figure out how to use it, Mom would have a better argument to use a prepackaged base.

Dawn knew she was a control freak. There were just so many potential pitfalls in the making of ice cream. Chocolate, for example, had to be beaten longer than vanilla because of the higher fat content. But too much air and you ended up with fluffy ice cream.

Mom didn't get any of that. She thought you could just dump the mixture into the machine and call it a day. So, so wrong.

Mom kept prodding Dawn to move on from the formation of the base recipe and try some flavor variations, or at least consider add-ins. But she didn't understand all the near disasters that awaited the impatient ice cream maker. Because the most important quality of all was patience.

Brynn had called on her way while on the train to work this morning and Dawn had given her an earful. "My mother is making me crazy."

"That's because your mother is the yin to your yang."

Dawn rolled her eyes. "I've never understood that saying."

"It means . . . you balance each other out."

"It's not easy when we try to work together. Mom jumps into everything and wants to take all kinds of unnecessary risks."

"And you're so thoroughly cautious that you take no risks."

True.

"Until now. You're doing something so adventurous that it's got everyone buzzing."

Dawn twirled a lock of hair. "Yeah?"

"Yes! A bunch of us are already planning to make a field trip to the Creamery on the opening day."

Really? That sounded rather nice to hear.

"So stop trying to turn your mom into you. Appreciate your oppositeness." The screech of metal brakes meant Brynn's train had arrived at her station. "Gotta run. Talk soon."

Hmm. So her Boston friends were buzzing about the Creamery. Dawn smiled.

Last night she had prepared another vanilla base and let it cool overnight in the refrigerator. She poured the mixture into the machine, set the speed, set the timer for eight minutes. She listened to its steady whirl, pleased. In just a week's time, she was developing a familiarity with this machine, listening carefully to know what each sound of churning meant. When the sloshing changed to sound like wet towels in a dryer, she knew the ice cream was nearly ready.

While the Emery Thompson churned away, she grabbed an empty container and set it on the counter near the machine. Seven minutes later, she turned off the machine, waited a minute, and opened the gate to allow a dribble of vanilla to slide down the metal barrel. It came down too fast. "Not ready," she said to no one in particular and started the machine up again.

After another minute, she pulled the gate. This time the sample that slipped down the barrel was firmer, thicker, not gloppy. She grabbed a metal tasting spoon. The ice cream had a soft-serve consistency—smooth in the mouth, sweet on the tongue. The vanilla flavor was perfecto. Spot on. She filled the container, quickly covered it and transferred it to the freezer, where it would harden to the perfect consistency—and left the kitchen with a pleasing sense of satisfaction.

As Mom was leaving this morning for Truro, she pleaded with Dawn to add crumbled Girl Scout cookies or crushed-up pretzels or some kind of berry into today's vanilla mixture. "Anything," Mom begged, like it was simple. But depending on the add-ins, Dawn would have to tweak her base recipe. Too salty? Too sweet? And add-ins had to be cold, if not frozen, before mixed into the ice cream base. Oh, no. Add-ins were *not* simple.

All these steps, all the attention to detail in the process of ice cream making . . . Mom just did not appreciate. The most important thing Dawn expected from her ice cream was consistency—because she couldn't expect it from the rest of her life.

*   *   *

It wasn't until an hour later, when Marnie started unpacking the car, that she realized several of the missing shingles on the side of the Creamery's exterior had been replaced. When had *that* happened? The new cedar shingles—almost bright yellow—stuck out like a sore thumb against the existing gray-weathered shingles.

Out of nowhere, Nanette appeared at her side. "Hon, the Creamery is looking great, just great. That Lincoln Hayes . . . he's too good to be true. But then . . . I don't have to tell you that, do I?" She gave her a knowing wink and dashed back to her T-shirt store across the street.

Ignoring Nanette's insinuation, Marnie stood back to take a fresh look at the building. It was then she realized that the trim around the front door had been sanded and painted. When had Lincoln done all this? She was all for making improvements—and she had to admit that the weed removal, the fresh shingles, the paint trim, the roof repair, they were adding up. The Creamery was starting to look like someone cared—but she had wanted everyone to stick to the interior. She hoped to stay under the radar a little longer as she waded through paperwork for submitting permits to the Historical Commission—it was endless! And she had no desire to ruffle Mrs. Nickerson-Eldredge's feathers. Kevin had warned her.

She heard voices and realized Dawn and Lincoln were coming around to the front with ladder and shingles. She slipped into the house before they spotted her, pulled her cell phone out of her pocket, and scrolled through her favorites list to find Kevin's number. "Hi. Dawn doesn't know I'm calling—"

"Is she all right?" There was alarm in his voice.

"Dawn? Yes. She's fine." Outside the window, Marnie saw Dawn pass a box of nails to Lincoln on a ladder. It occurred to her that Dawn did seem fine lately. This ice cream shop was helping her. It was helping all of them. And they weren't using a nail gun on the new shingles—only hammers. "I'm calling about the Creamery."

"Shoot."

"What happens if we get a little ahead of the Historical Commission's OK to work on the exterior?"

"Describe what you mean by getting a little ahead of the commission."

"Paint, for one thing." She hastened to add, "The only paint that's been brushed on so far is for the door trim, and it's a shade of white that the Historical Commission has approved for other buildings on Main Street. I know that for a fact." She'd been making friends with other shop owners. Trying, anyway. Some welcomed her; some were skeptical of newcomers. One thing they all had in common—no one had liked Bonnie's ice cream.

"Then what's that sound of hammering I hear in the background?"

"That's Dawn. She's nailing new shingles on the siding."

"Dawn? Your daughter? The one who thinks manicures and pedicures are more vital than food?"

Marnie smiled. Kevin knew Dawn so well. Their breakup had grieved her. She would've liked to know, from his perspective, what had gone wrong between them, but she was Dawn's mother, first and foremost. She shouldn't even be calling him with questions about the Creamery, but he was an excellent resource. "So what might happen if we get ahead of approval?"

"You can be fined for violations. As small as one hundred dollars a day for anything that isn't code compliant. There can be big fines too. I was just reading about a contractor in Salem who was fined $5,000 per day."

Oh no. Dawn would flip. She was all about the bottom line.

Marnie bit her bottom lip, then she relaxed. Mrs. Nickerson-Eldredge hadn't come around since that first day. Over a week now. Maybe Dawn was right. Maybe she was all bark and no bite.

"When did you file?"

Marnie swallowed. "File?"

"File applications. Apply for approval." When she didn't answer, he said, "Marnie . . . have you not submitted any applications yet?"

"I'm trying to make sense of the paperwork . . ."

He coughed a laugh. "Yeah, I get it. It must seem like Greek."

"Yes! Exactly that. A foreign language. Kevin, do you think the Historical Commission would deny us? All we're trying to do is repair the building. No additions. No remodeling."

"Hard to say. Safety issues are one thing, aesthetics are another."

"I've been trying to keep them to the interior, but each time I leave the building on an errand, they end up outside, doing something they shouldn't."

"Who do you mean? Have you hired a crew?"

"Heavens, no. We can't afford that. I just meant Dawn and Lincoln. He's a . . . new friend." When a moment passed in silence, Marnie said, "Kevin, do you think the Historical Commission could make things difficult for us if we just keep going? Dawn is determined to open the doors by Memorial Day weekend."

"Yes."

"Oh." That wasn't what she wanted to hear.

"So this Lincoln guy . . . you say he's a new friend?"

"Yes. He's helping us out each day. A great guy. Really, quite wonderful." Through the window, she saw him walk past the yard with a box of shingles propped on his shoulder. Not bad for a guy his age. Not bad at all.

Behind him trailed a small cowboy. "And then there's Leo,"

Marnie said with a smile. "He's completely smitten with Dawn. He's crazy about her ice cream."

Silence. "If these guys are so great, maybe you should ask them for help with the permitting process. Look, Marnie, I'd better get back to work."

"Oh . . . of course," she said, a little flustered by his abruptness. "Sorry if I caught you at a bad time. Thanks, Kevin."

He hung up before she finished saying his name. Slowly, she tucked her phone in the back pocket of her jeans. She'd been floating along pleasantly in a haze of happy progress. And she just landed on the ground with a thud.

* * *

Dawn hit her thumb so hard with the hammer that she had to stop to get ice for it. It was throbbing. She was pretty sure she'd lose her nail, too, which only added to her pain. In most matters, Dawn was pragmatic and practical, not an overly girly girl, but she did take good care of her hands. And toes. While icing her thumb in the kitchen, she checked her phone messages. A new text message from Brynn.

Who are the new guys?

New guys? Dawn texted back:

I don't know what you're talking about.

Aren't there great new guys in your life?

Only new anything in my life is a hammer. And blisters.

She was just about to ask Brynn why in the world she thought there were new men in her life when the door opened and Mrs. Nickerson-Eldredge stood at the threshold, frowning mightily, hands on her bulbous hips.

Chapter
FIFTEEN

Bad ice cream is better than no ice cream at all.

—Anonymous

Wednesday, April 30

If Dawn felt confused by Brynn's texts, she felt outraged by Mrs. Nickerson-Eldredge's visit.

The dour woman swept the interior of the Creamery with a dismissive glance. On the second sweep, her beady eyes zeroed in on Cowboy Leo, who'd been shadowing Dawn all afternoon. "Surely your mother is looking for you."

Spurs jangling, he scooted out the door.

"I've never met Leo's mother," Dawn said, trying to ease the tension that filled the Creamery with Mrs. Nickerson-Eldredge's presence. It was like the molecules in the room had started to vibrate. "Does his family live around here?"

"I don't know nor do I care. I don't particularly like children."

A revelation, Dawn thought, that came as no surprise. But

she knew that wasn't the message Mrs. Nickerson-Eldredge had come to deliver. She braced herself.

"You must cease and desist on any further work of improvements on the Main Street Creamery."

BOOM. There it was. Stunned, Dawn found herself unable to respond. "What? Why?" she finally managed. "Surely, you're joking."

"I never joke."

Dawn pushed a stray lock of hair away from her forehead and held her hand there, a dozen responses battled themselves out in her brain. "Tell me what we did that was so wrong?"

"The Historical Commission has not given you approval to paint the exterior."

"The trim! The chipped and flaking trim. We've only repainted what's already been painted. Same color as the trim on every shop in Chatham! Lincoln triple-checked before he bought the paint. He even took Nanette's paint can with him to the hardware store."

"I repeat," she said, her mouth puckered so tightly it all but disappeared. "You need approval from the Historical Commission to paint any part of the exterior."

Dawn's fists curled in frustration. "My mother bought this building, lock, stock, and barrel. She should be able to do what she wants to do with the place."

"Bah! The village of Chatham is not the state of Texas. We have traditions to uphold here. 'If you don't know history, then you don't know anything. You are a leaf that doesn't know it is part of a tree.'"

Dawn's face scrunched up in confusion. "Excuse me?"

"It's a quote by Michael Crichton. It means that in this town, we work together to preserve the history. To respect those who came before you. You and your mother are flagrantly disregarding any respect for our town."

"That's not true! We're updating a tired, neglected old building."

"That tired old building has meaning and purpose that started long before you arrived and will be here long after you leave." Her gaze sharpened as she studied Dawn's face.

It was almost as if Mrs. Nickerson-Eldredge sensed Dawn's plan to sell the refurbished building after Labor Day. Stay calm, she told herself. Try logic. "Well, in the meantime, life can't just stand still. There must be some middle ground of preserving the past while living in the present."

"Indeed. That's exactly what the Historical Commission aims to do."

"Really? Because all it seems to do is to stop progress from happening." There was a long pause, a glare turned into a glower, and Dawn realized she had probably said too much.

"Let me make this perfectly clear," Mrs. Nickerson-Eldredge continued with the same angry edge. Maybe even ratcheted up a few notches. "You may not do anything to the exterior of this building unless you have approval from the chairman of the Historical Commission."

"And that would be . . ."

"Me." She ended the visit on that sour note.

Dawn went to the open door and watched Mrs. Nickerson-Eldredge march away. Such a busybody! She was as annoying as an angry hornet. As interfering as an IRS auditor. As unwanted as rain at a picnic.

Halfway up on the ladder, sanding window trim, Lincoln looked down at her. "I take it that the visit didn't go well?" he said.

"What is her problem? It's like she's doing everything she can to drive us out."

Lincoln was quiet for a second. "She can be a little stodgy, but don't take her personally. The Historical Commission has done a lot of good for Chatham. They've kept out retail chains that would make this town look like any other place on a busy route. They've been able to keep Chatham's distinct personality."

Dawn sighed. "So Mrs. Nickerson-Eldredge treats every newcomer the same?"

Lincoln turned around on the ladder to catch a glimpse of her before she got in her car. "That's why Bonnie gave up."

"Hold on a moment." Dawn put her hands on her hips. "Lincoln, exactly why did the Main Street Creamery fail? Was it because of Bonnie's bad ice cream or was it because the Historical Commission made things too difficult for her?"

He climbed down the ladder. "I think it mostly had to do with Bonnie's terrible ice cream. Once an entire Little League team ended up with food poisoning." He folded his arms against his chest. "It'll be different for you. Your ice cream is incredible. Memorable."

She gave him a weak smile. "But how are we going to open up on Memorial Day when Mrs. Nickerson-Eldredge won't give us the green light to improve the building?" A chilling thought occurred to Dawn. "Surely, Mom has submitted every-thing to the Historical Commission." The whole topic had completely slipped her mind. All that she thought about lately was making ice cream.

"I did ask her about it the other day. She said she had every-thing under control."

Oh no. Dawn had made a cardinal mistake. She neglected the review process that was a critical component in finance and accounting. She should have been following up on her mother's big, lofty, empty promises. Should have tracked her like a dog after a slippery fox. Dawn slapped her hand against her forehead. She was slipping. As soon as Mom came home, she would deal with this matter.

Across the street came Nanette, sniffing the air. "Any chance I smell brownies baking?"

"Good olfactory skills." Dawn looked over her shoulder

toward the Creamery. "They're cooling on the kitchen counter." She'd whipped up a batch after talking to Brynn this morning. She thought if she added chunks of brownie to vanilla ice cream, it might appease Mom's relentless pressure to try new flavors.

Nanette's eyes went wide. "Why, I've had the worst craving for chocolate all the day long." She smoothed her hair up the back of her neck. "Dawn, honey, I don't suppose you'd let me sample a brownie?"

Dawn smiled. "I think they've cooled by now." She glanced at Linc. "What about you? Interested?"

"Absolutely. It's been torturous to smell them baking. But you two go on ahead. I'll finish up out here and come in to wash up."

That was one thing Dawn appreciated about Linc. He was thorough and diligent, finishing what he started. Unlike her mother, who had a dozen started projects inside the Creamery and few finished ones. Inside the kitchen, she found a clean knife and made a cut in the brownies.

Nanette put her hand over Dawn's. "A little bigger sample, please."

Dawn moved the knife over an inch. She cut the brownie and lifted it with a spatula to set on a paper napkin. "Enjoy."

"Oh, I will," Nanette said. With the first bite, she closed her eyes and looked like she might float away with happiness. "The best in the world, Dawn. I mean it. The *entire* world!"

Dawn sure hoped so.

Nanette polished that brownie off and looked longingly at the pan.

"Could I talk you into another?"

"Oh, Dawn, honey . . . I thought you'd never ask. If this is anything as good as your ice cream, the Main Street Creamery is going to be an enormous success."

Slowly, cautiously, Dawn was starting to warm up to Nanette. While the tiny, talkative woman was a very meddlesome neighbor, she was rooting for the Creamery to succeed, unlike Mrs. Nickerson-Eldredge. Frankly, unlike a lot of other locals, who gave Mom and Dawn a cool and distant welcome. Over her third brownie, Nanette explained that you had to be born on Cape Cod to be truly accepted here. If not, you were viewed as an imposter. A wannabe.

"Hon, have you given any thought to changing the name of the Creamery? Maybe to give it a little, you know, distance from Bonnie's version of ice cream?"

"I don't think so."

Nanette carried on like Dawn hadn't responded. "I was thinking on it last night, when Michael was snoring so loud the windows were rattling. Here it goes. Ready? 'Ma & Me.' Get it? It's a play on a mother and daughter in business together. Catchy, huh? I think it would make folks stop in their tracks and come right on in. You see a lot of 'Father and Son' businesses out there, but you don't hear much about mothers and daughters. Frankly, there's probably a reason for that. I never had a daughter, but from what I see in my shop, most mothers and daughters couldn't work together well." She rolled her eyes. "The way those daughters talk to their mothers." She shuddered.

"Thanks, Nanette, but it's pretty hard to beat Main Street Creamery. Kinda says it all." Dawn thought about trying to explain to Nanette that she wasn't going to be staying in Chatham after Labor Day. That she highly doubted Mom would be here after Labor Day, that she was hopeful the Creamery would be sold to another naively enthusiastic ice cream maker, thus the marketing concept of a mother-daughter team would be short-lived. But one thing she had discovered about Nanette—she liked to hear herself talk. And she did love to impart local lore.

"Nanette, do you know anything about the Nickerson legacy in Chatham?"

Nanette gasped. "Do I ever!" She leaned forward as if sharing state secrets. "Here's the answer you'll get if you ask Mrs. Nickerson-Eldredge." She dropped her voice an octave and took on a serious narrative tone. "William Nickerson was born in England, became a worster—"

"A what?"

Nanette's voice slipped back to normal. "A worsted weaver. Just a fancy way of saying he was a tailor." Her voice dropped an octave again. "William Nickerson married Ann Busby and emigrated with their four children to the Plymouth Colony aboard the ship *John & Dorothy* in the year 1637. On the same ship was Samuel Lincoln, ancestor of Abraham Lincoln, but that's neither here nor there. William Nickerson spent a few years in Salem and then moved his family to Yarmouth. In 1656, he pulled a cart along an old Indian trail on land occupied by Mattaquason, the Mononmoyick sachem . . ." She paused. "You know what a sachem is, don't you, hon?"

Dawn nodded.

"He offered Mattaquason a bunch of stuff, like a shallop and shillings and tools in exchange for four square miles of land. As a result, William Nickerson became the first white settler of Chatham and died at the ripe old age of eighty-five. No other colonist owned as much land as did he." She slapped the kitchen counter with the palms of her hands. "Now the real story," she said, in her breathy, nasal Nanette voice. "William Nickerson was always causing trouble or in trouble or looking for trouble. He'd trade for land from the Indians without getting approval from the Plymouth Colony. He scoffed at religion and disrupted town meetings. He didn't care. Didn't want anyone telling him what to do or how to do it."

She stopped to take another bite of brownie and talked around it in her mouth. "And Nickerson liked to sue people. A regular hobby. He would pay folks to make tar on his property, then he would sue them for leaving wagon wheel tracks in his field." She took another bite. "Then there was the time when the constable came to collect taxes, and he and his sons attacked the poor fellow. That got 'em a little 'time for reflection' in the stocks." She polished off the last bite. "There's lots more scuttlebutt on the Nickerson legacy, but it'll have to wait. I left the store long enough." She rose from the table. "So, speaking of Chatham's glorious history . . . I hear you've ruffled Mrs. Nickerson-Eldredge's feathers."

Dawn snapped her head up. "Who told you that?"

"My Michael. He ran into Mrs. Nickerson-Eldredge at the pharmacy when he was picking up a prescription." Nanette's sparse eyebrows lifted. "She was not a happy camper, my Michael said."

"Oh, right." Small towns were like this. Everything was news and nothing was private.

"Hon . . . just a word to the wise. She's a lot like old William."

"How so?"

"Not someone I'd want for an enemy."

Neither did Dawn, but why was the Creamery suddenly everybody's business?

● ● ●

Marnie stopped by the flower shop to pick up a bundle of pink tulips for Mrs. Nickerson-Eldredge. They had some fence-mending to do with her. When Dawn told her about their conversation, Marnie stared at her, then laughed. Dawn was an accountant, a rule abider, and yet here she was pressuring this firm elderly woman to bend the rules. "You're becoming your mother!"

Dawn didn't like that. Not at all.

Marnie wasn't offended. She would've cringed if her mother had told her that same thing. They were complete opposites, she and her mother. Just as Dawn and Marnie were opposites.

Maybe that's the way it went, generational flip-flops of personality traits.

Then Dawn asked her if she had submitted the paperwork for the Historical Commission and it was Marnie's turn to bristle. "Remember our agreement? You take care of the back of the house, I'll take care of the front of the house."

Dawn's eyes narrowed. "You didn't answer my question."

What was it about daughters that they could practically sniff your thoughts? "Dawn, I don't interfere with your ice cream."

"Yes," Dawn said smugly, "you do."

"That reminds me. I have a great idea. Since you aren't going to branch out from vanilla, what if we let the customers choose the add-ins? We could have rows of candies and sprinkles and chocolate chips and gummy bears and marshmallows and crumbled graham crackers and mint brownies and all kinds of other treats."

Dawn rolled her eyes and shook her head, both. "That might be the worst idea I've ever heard of."

"What? Why? I thought it could give customers a unique experience. Everybody loves to have choices."

"You can't trust customers to choose the best add-ins. Imagine someone adding gummy bears to mint brownies." She shuddered. "No. That is a terrible idea." She pointed to Marnie. "You keep to the front of the house." She took in a deep breath and clasped her hand to her chest. "And I will branch out from vanilla."

At long last! Swallowing a smile, Marnie grabbed her purse and headed to the door. "I have a few more errands to do. Be back soon."

First stop: flower shop. After she paid a fortune for the prettiest flowers in the shop, she squinted at the address Lincoln had written down for her on a piece of paper. She was starting to know Chatham well enough that she could find the address without consulting her phone's GPS.

Marnie pulled into the driveway of a classic Cape Cod house, silvered shingle siding, white trim, a blue door, and a row of hydrangeas edging the house, just starting to leaf out with their big green leaves. Sun-bleached and broken scallop shells lined the driveway.

You could tell a lot about a person by their home. This yard told Marnie one thing—meticulously tidy and well-tended, the recently mowed lawn had been shaved to a half inch. The NO SOLICITORS sign told her something else.

She saw a curtain move at the window closest to the door and realized she was being watched. She saw the curtain move again. So quirky! But Marnie wasn't put off by quirkiness.

She knocked on the door and waited. Knocked again. And again. She saw the curtain move again, ever so slightly. She knocked harder. "Mrs. Nickerson-Eldredge! I know you're in there. I have something for you."

"Leave it on the doorstep."

Braving it, she sucked in a deep breath and tried again. "I'd like to talk to you for a minute."

The door opened a crack to reveal an eye. "What do you want?"

"We seem to have gotten off on the wrong foot."

"I told your daughter how to make amends."

"Yes. The approval process with the Historical Commission. You see, I'm working on the paperwork. It's quite complicated, as you know."

"Hire a historical architect."

"The thing is, we're not trying to build anything. Or remodel anything. We're just trying to repair a little roof damage, paint the trim. That sort of thing."

"Then hire a preservation contractor."

"Is there such a thing?"

"Of course there is."

It was very odd to talk to an eyeball peering through a

small opening of the door. "Mrs. Nickerson-Eldredge, couldn't I come in for a moment? To get your advice on the matter?"

"No. Go through the proper channels of the Historical Commission."

"Aren't you the proper channel?"

A long pause. "There is an application process for the Historical Commission. That is the proper channel."

"Why can't the Historical Commission"—Marnie wiggled her hand in the air—"bend a little?"

"Like Procrustes?"

"Who?"

"Greek mythology. He shortened or stretched his guests to fit his bed."

"Yes! Then . . . be like Procrustes. Make a little allowance for us."

"You've missed the whole point of the myth." She started to close the door.

"Wait!" Marnie held up the pink tulips, wrapped in brown paper and tied with a pink ribbon. "I brought you flowers."

"I do not accept bribery."

"Bribery? No, not at all. They're just . . . flowers."

"Hunting me down at my own home? Plying me with gifts? I would call that bribery." And the door closed tight.

That woman! Marnie left the tulips on her doorstep and started toward her car, then reconsidered and picked them up. She had a hunch Mrs. Nickerson-Eldredge would just toss them out. As she sat in the car, fuming, she saw the curtain move again. She backed the car out of the drive, hearing the crunch of scallop shells under the tires.

Somehow, someway, she was going to befriend that woman.

Chapter

SIXTEEN

Ice cream—the great melter of all resolve.
—Dr. Idel Dreimer, poet

Thursday, May 1

All things considered, Marnie could sense the rebirth of the Main Street Creamery was working its magic. They were deep into week two and much progress had been made—thanks, in large part, to Lincoln Hayes. She enjoyed working with him. They made a great team.

On Thursday afternoon, Dawn had gone to Hyannis to seek out yet another source for vanilla beans, so Marnie had made the most of her absence. Working quickly, she mixed three flavors of ice cream using the prepackaged vanilla bases that she'd hidden in the refrigerator: Cinnamon Streusel Swirl, Meyer Lemon with Pomegranate Molasses, and Black Coffee. When Lincoln came in for a break, she lined up three pint-sized containers of ice cream in a row. There hadn't been time to harden them, so they had a soft-serve consistency. Not ideal, but it was the flavor she wanted his opinion on.

She took a metal spoon and scooped a taste out of the first one, then handed it to Lincoln. With great care and thought, he tasted and swallowed, ending by closing his eyes. When he opened them, he said, "I am transported back to the summer of 1999. I was in Vietnam, hurrying down a busy road, smelling the scent of French bread baking in ovens . . . and suddenly, the scent of cinnamon mingled into the sweet air. I stopped and went straight into the bakery, and had the most delicious pastry I've ever tasted."

Marnie grinned. "Such is the power of scent. It's like a time machine. It can transport you to other times and spaces, all through your nose." She tipped her head. "What were you doing in Vietnam?"

"Sourcing raw materials for my business."

"Fragrant cinnamon?"

"Different kinds of materials. But I did bring back some fragrant cinnamon."

"What kind of business materials did you bring back from Vietnam?"

He glanced at her. "Computer thingamajigs." He dropped the spoon in the WASH tin. "Have you been to Vietnam?"

"No. I haven't traveled to Asia. It was on our someday list. Mine, anyway. Philip wasn't much of a traveler. Unless it had to do with Dawn. For her, he'd go anywhere." She lifted another spoon. "Just like wine, we'll go from less complex to more complex flavors. This one is Meyer Lemon with Pomegranate Molasses. Inspired by a documentary I saw on Afghanistan. Pomegranates are a big deal over there."

He tasted and his mouth puckered up. "Tart and tangy."

"Too much?"

"Maybe a smidge too tart." He grabbed a glass of water and gulped it down.

Marnie frowned. "I was afraid of that. Okay . . . that one goes back to the drawing board. Try this one." She handed him a spoonful of Black Coffee Ice Cream.

He swallowed, eyebrows lifting. "Marnie . . . this is incredible. I've never had coffee ice cream that doesn't have a slightly bitter aftertaste."

She was pleased he noticed. Dawn always made Marnie feel like she didn't know the first thing about ice cream. She did! As long as it started with a prepackaged base. "I got some just-roasted coffee beans from Monomoy, still warm—and steeped them in the warm cream. The butterfat fuses with the oils in the coffee, sort of seals the coffee flavor into the cream, and then those flavors are released as the ice cream melts in your mouth."

He picked a spoon from the CLEAN tin and dug another spoonful out. "You should call this Monomoy Coffee Ice Cream. It'll make you a favorite with the locals."

She tapped her temple with her finger. "Smart. You should've gone into marketing ice cream instead of computer thingama-jigs."

He grinned.

Suddenly, she had a lightbulb moment. If Dawn was so insistent on creating her own base and not using a prepackaged one, then why not run with the concept? Create a mantra of everything homemade, sourced regionally.

In fact—Marnie's mind started to spin—why not celebrate the region? Focus on the treasure of living in a small town. Especially during the off-season times, when the population dropped dramatically down to the local residents. But six thousand people was still a lot of people, and Marnie was sure that most of them loved ice cream year-round. So what if she made a point to give hyper-local names to flavors? Lighthouse Lemon Coconut. Oyster Bay Banana French Toast.

She leaned forward on her elbows. "Linc, what if the special flavor of the day was always some kind of nod to Chatham? Think of all the historical buildings that could be paired with ice cream. The Chatham Windmill, the Atwood House, the Mayo House. Marconi Wireless."

"My first thoughts are mayonnaise and macaroni pasta."

She pulled a face. "How about this? Marconi Wireless Chocolate Macaroon."

He grinned. "What flavor would you create for the Eldredge library?"

"Maybe, um . . . Eldredge Egg Nog and . . . um . . ."

"Rum."

Marnie smiled. "Bingo. And then . . . there's celebrating the land. Crows Pond Black Licorice. Cranberry Bog Cheesecake. And beaches."

Thoughtfully, he rubbed his chin. It was a nice chin, with a cleft in the middle. "How would you make an ice cream inspired by the beach? Sounds gritty."

"Smashed graham crackers for the sand. Marshmallows for the seashells. Chocolate bits for the seals."

"Okay," he said, "okay. I'm catching your vision. Here's another idea. What about also celebrating Chatham's salt-making history? And then fishermen and shipbuilders need a shoutout too."

She grinned. "Saltmakers' Caramel. Coconut Ginger Cod. Shipbuilders' S'mores."

"Marnie, you should be running a company."

"Ah, but I am! I'm the CEO, president, and janitor." She spun around to find her notebook and a pencil. Slapping them in front of him on the table, she said, "Write down every monument and building and beach and . . . anything that comes to mind. Anything that makes Chatham unique."

A sly look came over him. "Starting with the Nickersons?" He pointed to the Meyer Lemon with Pomegranate Molasses container. "Maybe that could be theirs."

She laughed, and he laughed, and they polished off all three containers of ice cream and cleaned up the kitchen before Dawn came home with her rare vanilla beans.

● ● ●

Signs were everywhere. Dawn knew Mom had been messing with the ice cream machine. The interior had drops of hot water from a recent cleaning, there were odd ingredients in the refrigerator (pomegranate molasses—what was *that*?), and the dishwasher was running.

Well. Never mind. Mom could try out her prepackaged base and toss in her strange add-ins, but it wasn't changing Dawn's strategic plan for the Creamery. Today, she had brought home the extremely difficult to find Vanilla planifolia from Papua New Guinea—a vanilla bean with a higher vanillin content than other beans. Extremely expensive too.

She smelled the bean. It had a slightly smoky profile, with hints of dark chocolate.

"What's that?"

She found herself staring down at the face of Leo, looking up at her in that solemn way of his. He wore a cowboy hat that tied underneath his chin.

"Oh, hello!" she said, smiling. "How'd you get in?"

"Door was open."

She held out the vanilla bean for him to sniff. "This, my friend, is the reason that people will try my ice cream once and insist on returning for more. Every single day, lines will be snaking out the door with customers who simply must have my vanilla ice cream. They will drive long distances to eat it. This . . . is what makes all the difference."

"But what is it?" The vanilla bean was longer than his little round face. Earnestly, he looked it up and down, as if trying to imagine what magic it could possibly bring to milk and cream and eggs and sugar.

"It's a vanilla bean. From the orchid family. One of the most expensive spices in all the world. Second only to saffron."

He scrunched up his face. "It looks like a shriveled-up worm."

It did, actually.

"Can't you just make regular vanilla ice cream?"

"Oh no," Dawn said. "I can't." Mom could, but she couldn't.

"Do you have a boyfriend?"

She stopped what she was doing. This was the first time she'd been asked that question since Kevin broke off their engagement. She was glad it came from five-year-old Leo and not nosy Nanette. "I did. But now I don't."

He smiled.

"Leo, how would you like to help me make some ice cream?"

Before she finished the sentence, he had pulled a chair against the counter to step on it. "I can crack eggs without hardly any shells getting in the bowl."

Surprised by his zeal, she decided to roll with it. "First things first. We wash hands with soap and water." Lots of soap. He might be a cute little cowboy, but she wasn't taking any chances on germs.

* * *

Friday, May 2

On Friday afternoon, Marnie drove to Brewster to pick up a table and two chairs from an older couple who were planning to move to a retirement facility, and they talked her into buying a few more knickknacks than she needed. But she was happy about the table and chairs—a little elbow grease and they would be just the thing.

She made a stop at the iconic Brewster General Store and tried out a scoop of their vanilla ice cream. Excellent, quite good, with a nice melt-in-the-mouth feeling, not icy. Dawn's vanilla flavor was definitely better, but this was good.

Marnie bought a large wooden-framed chalkboard to hang in the front room. On it, she envisioned a list of all the flavors the Creamery offered for the day . . . assuming Dawn would make good on her promise to move past vanilla. Adding chunks of brownies to vanilla ice cream didn't count.

Her mind traveled back to the flavor brainstorming session with Lincoln. It was so much easier to work with Linc than Dawn, who challenged Marnie on nearly every decision. They just couldn't seem to work together easily. They never had. As she wandered the aisles of the General Store, she thought back to Dawn's Girl Scout Brownie troop. Marnie had volunteered to be the leader. Big mistake. No matter what Marnie had planned for the girls, Dawn would try to improve it or correct her. She was only seven years old and she was already editing her mother. The only way Marnie had ever figured out how to work with Dawn was to work around her. Like they did now. Dawn was fully occupied in the kitchen, the "back of the house." Marnie stayed out of her way. Separate rooms, separate tasks.

Well, Dawn could keep her vanilla and chocolate, but Marnie was going to keep up the pressure on her to try untraditional innovations—crave-able, creative, bold flavors. Funky flavors for vegans, like Spinach. Maybe she'd branch out to sorbets. Spinach and Lemon Sorbet! On second thought . . . scratch spinach. It might be flavorless, but there was a limit to what kinds of vegetables you could add to ice cream.

What about . . . Basil and Lemon Sorbet? Avocado and Lime? Carrot and Pineapple?

And then there were seasonal twists. Pumpkin Gingersnap. Apple Cinnamon Crumble. Chai Cheesecake. Oh, the possibilities were endless!

Pleased, so pleased, so filled with excitement and enthusiasm for the Creamery, she left the store and started back home on the Brewster-Chatham Road. Indulging a whim, she turned onto the Orleans-Harwich Road to wander along less traveled roads. She wanted to get to know this place, inside and out. Living in a place was different than vacationing in it. Chatham was now her home.

And suddenly she was lost. But she wasn't worried, because she noticed that the sides of the road showed more sand than dirt and she knew she was heading toward the beach. How lost could she get if the Atlantic Ocean bordered one side? A few more turns and there it was—the water. It looked surprisingly calm and quiet. Low tide, she gathered.

She parked the car on a side street and walked down to a sheltered cove. She took off her shoes and wandered along the water's edge, looking for shells to add to her collection. The water covered her feet and she paused for a moment, loving the cold sensation, listening to the steady rhythm of the waves hitting the sand.

"Marnie!"

She spun around to find Lincoln walking toward her, his dog Mayor darting after seagulls. She watched him toss a piece of driftwood in the air and Mayor went racing after it.

"What are you doing along Pleasant Bay?"

Oh! So that's where she was. Pleasant Bay was north of Chatham Harbor. "I've just come from Brewster"—she pointed behind her—"and thought I'd get a walk in before the day's over."

"Mind if I join you?"

"I don't mind. But what are you doing here?"

His thumb jabbed the air above his shoulder. "My cottage isn't too far from here."

She glanced behind her and saw no cottages, only grand historic homes, built from whaling fortunes long ago. Before she could ask him anything else, he said, "A moment ago, as you were facing the water, what were you thinking?"

"What I always think when I'm standing on the beach. Any beach."

"Which is?"

"That it must be the most beautiful place on earth. Don't you agree?"

"I do." Their eyes locked for a moment, until Mayor dashed up to Lincoln with the stick of driftwood in his mouth. Linc tossed it far up the beach and the dog tore after it. "Shall we walk?" They started along at a nice leisurely pace. "Is that a conch shell in your hand?"

"Actually, it's a whelk. In fact, it's a knobbed whelk. The Latin name is *Busycon carica*. You can tell it's a knobbed whelk by the nine little knobs on the shoulder of its body whorl." She gave him a smile, suddenly shy. She seemed to open up like this with Lincoln; she didn't know why and she couldn't seem to stop. "I'm talking too much," she said.

"Never!" he said, and she could tell he meant it. He touched each one with the tip of his finger and counted. "You're right. There's nine."

"If you like learning about shells, I can loan you a shell guide."

"I never paid much attention to them. But, like so many things, it's high time I start."

She wondered what he meant by that. It felt as if she'd only scratched the surface in uncovering who he was. With that came the knowledge that she wanted to know more. They walked along for a while in companionable silence.

"So what did you do before you bought the ice cream shop?"

"I planned parties. Mostly for friends. Philip, my husband, was an electrician. Dawn's the first in our family to go to college. She's the educated one."

He stopped and his gaze intently rested on her. "And yet . . . you know the Latin name for a knobbed whelk."

Suddenly Marnie felt heat creep up her neck. "What plans do you have for the weekend?" she asked, breaking the spell by deliberately pulling her eyes away from him.

"Well, tomorrow is Saturday. As in, the day for the cancer support group." He paused. "Have you considered coming back? Give it another try?"

Argh. She walked right into that trap. He wasn't going to let up, so maybe she needed to try candor. "Linc, I have to be honest. That time I came to the group, there was something you said that bothered me. You said that cancer is a wonderful teacher. I think you're wrong. Cancer is diabolical. It's a terrible thing. Something to get rid of and never think of again. It wants to consume its victims. I won't let it."

"So if you come to the support group, then you think you're letting it win?"

"Not win, exactly. I'm just allowing it more . . . space . . . in my mind. In my life."

A thoughtful look came over his face. "I agree with you that cancer is a terrible thing. And all of us want to get rid of it. But it's just not that easy to never think of it again. Didn't you notice, after you had surgery? Waking up, thinking it was over and done with. But it wasn't done with you yet."

She couldn't deny that. She'd even thought she could leave all thoughts of cancer back in Needham, but they wouldn't stay there.

"If you know the Latin word for a shell, then you must enjoy knowing about words. Do you know the definition for *support*?"

"My first thought is . . . to carry."

"Yes, that, and much more." He pulled out his phone and googled it. "'To carry the weight; to maintain position so as to keep from falling, sinking, or slipping, to be able to bear—withstand; to keep from falling or yielding during stress.'" He put his phone in his back pocket. "Believe me, every single description applies to the experience of belonging to a cancer patient support group."

"But everyone's situation is so different."

"Yes, cancers are different, and every case is unique and distinct. But the feelings, concerns, and fears that we have are all very much alike. Whatever you're feeling, one hour with a cancer support group will convince you that you're not alone. Others have felt the way you feel, and they have survived."

They walked along in silence for a while. Mayor dashed past to chase a seabird, kicking up sand behind him.

"Why does Dawn want you to go to a support group?"

Ah, so the two must've talked. Marnie frowned and bit her lower lip. "She thinks I bought Main Street Creamery to avoid accepting the fact that I had cancer. That it's just a distraction." She glanced at him. "She's not entirely wrong. I needed something new in my life. I've planned enough parties for other people."

"I don't know if this rings true for you, but the group talks about how they feel increasingly left out of the conversation with those who didn't have any experience with cancer. The things that are on people's minds seem trivial compared to dealing with cancer treatment."

Trivial was just the word for it. Marnie's mind traveled to how she had isolated herself after her diagnosis, hardly even opening up to Maeve. She just didn't want to hear about anyone's petty grievances or travel plans. She had buried her husband unexpectedly, and less than a year later, she was undergoing surgery for breast cancer. It was easier to live in Chatham, where she had no expectations of others, and they had none of her, and all she was trying to do was sell ice cream. She glanced at Linc. "If not trivial, I felt annoyed at how some people thought they had such control over their lives."

His chin dipped in a nod. "I suppose you could've put me in that camp until cancer stopped me in my tracks. It was a major wake-up call."

Marnie stopped. That was the very first time Lincoln volunteered anything personal about his own experience with cancer. The very first time. It had always been general, big-picture, airplane view. "So what happened?"

"That's a long story. Let's save it for another day."

"I'm not in any hurry. And I'd like to hear it."

He looked at Marnie for a long while, then opened his palm to indicate they should sit down. After settling on the sand, he asked if she was comfortable, and then he kept his eyes on Mayor at the water's edge, sniffing to his heart's content. "I was on a frantic sprint from extra-innings adolescence to sobering adult responsibility. I'd had this idea and started a little company. I had some success early on when a large company bought up my company, but instead of taking the opportunity to slow down or take a break, I started another company with another idea. Then that got bought up. And again, instead of stopping to catch my breath, I doubled my efforts. There was always one more thing to achieve, one more goalpost to aim toward."

Down by the water, Mayor stopped, looked up, as if he'd just now remembered he had an owner somewhere on the beach. He charged toward Linc, kicking sand up behind him. Linc reached out his arms to shield Marnie from the dog's body block. He grabbed Mayor's collar and made him sit.

"I've never heard you mention if you had a family."

Linc leaned forward, resting his elbows on his knees. "I married a lovely woman who worked at my company, and we had two children. Twins, in fact. A son and a daughter, both grown. I completely missed their childhood—traveling or preoccupied. Both, usually. I can't remember attending a single thing they did—not a Little League game, not a piano recital. It was like they were born one day, and suddenly grown the next." He paused, stroking his hand down Mayor's back. "And when both kids went off to college, my wife decided she was ready to go too. I came home from an overseas business trip and found a note from her, tacked to the refrigerator."

Marnie's back straightened in surprise. "She left you?" Like *that*?

"She did. She divorced me on the grounds of neglect. That was her sole complaint and I couldn't dispute it—I was never abusive, never unfaithful. We never even argued. But she was right about being neglected. Taken for granted. Forgotten. We had a very amiable breakup. She took the Boston house and I took the Chatham cottage. She ended up marrying a guy who works in a library. No travel in his line of work. I think she found the happiness she was looking for with him."

She heard a slight tremor in his voice and reached out to rest a palm on his back. "That must have been a sad time for you." Everything you were sure of could be swept away in a moment. That, she knew.

"I wish I could say it was. But I'm ashamed to say I barely blinked. I just dug in deeper to my work. I kept going on a frantic sprint to . . . nowhere. That should have been my wake-up call, but I missed it. I think God was trying to get my attention and finally had to use a megaphone."

Linc reached for the dog's big head and rested his hand on it. Mayor opened lazy eyes, got up, stretched, then curled into a ball, chin on paws, and closed his eyes.

"One morning, while shaving, I noticed a funny lump on the side of my throat. When I went to the doctor, he sent me over to the hospital to take some tests, and the next thing I knew, I was getting prepped for surgery for thyroid cancer. As I was filling out the hospital admission papers, there was a line that asked for an emergency contact. That was the moment when I realized I had no one to put down. My wife had divorced me and, in a way, my children divorced me too. I'd never had time to make friends. There was not a single person in my life whom I could call and ask for help. No one . . . but God. *That* was my wake-up call. I sold my business and retired and moved to Chatham, and I promised myself that I would spend the rest of my life working on the building up of relationships. All kinds. Whomever God brings into my path."

"So that's what you do with your days?"

"That's it."

"Sort of a leisurely slide into retirement?"

He coughed a laugh. "Not in the least. I'm busier than I've ever been, but in a different way. I volunteer as many ways as I can. Every single day."

"So you do more than lead the cancer support group?"

"That's just on Saturday mornings. And I don't limit volunteering to Chatham. I go all over the Cape. Monday mornings, I volunteer at the food pantry in Hyannis, Tuesdays I go to the senior center in Falmouth, Big Brothers program in Sandwich on Wednesdays, on Thursdays I drive up the Cape to Provincetown for the AIDS support group, on Fridays it's back to Hyannis with the homeless shelter. There's other places too. The Cape has all kinds of volunteer opportunities. More needs than anyone realizes, but my criteria is that the organization has to be people-focused. Mrs. Nickerson-Eldredge has been upset with me for not volunteering some business skills to the Historical Commission."

Ah! Now Marnie understood why Mrs. Nickerson-Eldredge had only harsh words to say about Lincoln.

"Is it working? Are you happy?"

"Happier than I've ever been. Content. Fulfilled might be the best word for it."

"What about your kids? Are they part of the new and improved Lincoln Hayes's life?"

"My daughter and I are making some progress. My son— he's still distant. I don't blame him. I wasn't there for him when he needed a father."

"Is a boy ever too old to have a father?"

He shrugged with a sigh. "I hope not. But, Marnie, this is where cancer changed me, thoroughly and completely. It really was a gift. Not an easy one to accept, but it taught me to not take my life for granted. To not take the people in my life for granted. I wouldn't wish cancer on anyone, but I wouldn't trade it, either." He rose to his feet and offered a hand to help her up. "You know, even God thought support groups were important. That's why he made families."

Oh man. How could anyone argue that? "I give up," she said with a laugh. "You win. I'll come to the group tomorrow morning. I'll give it one more try." Just one. Just to appease him.

He smiled. "Good." He squeezed her hands. "If you still feel that it isn't helpful to you, I won't ask again."

But she wondered. "Are you sure you wouldn't feel offended? After all, I don't want you suddenly quitting on us prior to the big Memorial Day opening. Even if you won't accept a salary, you're still considered our top employee."

Humor brightened his eyes. "No. I won't take it personally. And I won't quit Main Street Creamery if you don't come back. The support group is there for those who need support. If you don't need it, then so be it."

Marnie suddenly realized he hadn't let go of her hands from helping her up. Heat started to radiate from her neck, creeping quickly upward. Horrible hot flashes! Such a nuisance. Pulling her hands from his, she said, "I'd better get Dawn's car back to her before she sends out the police. She has no confidence in my sense of direction. See you tomorrow morning, Linc." Marnie started down the beach.

"Um, Marnie. I think your car is parked in the opposite direction."

"So it is." She spun around and went the other way, face flaming.

Chapter
SEVENTEEN

First love is like vanilla ice cream. There may come many eclectic flavors, but there shall be only one classic.

—Akshar

Saturday, May 3

As part of her new routine, Dawn would wake early and go for a run. Calling it a run was generous—more like a very slow jog. Weather permitting, she would head due east and make her way down the beach. It was less than a mile between Main Street Creamery and Lighthouse Beach—the best beach for running.

Chatham had six separate beaches. The constantly changing erosion of the barrier beaches and the mainland made it impossible to run along the water from North Chatham to South Chatham, so distance running required weaving through narrow streets. Dawn hadn't run in years, not since college, but now that she was making it a habit, she had to admit it felt good. Maybe not while she was doing it, but afterward. The fresh air, heavy with the salty tang of the ocean, invigorated her, and she felt proud of herself for sticking to a regular schedule of exercise.

Her dad had always kept fit, especially important in his work as an electrician, where he had to climb telephone poles or crawl around under the foundation of houses in dark basements. She found herself thinking more and more about her dad. Curiously, thoughts of him didn't provoke the sweeping sadness they normally had. She could almost sense his pleasure in this crazy venture—making the ice cream, working in tandem with Mom. She was right. He would've loved every single minute of it.

And Dawn was loving it too. She had a reason to set the alarm and get out of bed in the morning. She was needed, broken as she was, and knew just what her purpose was. Because, quite frankly, Mom would make a mess of this business if it weren't for Dawn. She never finished anything! She'd started painting in every room, upstairs and down, and had yet to complete four walls in any room. There was always a table or chair for sale in some other town that required her to dash off.

On this Saturday morning, Dawn jogged down Main Street to warm up, onto the beach, then broke into a run as soon as she reached the waterline where the sand was packed hard. Even though she'd been trying to run each day, she hadn't turned the corner yet when it felt easier. Within minutes, her muscles started to burn. Wheezing for air, she fought through the feeling that her lungs were about to explode. *I can do this. This is good for me. It'll get easier.* She ran on, determined. *This is all part of the new me.* She went as far north as she could, which wasn't terribly far, then turned around to head back—and nearly stumbled when she saw a familiar figure approaching her. At first she thought her imagination was playing tricks on her, but it wasn't.

It was *him*. Kevin.

He was here? As in *here*? Confusion brought her to a sudden stop only a couple of yards away from him. Breathing hard, her heart pounded, and it wasn't just because she was out of shape. She was completely unprepared for the impact of seeing him again.

"What . . . are you . . . doing here?" she asked, panting, keeping her distance. She smoothed a stray strand of her hair up toward her ponytail, trying to act nonchalant about unexpectantly bumping into the man she had so nearly married.

For one elongated moment, they simply stared at each other. Kevin broke eye contact first. "I was driving down Main Street and happened to see you heading toward the beach."

"I meant . . . what are you doing in Chatham?"

"I thought I'd just check up on you. Make sure, you know, you're doing well."

"I'm fine," she said crisply. She was fine up until a minute ago, she thought. Even now, after all that had happened between them, the sight of Kevin still had the power to mesmerize her. Old habits died hard. She'd almost forgotten how handsome, how appealing he was. She took in his concerned brown eyes and dark hair—longer than he usually wore it. So long it curled around the collar of the oh-so-hip charcoal gray Patagonia jacket she'd given him two Christmases ago. And he'd shaved his beard!

She felt the opposite of hip. Frumpy. Dowdy. Plain. Sweaty. She wore yoga pants and a baggy paint-splattered T-shirt. She'd gained back the weight she'd lost to fit into her bridal dress. She hadn't had her hair trimmed or highlighted since before they'd broken up. Each morning she just gathered it up in a ponytail to keep it out of the way.

"This isn't like you, Dawn."

She felt Kevin's concerned eyes on her and tried not to let the panic show. "What isn't?"

"Dropping out of work. Starting an ice cream shop." He

looked her up and down. "Even . . . running on the beach. You hate to exercise."

She lifted her chin with an edge of defiance. "Maybe you don't know me like you thought you did, Kevin."

"Well, you've never exactly been the spontaneous type. Especially if something came between you and your job."

She darted a glance at him. Was he criticizing her? Pointing out her tendency toward workaholism? He had asked her, repeatedly, not to work so hard. She had always promised him she would slow down, just as soon as she made partner.

Or was that a jab at their honeymoon?

Kevin had wanted them to take three months' leave after their wedding and travel the world. She refused, insisting that she couldn't leave work for such a long time. You know, so close to becoming partner and all. It was her top priority.

But that wasn't all there was to it. She didn't want to travel because she felt panicky at the thought of not knowing what to expect. A predictable pattern to her days, to her life, became critically important to her after her dad's sudden death. So she talked Kevin out of a three-month around-the-world tour and into a one-week honeymoon on Cape Cod. She knew he was disappointed, and yet she couldn't even tell him her reasons.

"Is this really what you want to do? Manage an ice cream shop on Cape Cod with your mother? The two of you are as different as night and day. Fire and ice. Oil and vinegar."

"Right, right." She put her hand up to stop him. "I get the metaphors. So that's why you drove all the way down here? To question my sanity?"

"I don't know. I woke up early this morning and I just felt . . . I guess I felt really worried about you."

Pity? He pitied her? Humiliation swept over her. "Look, Kevin," she said, head held high, cheeks aflame with emotion. "As you can see, I am just fine. You can head back to Boston without any misplaced feelings of guilt."

His gaze settled on her face. "Dawn . . . I handled things badly."

And he'd done a fine job of it, she thought. "Well, you were abundantly clear." She took in a deep breath. "Frankly, you did me a great favor by breaking the engagement. Really, I should thank you." *Liar.* He had broken her heart in a million pieces. *Stop talking, Dawn. Stop talking.* But she couldn't. "I'm happier than I've been in a very long time."

Emotion filled his eyes. Anger? Or was it hurt? She couldn't tell. She felt the sting of tears prickle her eyes and started to walk away before she totally lost it in front of him.

"Hey, Dawn!"

She slowed but didn't turn around.

He came up behind her. In a soft voice, he said, "Do you mind if I check out the ice cream shop before I leave town? I'm just . . . curious."

"Suit yourself."

"So you really don't mind if I stop in to say hello to your mom?"

"She won't be back until ten-ish." Dawn lifted a hand in a casual wave, though she felt anything but casual. "All in the past," she whispered to herself as she jogged away from him, tears spilling down her cheeks. "All in the past."

● ● ●

Marnie sat in the same chair, closest to the exit, of the Cancer Room—knowing full well she shouldn't call it the Cancer Room but that was how she felt about it—and tried to distract her mind from thinking about cancer. Instead, it was like a blaring neon sign kept going off in her head: Cancer! Cancer! Cancer!

Being here took her right back to those days just after she was diagnosed, before she had the surgery, and she hadn't told anyone, other than Maeve O'Shea, that she had breast cancer.

It was the most challenging time in her life. The nights were the hardest. Those were the times she was most aware she was all alone, without Philip to lean on. Maeve had told her to call, day or night, and often reassured her that there wasn't anything she wouldn't do for her. Maeve was a wonderful friend, but Marnie didn't call her in the night. She couldn't do that to her, not to anyone.

It was a terrible time. And also a deeply spiritual time. She'd had to develop a complete and thorough dependency on the Lord during those weeks, and it made the situation tolerable. Manageable. Day by day, she leaned on God's strength to get through the treatments. Throughout the day, she would return to the Bible like it was a spring of fresh water and she was parched for thirst. In it, she'd find the sustenance she'd need to get through a few more hours, to redirect her thoughts and allow her to focus on the task at hand. There was a sweet intimacy to discovering how faithful the Lord was, giving her strength as she needed it.

Still, she wouldn't wish cancer on anyone. And being here, right now, brought it all right back.

Up front, Lincoln rose to start the meeting. He looked at Marnie sitting across the circle and winked a hello. She smiled in return, but it was a halfhearted attempt. Her insides were churning and she felt the warning signs of a hot flash coming. The back of her neck started to burn, soon her face would be flush with color. She tried to stay in the chair—tried to break it down to five-minute segments. Surely, she could stand anything for five minutes. She got through one minute, then two, and felt herself calming down.

Then a pretty young woman with a toddler in her arms rose from her seat. She wore a telltale scarf around her head. "I've finished chemo and am now undergoing daily radiation treatments over in Hyannis," she said in a matter-of-fact way. "Does anyone have advice for handling the skin burns?" Even from across the room, Marnie could see the red blister that had formed at the base of the young mother's throat.

Marnie visibly cringed, instantly transported back to that time. She remembered how her skin had turned angry red during radiation, itching like pins and needles. She had to wear turtlenecks so Dawn wouldn't notice the redness, but the weight of the turtlenecks against her skin made it worse. She had tried all kinds of skin creams. One would work one day but not the next. She remembered how she counted down the thirty daily doses of treatment, rejoicing each time she passed a milestone. One week done. One third of the way done. One half. And then, down to single-digit days. Walking out of the thick-walled radiation room on that last day was one of the best feelings she'd ever had—because enduring those thirty days of treatment were some of the hardest. And, unlike so many others, she hadn't had to undergo chemo. She couldn't even imagine having to cope with both treatments.

She pressed a hand to her chest. Her heart was racing. She felt as if she couldn't breathe.

Too much. Marnie couldn't go back to that hard experience. She bolted and slipped out the side door.

She had only lasted four minutes.

Chapter
EIGHTEEN

Don't let your ice cream melt while you're counting
somebody else's sprinkles.

—Akilah Hughes, comedian

Saturday, May 3

Unsettled by the appearance of Kevin, Dawn ran farther than
she ever had, as far as she could go until stopped by a fence
with a stern warning to turn back because of the strong current. She leaned over to put her hands on her knees, catching
her breath, brushing her hair away from her face, her mind
absorbed with Kevin.

He seemed different. Why had he shaved his beard? It had
been a point of contention between them, because she had
thought the beard gave him a serious professional look and he
had felt as if it made him look like an absent-minded profes-
sor. The real reason she liked his beard was that Kevin had a
youthful look, more than she did, and she felt as if, without
the beard, she looked older than he did.

Why? Why had he come? Why now?

He said he was worried about her. Trying to see the situation objectively, Dawn had to admit she believed him. Kevin always told the truth. He probably was concerned about her. But it felt patronizing to be worried about, humiliating, especially when she knew what she was doing. She was helping her mom, she was fulfilling a dream of her dad's. And quite frankly, she liked being here. She liked making ice cream each day, and she liked living near the beach. Running each day along the ocean instead of running to catch a train. There'd been too many days at the accounting firm when she never even saw sunlight—she arrived at work at dawn and left after dusk. So many days spent inside an office building, poring over figures, trying to find mistakes. And there were always mistakes to be found.

Now that she had a little fresh air in her brain, she was starting to rethink her career choice. About what it would mean to become partner, how it would set the course for the rest of her life. Yes, she would be financially secure—the importance of which her father had stressed on her. But she wasn't sure that spending a lifetime looking for other people's mistakes was such a good thing for her. While it was an important job, and a financially desirable one, and she was good at it . . . she was starting to see how it had shaped her thinking. She was so reluctant to make mistakes herself, to risk any change.

She straightened, staring out at the ocean.

Is that why I can't stop making vanilla ice cream? Am I just that afraid to make a mistake?

There was something else that had been needling her. Brynn had made a comment that Dawn was trying to turn her mom into herself. At work, she'd often been praised for training her direct reports to become mini-Dawns. She justified it—this was her job, this was what she was good at. But her success came at the expense of others' feelings. Of their individuality and uniqueness.

She covered her face with her hands. *Oh my goodness.* It

occurred to her that she treated her mother like she was an employee, dismissively, as if Dawn's way was always better. She treated Kevin the same way. She knew she did. She could think of dozens of examples—from which restaurant to try out to which route to get there.

She felt herself choke on the truth, even harder to think than to swallow. No wonder he felt as if he couldn't talk to her. He was right! There was no real conversation. She was right and everyone else was wrong.

She was just like her dad.

* * *

Marnie walked back to the Creamery at a record pace, eager to get her mind on something besides cancer. She almost felt angry with Lincoln, a man who had been so good to her but who kept pushing her to come to the support group. Why? Why did he persist? She didn't need it!

Rounding the corner, she stopped short when she saw Kevin Collins walking around the Creamery, hands behind his back, head tilted up toward the roof. *Kevin? Here!* Had he come to patch things up with Dawn? *Oh, wouldn't that be wonderful!* But if so . . . where was Dawn? Nowhere in sight.

"I think you might be the last person I'd expect to see here today," she said as she approached him.

He spun around, a sheepish look on his face. "Morning, Marnie. You're looking well."

She walked up to him and wrapped her arms around him in a bear hug and squeezed. She couldn't help herself. She'd missed him. His even-tempered personality had never failed to lift her spirits. Releasing him, she said, "Have you seen Dawn?"

"Yes. Down on the beach. She was taking a run."

Oh. By the measured way he said it, lacking warmth, Marnie sensed that whatever had gone on between them hadn't gone well.

"I just thought . . . maybe I'd come and see about this historical building you bought yourself." Kevin glanced up at the roof. "Would you mind giving me a tour?" Quickly, he added, "Dawn said it would be all right."

Marnie looked at him, then over his shoulder at the Creamery. "Kevin, I would consider that a gift sent straight from Above."

Inside, Marnie showed Kevin around the shop—the front room, then the kitchen, the upstairs. He acted like a doctor examining a patient: carefully lifting and closing windows, knocking on walls and listening. The center wall, the one behind the display case for ice cream, was the one that intrigued him the most. He kept returning to it. Why, Marnie had no idea.

He asked her all kinds of questions, most of which she couldn't answer. At one point, she left him to his inspection to make coffee in the kitchen. Pouring two cups, she brought them out to the front room, where Kevin stood gazing at the floor, then his eyes landed on the wall. He accepted the coffee with a grateful nod and walked slowly toward the wall, then back again. "Marnie, have you noticed how the floor sags here"—he pressed the floor with the toe of his shoe—"and here."

She looked down at the floor. "Now that you mention it, I guess I can see it slants down a bit." Now she realized why he had rolled a marble on the floor. It had instantly rolled downhill.

He knocked on the wall. "Hear that?"

"What?"

He knocked on the wall a few feet away. "Here, it's hollow. Here . . ." He went back to the center. "It's muffled." He dropped his arm and turned to her. "I'm fairly confident there's a fireplace behind the wall. Didn't you ever notice there's a chimney in the middle of the roof?"

Marnie practically spit out her mouthful of coffee. How many times had she looked at that roof? Been up on it to examine the hole made by the firemen? Same with Lincoln and Dawn. Not one of them had considered a fireplace below.

She walked over to the wall and knocked. One knock was hollow, the other struck a muffled tone. Chills of delight slid down her arms and legs. Then horror. "You don't suppose a body's hidden in it, do you?"

He grinned. "Doubt it." He walked over to the doorjamb that separated the front room from the back of the building. "You never noticed how thick the wall is?"

No, she hadn't. The stairs were behind that wall, and under the stairs were storage cabinets. The only thought she'd ever given to the center wall of the building was that she appreciated someone had squeezed in every square inch of storage space. "Why do you think the fireplace was covered up?"

He scratched the back of his neck. "I've been reading some books about colonial architecture. There used to be something called a window tax. Instead of paying the tax, homeowners would board up the windows."

"And live in the dark?"

He shrugged. "More like . . . choose to live in the dimness. They preferred that to paying taxes. Stubborn folks."

"But surely a fireplace wouldn't be taxed." It would've been the only source of heat, of cooking, in a small house like this.

"No, it wouldn't have been taxed. But my guess is, there must've been a problem with it. The flue could be cracked, or blocked. Maybe they didn't want the draft from the fireplace drawing away all the warm air. If it was done correctly, which I doubt, there should have been ventilation added so that the chimney doesn't attract dampness."

Oh no. Marnie didn't even want to think about that. "Can we reverse it?"

"Yeah, it can probably be reversed, for a price. Most likely, only the opening would've been bricked up. If it's bodged, it may have been closed off with a wooden panel."

Bodged. Construction lingo for patched. Marnie smiled. Philip used to use that word when he described someone's DIY wiring. She looked around the room, the entire front room, then brought her hands together as if in a prayer. "Kevin, this could be wonderful news. It's just what this room has been lacking—a visual focal point."

"You really want to open it up?" His gaze swept the room. "Are you sure you want to reverse it? There's probably a reason it's boarded up."

"The brick face would be the same as the chimney, wouldn't it? Original to the house, right?"

"It could be expensive to repair if there's something wrong with it. Cracks. Missing bricks. Broken flue."

"But . . . I don't have to have a fire in it, right? It could just be for looks, couldn't it?"

He hesitated. "True. But maybe you should run it by Dawn first."

No way. Dawn would put the kibosh on the whole plan. Not if it cost money.

"Before I go . . ."

There was a look on Kevin's face that made Marnie instantly uneasy. She put her hands up in a stop. "I can't, Kevin. I can't discuss anything about Dawn. Whatever happened is between the two of you. Please don't put me in a tight spot."

"I was going to say," he said in a firm voice, "before I go, let's go outside and I'll show you areas where the Historical Commission might raise red flags when they review your applications."

Avoiding his eyes, Marnie looked down at her feet.

"You have filed the applications, haven't you?"

Slowly, she said, "You see, they're very lengthy. Very detailed." She chanced a quick glance at him. The look of alarm on his face was worrisome.

"Marnie, you've already started exterior work. I can see it. Anyone can."

"Repairs. That's all we've done. Surely they can't find fault with someone fixing a hole in a roof."

"It's more than the roof. The siding is full of new shingles. And do you really know what you're doing? To the best of my knowledge, you and Dawn have never picked up a hammer before."

"Lincoln has. He knows what he's doing."

Kevin frowned. "The Historical Commission doesn't care. They want those applications in first."

"It's just that the summer season . . . it's fast approaching. We absolutely, positively have to open the Creamery by Memorial Day."

"That's not far off." He ran a hand over his head. "Marnie, there's no way you can do all you need to do by then."

"But we can! Dawn's got it all figured out. On a spreadsheet." Marnie glanced at the fireplace. "A few things might have to wait, but we're on track. As long as the Historical Commission doesn't create any . . . hurdles . . . then it'll all be fine. And Kevin, you won't believe how delicious Dawn's ice cream is. It's never been better." Vanilla, anyway.

He tipped his head slightly, and she wondered what was running through his mind.

Then he let out a sigh. "Let me see the paperwork."

She smiled. "I'll be right back." She dashed upstairs, offering a prayer. *Thank you, Lord, thank you, Lord, thank you, Lord.* Followed by, *Please Lord, please Lord, please Lord. Don't let Dawn be upset.*

Chapter
NINETEEN

Saturday, May 3

Sweaty from her run, Dawn turned the bend on Main Street and nearly bumped into a baby stroller when she saw Kevin's car parked out front of the Creamery. And then she saw him, standing next to Mom, in front of the cellar door.

She stopped, watching them. Watching him. Her heart started pounding and her breathing went shallow.

What was *wrong* with her? She was over Kevin. Absolutely positively determined to be over him. Now she was getting all tingly and nervous at the sight of him.

Dawn wondered what they were talking about, because Mom seemed animated, arms waving, her face lit with excitement. Kevin bent slightly toward her as he listened carefully to what she had to say. Then he reached down to yank open the cellar door. Three hard yanks, and down the stairs he went, Mom following behind like a puppy. Dawn shivered. She didn't have the stomach for spiders and cobwebs and creepy things like Mom did. For all Mom's hippie-joujou stuff, she was fearless. For all Dawn's logical-rational-literal stuff, she was afraid of the dark.

She wiped a drip of sweat trickling down her forehead. Yikes! She looked terrible. She darted into the house and bolted up the stairs, taking them two at a time. In record time, she took a cold shower, dressed, combed out her long hair, put on some mascara and lip gloss, and went downstairs. She came through the kitchen door to the front room, to where Mom and Kevin stood talking.

Kevin saw her first. Their eyes met, and held. She was the first to look away.

Mom spun around. "Dawn! You won't believe what Kevin has discovered."

He took a few steps around the display case and put his palm against the wall. "Behind this wall is a fireplace."

Mom was beaming. "Have you ever noticed there's a chimney in the middle of the roof?"

Dawn's mouth formed a circle. There was! Right smack in the middle of the roof.

"How many times have we seen it and yet it's never occurred to any of us—not you, not me, not even Lincoln—that if there's a chimney, there must be a fireplace."

Dawn stared at the wall. The minute you walked into the Creamery, you wouldn't think about a fireplace because there was none to see. Only a large room with windows and that big clunky ice cream display case.

"Someone," Kevin said, "boarded it up."

"Boarded up?" Dawn said. "But why?"

"That's why we went down in the cellar," Kevin said. "To see if something might be structurally wrong with the fireplace."

Dawn hated to ask. "And?"

"The fireplace looks to be in good shape," Kevin said, "but . . ." He exchanged a hesitant look with Mom. "We found something else."

"There's a tiny glitch," Mom said.

Dawn's eyes darted from one to the other, trying to figure out what was going on. "What . . . kind of a glitch?"

Kevin cleared his throat. "There's a car jack holding up one of the piers underneath the house."

Dawn cringed. Visibly cringed. The foundation! She should have insisted on an inspection before Mom bought this old building. It would've been the first thing her dad checked. And it was an elevated foundation, with visible piers. She knew better! But it had all happened too fast.

"It's fixable," Mom said quickly. "Kevin said so."

"It is. But it does need to be fixed. Soon." He hastened to add, "It's not affecting the foundation of the house. The perimeter looks to be in pretty good shape, considering the age of the building. The problem is just one of the interior piers."

Dawn bit her lip. "It sounds expensive."

Kevin rocked his hand in the air. "Yeah, it can be. But there are some mechanical supports that aren't too expensive. They act a little like the car jack, but they don't move up and down."

Mom had lost interest in the broken pier. She was knocking on the wall, listening to it. "Amazing, just amazing. I can't wait to see what that fireplace looks like."

Dawn's jaw dropped. "No way. You can't possibly be thinking of tearing down that wall."

Mom spun around. "But it will add so much to this room. A focal point and a place to gather on cold days and . . ."

"Mom! We are selling ice cream. *This* summer!"

"Yes, but we're also trying to create a community gathering place. We can do both, Dawn."

"If you open up that wall and discover a monstrosity . . . we don't have the time or the budget to hide it again."

"It definitely won't be a monstrosity. Kevin assured me of that."

Dawn glared at him. "How could you possibly know that?"

"The brick below the building is consistent with the chimney," he said.

"There's a reason it was boarded up. What if bricks are missing? What if the air thingy . . ." She waved her hand up and down, struggling for the right word.

"The flue," Kevin said.

"What if it's broken?"

Kevin shrugged. "Just close the damper and use the fireplace for looks."

"You have to admit, Dawn, that a fireplace would be amazing in here." Mom tapped the case. "The ice cream display case really should be against that wall, not this one, so it's a straight shot to and from the kitchen."

It should. It actually would improve the workspace to move the display case. Dawn had already given it some thought. Better still, to chuck it and find a smaller one, called an ice cream cabinet. This large old one looked like something that belonged in a Baskin-Robbins store. Dawn's five flavors would look ridiculous in it.

But open up the wall for a fireplace in who knew what kind of condition when they were only four weeks away from the Creamery's grand opening? This was how Mom's big ideas usually ended up going terribly wrong. "Let's see what Lincoln has to say. He can be the tie-breaker again."

"Right," Kevin said in a flat tone. "He sounds like a great guy."

Dawn darted a look at him. *Weird.* That was exactly what Brynn had texted to her yesterday. Something seemed fishy. She studied him closely. Why was Kevin really here? Why did Mom seem so at ease with Kevin's visit? Her eyes narrowed at her mom. Had Mom asked Kevin to come? No . . . she wouldn't have. She didn't dare. Or did she? She opened her mouth to ask just as the door opened and in walked Lincoln.

"Marnie, four minutes?" Linc said, frowning. "That's all?"

Four minutes? Dawn wasn't sure what he meant. "What's four minutes?"

The door, left ajar, was pushed open. In came Leo. "I got spurs. For my boots." He wiggled his feet to jingle the spurs.

"Lincoln! Leo!" Mom said, delighted. "Come! Listen to the wall."

Lincoln's face scrunched up in confusion. "The wall?"

Kevin looked at Lincoln, then at Dawn, then at Marnie, then back to Lincoln. "You're . . . Lincoln?" He pointed to the little cowboy. "And he's Leo?"

"I am," Lincoln said, extending his hand to Kevin. "And you're . . . ?"

"Kevin."

Mom must have told Lincoln the backstory between Kevin and Dawn, because he took it all in stride, then turned and walked straight over to Mom and her wall. Leo paced back and forth in front of Dawn, showing off his new spurs.

Kevin's eyes were on Mom and Lincoln, heads together, knocking on the wall, with a curious look on his face. Almost pleased.

* * *

Old houses, Marnie was discovering, held secrets in their walls. And in their cellars. Secrets just waiting to be revealed.

Marnie couldn't have been more delighted with Kevin's unexpected visit at the Creamery today. It was . . . illuminating, for so many reasons. First, the fireplace. What a boon! How had they missed it? Yet, how wonderful that they missed it! How wonderful that Kevin, of all people, was the one to notice it. *Thank you thank you thank you, Lord!*

Second, Kevin took over the paperwork for the Historical

Commission. When Marnie showed him the pile of papers, he skimmed through them. He understood the complex language that stymied her, and clarified what she'd needed to do. *Thank you thank you thank you, Lord!*

Third, he found the car jack barely holding up the pier. Marnie didn't elaborate to Dawn, but it was nearly slipping off the pier. Even she could see the potential problem that jerry-rigged car jack posed. When she quietly described it to Lincoln, he lost interest in the missing fireplace and said he was going straight to the hardware store to see what kind of metal supports they had in stock. Clearly, Kevin shared his concern. He offered to accompany Linc to the hardware store to explain the pier situation. From there, he said, he'd leave to return to Boston.

Fourth, Marnie knew, just knew, that Kevin had come to Chatham this morning because he still had feelings for Dawn. Why else would he have come?

Yet gone was the warmth and affection that had once flowed between them, gone was the light teasing and inside jokes, and in their place was a mutual guardedness. The two hardly spoke to each other, casting only furtive glances when no one was watching . . . but Marnie. Dawn didn't try to stop him from leaving, barely lifted a hand in a goodbye. She seemed almost bewildered by Kevin's presence. The distance between them seemed palpable. Wasn't that, too, a sign that things weren't finished between them?

As soon as the door shut, Dawn went upstairs to dry her hair. Marnie rapped on the wall that hid the fireplace. By the sound she heard from knocking, she could tell where the fireplace started and ended, and marked the edges with a piece of chalk. She should wait to do anything. Wait for Lincoln to return and get his opinion on unveiling it. Marnie knew how Dawn felt—it was a terrible idea, it was risky, it would delay other more important tasks—and she was right. Really, Marnie should wait.

She was tired of waiting.

Curiosity took hold and got the better of her.

She heard Dawn's blow dryer turn on.

Then she picked up a sledgehammer and started whacking away at the wall that covered the fireplace.

● ● ●

There were so many things bothering Dawn that she didn't know where to begin. First off, her mom was certifiably crazy. Busting up a wall on a whim! The entire downstairs was dusted in drywall plaster, including the kitchen, which meant Dawn couldn't make the ice cream she had planned to make that afternoon—first time, a flavor other than vanilla. Instead, she was spending the afternoon cleaning up drywall dust, her mother's mess. Story of her life!

Then there was Lincoln. She thought she could count on him to offer a counterbalance to Marnie Dixon, a cool, logical head, someone to talk her off the ledge the way Dad used to. Instead, Lincoln walked in the door of the Creamery and saw what Mom had started. His eyes widened briefly, then the smile on his face grew huge. Next thing, Lincoln had picked up a hammer and joined the wall bashing!

Dawn had to admit that the exposed fireplace would provide an ideal focal point for the Creamery. The red bricks, in shockingly good condition, were clearly original to the house. On a hunch, Lincoln tugged at a corner of the hearth, pulling away the ugly but adequate indoor/outdoor gray carpet, and uncovered wide plank hardwoods. They pulled the carpet up from the entire floor, overjoyed to see the wood flooring. That floor, Dawn also had to admit, might've been worth the mess of the fireplace, as well as the delay to the daily punch list.

Still, she made Mom promise, three times, not to start a fire in the fireplace until they had it inspected by a professional.

"Besides, Mom, we're heading into summer." The mantel was missing, but Mom insisted that was an easy fix. Sure, for the right price, anything could be fixed. The problem was, they had no budget to fix it. Especially now that they had wooden floors to sand and stain and coat with polyurethane, then allow the floors time to harden and cure. All while the clock was speeding toward the day of the grand opening!

Still, once the mess was cleaned up, the front room was starting to look impressive. Dawn hadn't realized how cold the ugly gray carpet had made the room look. She could never have imagined the warmth brought to the room by a fireplace—even without a roaring fire or a finished mantel. Marnie Dixon had style, that Dawn could not deny. But no common sense! No thinking through consequences. So impulsive.

Dawn calmed herself down by reassuring herself that the exposed fireplace and floors could add value to the building . . . when it was sold after Labor Day.

As she wiped off drywall dust from the kitchen counters, she knew that the real reason she felt so agitated with . . . everyone and everything . . . was because of Kevin.

She didn't want him here, not at this special beach town that had memories unique to her family. Even though Kevin was raised just sixty-seven miles away, he'd never been to Cape Cod.

And now Kevin had come anyway.

Dawn would have a hard time shaking off the memory of first spotting him on the beach, the way she knew it was him long before she could make him out. There was something about the way he walked, and the way he held his shoulders, and swung his arms. She knew him as well as she knew herself. She thought she had, anyway.

Why did he have to come and ruin her beautiful beach? Why did he have to interfere with the Creamery? Why did he have to get involved?

More precisely, why did he have to come and ruin her recovery?

That was the real problem, wasn't it? If he kept coming around, she couldn't help but remember all the qualities she'd loved about him—his kindness, his humor, his sensitivity, and the way he'd made her spine tingle with little more than a look.

She'd been feeling so much better lately. She'd even told herself she was over him, but apparently that was simply because she hadn't been around him. Sighing, feeling a bit maudlin, she realized she was in danger of slipping back into that awful dark slump she'd been in since he'd broken their engagement.

She missed Kevin. She missed him terribly.

On Sunday morning, right after Mom left to meet Lincoln for church, Dawn opened the refrigerator to get out milk and cream and eggs for ice cream making. On the top shelf was a brown bag with a note attached:

Dawn: In this bag are organic ingredients I bought yesterday, plus a new recipe for ice cream. You've always loved ginger, and when I found this recipe online, I thought it might be just the thing to tempt you to move past vanilla ice cream. I would like you to try to make it this morning. The time has come, Dawn. The Creamery needs more flavors. I love you, Mom.

Seriously? Instead of spending yesterday afternoon looking for a company that had the time to sand and stain floors immediately . . . Mom went to the market?

Dawn took the bag out of the refrigerator and set it on the counter. She pulled out a large knob of ginger root, long stalks of lemongrass, and a small cellophane bag of Thai chili peppers. She read through the recipe once, then twice. She nixed the peppers and put them back in the fridge. But the recipe intrigued her. It needed tweaking, of course, but it had possibilities. Today was the fourth of May. Memorial Day weekend was coming quickly.

The time had come for Dawn to move on from vanilla ice cream.

A few hours later, when Dawn sampled the Ginger Lemongrass ice cream as it dripped down the barrel, she bolted upright, stunned, as if she'd just had an electric shock. The flavor was intense, a curious blend of sweet and tart, yet with a layered depth to it that she hadn't expected.

She filled a container, covered it completely with a film wrap so no air could touch its surface, and put it in the chest freezer. There was still ice cream left in the machine, so she put a bowl underneath the barrel and let the remnant slide out. Grabbing a spoon, she sat on top of the chest freezer and indulged. Licking the spoon like Leo did, she had to wonder, *Is this what I've been missing out on?* Vibrant tones that made her taste buds feel wide awake. Vanilla was a wonderful flavor, so pure and sweet, but it could be a little dull. With vanilla, a mouth knew what to expect with every bite. She swallowed another spoonful. Not this. Ginger Lemongrass surprised the palate.

A memory came to mind. There was a wonderful Indian restaurant around the corner from Dawn's apartment in Boston. She and Kevin went there at least once a week and, each time, she ordered the same meal—tandoori chicken over basmati rice with garlic naan bread. More than once, Kevin had encouraged her to try something new, just for the fun of changing things up.

"But why?" she countered. "If I know what I like, why not just enjoy it?"

He had seemed baffled by that response. "But what if there's something else you might like even better?"

"Not possible."

Running her finger along the bottom of the bowl this morning, she felt differently. It *was* possible. But it required risk.

A strange quiet filled the kitchen, an unusual stillness. Dawn froze, wondering what had just changed. And then the motor of the chest freezer sputtered to life and resumed its steady hum.

Dawn jumped off it. "Don't you DARE die on us."

It coughed.

She slapped her hand against the lid. "Pull it together. We need you to work."

It hummed.

Chapter
TWENTY

There is no sincerer love than the love of ice cream.

—George Bernard Shaw, playwright

Monday, May 5

"Marnie!"

The front door slammed and Marnie hurried out of the kitchen. There was Lincoln, holding a long, thick block of weathered wood in his arms.

"Look what I found. Wood from an old shed. I was driving along Route 28 and saw a farmer dismantling his old shed, stacking the wood. He was just going to burn it. Can you believe that? If I helped him, he said he'd give me all the wood I wanted for free."

She ran a hand along the wood. "But what do you want it for?"

"It's not for me. It's for you." His eyes shone with quiet joy. "It's going to be a mantel for the fireplace." He went over to the newly exposed fireplace and held it up against the brick. It looked . . . odd. Way too long, for one thing, and so chunky.

"A few adjustments, a little sanding and staining, and it'll look like it's always been there." He glanced over his shoulder at it. "Trust me."

She gazed at the wood for a long moment, squinting her eyes, imagining. Then she saw it, just the way he described it, looking like it had been there for two hundred years. She laughed appreciatively. "Now I see it." She smiled. "And I do trust you."

Dawn came into the room with her purse slung over her shoulder, her hair tucked under a knitted cap. She stopped short when she saw Linc holding the wood against the fireplace. "What in the world is that?"

"It's our new mantel," Marnie said.

"It looks . . . like something Paul Bunyan dragged in."

Marnie frowned at her. "Linc found a farmer who was dismantling his shed. That wood is probably as old as the house. You wait and see, Dawn. After Linc is done with it, it'll look like it's been here from the start."

The look on Dawn's face was one of doubt. "I'm off to the market," she said at the door. "Back later."

Linc set the soon-to-be-a-mantel down on the hearth. "I don't think your daughter holds much confidence in the power of imagination."

Marnie laughed. "Dawn's her father's daughter, through and through."

He brushed the dirt off his hands. "And yet she resembles you. There's no mistaking you're related."

"Dawn's like Philip in the way her mind works. The way she assesses things. Like the way she looked at this piece of beautiful old wood." Marnie crouched down by the wood to examine it. So many scars and scuffs. She ran a hand over it. It looked like it had been chiseled by hand. "She sees it in its literal form. A piece of old wood." She rubbed a knot in the wood, thinking that side should definitely face the front. "Dawn is a very black-and-white thinker."

He sat down beside her on the floor, resting his hands on his bent knees. "No gray?"

"No gray."

"The only problem with black-and-white thinking," Linc said, "is that there's just so much gray in life."

He ran a hand over knicks and cuts with a touch that was nearly reverent with its gentleness. "Hand hewn. Someone worked hard on carving this beam out of a log." Shoulder to shoulder, they studied the mantel with all its features and flaws, and a closeness stole over them.

Their eyes met. Met and locked, and Marnie felt her breath catch in her throat. A blush slid up her cheeks, warming them. *Confound it!* She neutralized it by jumping to her feet. "To celebrate your wonderful find, I have a surprise. I'm going to break out Dawn's first non-vanilla ice cream for you. Ginger Lemongrass."

She was halfway to the door when he asked, "Did Dawn come up with that flavor? Or did you?"

Marnie put a hand on the doorjamb and looked back. "Let's just say that I might have encouraged her to move on from vanilla. When I came home from church, Dawn had made this recipe. She seemed so proud of herself, Linc. You're going to love it. It came out better than I could've imagined." Even without the Thai chili.

"I don't doubt it." Linc patted his stomach appreciatively. "I'm going to double in size by the time the Creamery opens."

Hardly. He didn't have a spare ounce on him. She knew. She'd noticed. She'd seen him working outside without his shirt on.

"Well, you know how the saying goes," Marnie said. "'My head says to go to the gym. My heart says to eat more ice cream.'"

"In that case," Linc said, rising to his feet to join her by the door, "I'm going to follow my heart."

That annoying sensation of a hot flash started again in Marnie's middle, spiraling upward. She felt herself drawn to Lincoln, almost to the point of attraction, which she immediately dismissed. "I'll go get the ice cream," she said, flashing him a brief, nervous smile. Soon her face would be crimson. She strode to the chest freezer, opened it, and stuck her face inside.

● ● ●

Tuesday, May 6

Brynn
Kevin called. He said he drove to Chatham on Saturday. He sounded pretty amazed at all you and your mom were doing at the creamery.

Dawn
Oh? That's nice.

How was it, seeing him?

Pretty brief visit. In and out.

Really? He made it sound like it was a bigger deal.

Probably because of Mom. She had him exploring the foundation of the building.

Think you'll see him again?

What for? There's nothing more to say.

● ● ●

Wednesday, May 7

Marnie was in high spirits over the steady progress of the Main Street Creamery. Lincoln had taken ownership of the pier project and spent each afternoon underneath the house with his toolbox by his side. She could hear him tinkering away. Frankly, you could hear everything in this old building. Every time a faucet was turned on, every flush of the toilet, every squeak of a door hinge.

Dawn remained in the kitchen, focused on making ice cream. To Marnie's astonishment, she was moving steadily on from vanilla to experiment with new flavors. Today, she'd made an espresso coffee, flaked with roasted ground coffee beans. It was outstanding. Encouraged, she tried another flavor after stopping at the market and examining the fresh fruit. She came home with baskets of fresh strawberries, flown in from California, and this afternoon she created Strawberry Balsamic. It was . . . sublime.

Dawn's head popped around the doorjamb. "Mom, does the freezer sound funny to you?"

It had, actually. When Marnie came down to make coffee this morning, she noticed the freezer was making an odd clunking sound. Alarmed, she checked the temperature and was relieved that it was 0°F. The ice cream was hard to the touch. "I'll ask Linc to have a listen when he comes up for air."

"Marnie!" Lincoln's muffled voice floated up through the floorboards, from underneath the house. "I've found something interesting. Come down here when you can spare a minute."

She went outside and down the cellar steps to find Lincoln squatting by the fireplace floor, an old metal box in his hands. She had to crawl over to where he sat. "What's so interesting?"

He held up the box. "I found this in the ash dump."

"The what?"

"Behind the metal plate there." He pointed to the base of the fireplace. "It's called the ash dump. I opened it and found this in it."

"What's in it?"

"I don't know. Sure looks old, though. I'll need to go through my toolbox to find something to open it that won't harm the latch."

"Ooh, I love a mystery."

"I do too." Their eyes met, then she felt a spiral of warmth start up, knew a blush would soon be creeping across her cheeks. So annoying! Hot flashes came at the most unwanted times. She looked over at the pier. The car jack was gone, and in its place was a shiny metal support. "Lincoln! You fixed it. You're a miracle worker."

"It wasn't too difficult. I'm just going to check it over one more time, and then I think it's good for another hundred years."

Marnie thought she heard a knock above them. She tipped her head, listening, and heard it again. She crawled over to the cellar door. Up at the top of the stairs stood Mrs. Nickerson-Eldredge, smiling down at her with an icy look in her eyes, before she turned and walked away. On the top step was a white envelope. Marnie climbed the stairs and sat down, opening the envelope, her high spirits sinking fast.

"What is it?" Lincoln asked as he joined her on the top step and plopped down.

"It's a list of grievances from the Historical Commission about the work we've done." She turned to a second page. "What's this?" She held it out to him.

Lincoln skimmed it. "I can't believe it. It's a 'cease and desist' order." Then he took in a deep breath. "Oh boy."

"What?"

"You've got an appointment with the Commission on Monday morning to present your case."

"Present my case? Like . . . I'm a criminal? That's ridiculous!" She frowned. "What can they do to me? Toss me in jail? All I did was buy a piece of property and make improvements on it. How could that be a crime?"

"I'm on your side. But the Historical Commission seems to

have a vastly different point of view about such matters." He skimmed through the top letter. "Marnie, you did turn in the paperwork, didn't you?"

Kevin had filled it out and left it with her to turn in. She meant to drop it off earlier this week. She really did. But she got distracted with the fireplace, the progress they were making, the new flavors Dawn was coming up with. "I . . . forgot." The shocked look on Linc's face . . . it made Marnie cringe. "But what can they do to me? We've already done so much of the work. We're so close to opening day."

He pointed to a figure at the bottom of the letter. "Fines. They can slap fines on you if you continue any work. Accrued daily."

"Oh no," Marnie said. No no no no no.

*　*　*

Marnie planned to tell Dawn about the Historical Commission's grim notice but found she couldn't get the words out. She didn't have the heart. Lincoln kept giving her a curious look, as if to say, "Now?" And Marnie would shake her head, silently conveying "Not now." Not after seeing what Dawn had created in the kitchen.

Apparently, Dawn had liked Marnie's idea of creating ice cream flavors that identified with the town of Chatham and ran with it. The first ice cream she presented to them, like a chef at a fine dining restaurant, was called Chatham Beaches. It had a vanilla cream base, ribboned with salted caramel, plus an add-in of a crumbled-up homemade chocolate-covered shortbread. The second ice cream was Cranberry Bog. It was made up of an almond-flavored base with add-ins of gently simmered tart cranberries and thinly chopped roasted almonds.

Lincoln asked for seconds on both. When Marnie saw the pleased look on Dawn's face, she decided the Historical Commission's bad news could wait.

After all, Dawn was branching out from vanilla ice cream. Was that not a sign in itself that all would be well? She was starting to heal from the inside out. Everything, Marnie reassured herself, would turn out all right.

And suddenly a bloodcurdling scream came from the kitchen, where Dawn had been cleaning up. "MOM! The freezer! It died!"

* * *

Nanette let Marnie and Dawn borrow space in the freezer compartment of her refrigerator to store the ice cream containers, and when there was no more space to be had, she loaned them a cooler to keep at the Creamery to save what was still in the ice cream maker. As long as it hadn't been frozen yet, Dawn said, it could be kept cold. It was the change in temperature that worried her the most. Linc called a guy to come over and fix the freezer—he seemed to know all kinds of skilled guys who owed him favors and were willing to drop anything for him—but if Marnie's day had been sinking fast, the visit from the freezer guy only made it worse. He pronounced it DOA.

"See these?" A big man with a round belly, he held some pieces of copper tubing in the palm of his hand. "They've snapped right through."

"Can't you solder them back together?" Linc asked. "After all, you're the refrigerator guy. You can fix anything."

He shook his head. "That motor . . . it's too old to fix. Sorry, dude. You'd just be throwing good money after bad."

After Lincoln went home to feed his dog, Marnie went down to the beach for her evening walk. Her stomach had been churning over the letter from the Historical Commission, and now was twisted in a knot over the freezer. She didn't have the money for the outstanding bills waiting to be paid. She'd maxed out her credit card to get cash to reimburse Linc for the items he'd purchased—the POS system and Dawn's pasteurization machine. How could she afford a new freezer? Or the new ice cream cabinet Dawn had her eye on? Or the frozen food display freezer that Linc had suggested, for those moneymaking take-home pints? And now those daily accrued fines from the Historical Commission?

Lincoln had offered to loan her money, but she adamantly refused. She was the one who had delayed—*no, be honest with yourself, Marnie Dixon*—she had *avoided* filling out the paperwork that should've been filed with the Historical Commission. Mrs. Nickerson-Eldredge had warned her, many times. She was the one who had *neglected* dropping off the paperwork that Kevin had spent time completing. Dawn had warned her that the Creamery was a money pit. Marnie had waded waist-deep in trouble. She had created this mess and she needed to be the one to find a way out of it. She said a quick prayer, pulled out her phone, and dialed. "It's Marnie Dixon." She paused. "I wondered if we could talk."

After she finished that call, she held the phone in her hand. Guilt tapped on her shoulder, but she brushed it away. She wasn't doing anything wrong. There were hard decisions to make here. And she'd rather do anything than involve Dawn in those decisions.

She sat for five minutes, thinking and praying. Stalling. Finally, she took a deep breath and she made another call. "Dawn and I . . . we need your help."

● ● ●

Thursday, May 8

Dawn had spent thirty minutes begging the purchase manager of Chatham Village Market to consider stocking a certain hard-to-find organic cream she preferred for her ice cream. "At least for the summer season," she pleaded. After that, he could scratch the order. Finally, he agreed to stock the cream if she would agree to pay full retail price for it.

Ouch. That hurt. But she preferred that particular cream, and they would only deliver to Chatham if a ridiculously large product order was placed—far more than the Creamery would require.

As she returned to the shop, she found her mom bent over a dry sink on the west side of the store, scrubbing away. She stood when she saw Dawn. "Hi," she said with a bright smile. "Good news! Lincoln found a deal on a new freezer. One that will actually fit in the kitchen and not jut out. It's an upright. And . . . with it will come a smaller display case for ice cream. An ice cream cabinet, it's called. Plus a frozen food display freezer to sell take-home pints. He got a package deal, he said. Everything will get delivered this afternoon. And they promised to take away the old freezer and display case." She snapped her fingers. "Five birds, one stone."

Dawn set her bag of groceries on a tabletop. "The ice cream cabinet?"

Mom grinned. "The very one you wanted. It'll free up so much space in that front room. And the frozen food display freezer is tall and thin. It'll easily fit on the other side of the door, closer to the checkout counter. For impulse sales, Linc said."

"That's . . . amazing. How does Lincoln have so many connections?"

"No idea. But I'm grateful."

"How much will all this cost?"

Mom bent down to pick up her rag. "You know Lincoln. He negotiated a very reasonable price for us." She popped back up. "And we'll have a new freezer by day's end. Back in business."

"Mom, how much?"

"Nothing to worry about. I've kept a little slush fund for emergencies."

Right. That was the first Dawn had ever heard of a slush fund.

"Look at what I found at a tag sale in Hyannis. This old dry sink. Lined with copper! That's what I'm polishing. The copper is starting to gleam."

"You dragged it home from Hyannis all by yourself?"

"It's not as heavy as it looks. I thought we could use it for coffee fixings."

"Mom, nobody says fixings."

"What should I say?"

"I don't know. Accoutrements, maybe. Just don't say fixings." Dawn crossed the room to examine the dry sink. "Actually, this top shelf could be used for line extensions."

"What are those?"

"Ice cream toppings in jars. Sprinkles. Ice cream cups. Cute paper napkins. That sort of thing."

Mom's smile broadened. "I like the way you're thinking."

Dawn had to admit that she was enjoying the process of transforming this old building. And she loved making ice cream.

Mom bent over again to polish the dry sink's copper lining and Dawn went into the kitchen to put the groceries away. The laptop computer had been left open. As Dawn reached out to close the tabs, she noticed that the page was open to Mom's checking account. Dawn's eyes widened at the amount of the balance. Whoa! Whoa, whoa, whoa. Dawn felt tension drain out of her, like water down a sink. She hadn't realized how taut she'd been, how worried. She exhaled a deep cleansing breath. Everything was going to be okay.

Mom's little emergency slush fund runneth over.

Chapter

TWENTY-ONE

Ice cream is edible perfume.

—Jeni Britton Bauer, founder of
Jeni's Splendid Ice Creams

Saturday, May 10

Early Saturday morning, Dawn stood in front of the open refrigerator, wondering what had happened to the cream for coffee, until she remembered she'd used it up yesterday as she made new ice cream flavors. Highly successful ones, she reminded herself. She smiled and opened the newly installed freezer, pulling out a pint of Cranberry Bog. Why not? The almond extract flavoring would hit the spot in a cup of coffee. She grabbed a spoon and dug into it, deciding to sample it first, to see how it tasted after a hard freeze. She closed her eyes, letting the cold cream fill her palate. Oh, that subtle almond touch . . . it hit all the right notes. She dug her spoon in for another bite when she heard a polite knock at the door. Thinking it might be Lincoln or Nanette, she went to the door, holding the pint of ice cream in one hand. As she opened it, she gasped.

"You!"

Kevin stood a few feet away from the door, a leather messenger bag at his side. "Me."

He wore jeans and a sweatshirt, and hadn't shaved, so there was some stubble on his chin, making him look surprisingly sexy. A ray of morning sun shone down on him, giving him a nearly angelic look.

He grinned, a little devilishly. "Ice cream? At seven in the morning? Things must be worse than I thought."

Her heart rate accelerated. "What are you doing here?" She was surprised by how shaky her voice sounded. With her free hand, she brushed her hair behind her ear. Oh, how she wished she hadn't hit the snooze button today. She should've been on the beach right now, running.

He peeked around her. "The fireplace! Wow, wow, wow. It looks great. And that big ice cream case—that's gone." He noticed the ice cream cabinet against the other wall. "A lot has happened in a week's time."

"Why are you here?" she repeated, this time her voice a little less shaky.

"I've come to help."

"Help? But we don't need your help."

Mom came up behind Dawn. "Oh yes. We do. We really do. I'm sorry, Dawn, I'm so very sorry. But Kevin is the only one who can help." In her hand was a white envelope. "I'll get you a cup of coffee, Kevin, while you make sense of this."

He walked right in, set his messenger bag by the door, took a step, stopped, pivoted, and lifted Dawn's spoon out of the container with a big spoonful of ice cream. "Mind if I try it? I didn't get any breakfast."

Before she could answer, he swallowed down the ice cream and stuck the spoon back into the container. Halfway to the kitchen, he stopped and turned, a confused look on his face.

"It's not . . . it's not vanilla." He studied her curiously, as if he didn't recognize her. Then a soft smile curved his lips.

Mom popped her head around the kitchen door. "Dawn's been experimenting. You'll have to try the Chatham Beaches flavor." The two of them disappeared into the kitchen while Dawn remained at the open door, in her pajamas, wondering exactly what kind of trouble her mother had gotten into.

●　●　●

Marnie had a pretty good idea what was running through Dawn's mind as they sat at one of the tables in the front room and watched Kevin review the latest paperwork from the Historical Commission. After Dawn was told that Marnie had not filed any paperwork with the Commission—none—she avoided all eye contact with her. But she didn't blow up at her, not the way Marnie had expected she would. Then again, they were in triage mode right now. Completely dependent on Kevin to help the Main Street Creamery survive.

Or maybe Kevin was the reason Dawn remained calm. He had a reassuring attitude, and a way of conveying bad news in an upbeat way. Because there was plenty of bad news they had to face . . . and more to come.

Kevin read through everything, twice, making notes as he read. Marnie kept his coffee cup refilled. Dawn whipped together some avocado toast to share, which Kevin nibbled absentmindedly as he continued to decipher the forms. He finished the last page with a sigh and looked up. "Okay. Now I need a walk-through of the entire building, top to bottom, inside and outside. Describe what things had looked like a month ago, and how they have changed, and what materials you used." He stacked the papers in a neat pile. "Pictures too. Do you happen to have any before and after?"

"I do, actually," Dawn said. "On my phone. I've been sending them to Brynn each day."

"Great. Let's get those printed." He glanced around the front room, grabbed a notepad, and rose from the table. "Okay, start here."

"Well, besides the fireplace," Dawn said, "there used to be a hideous indoor-outdoor gray carpet throughout the entire front room."

Marnie looked at the wide plank floorboards that lined the room. She wondered which previous owner thought gray carpet would be an improvement over that gorgeous old wood. Bonnie, maybe? It seemed to match her style. "Linc found someone who could sand and re-stain the floors next week. To give them plenty of time to cure before opening day."

Kevin looked up from his notepad. "No."

"No?" Marnie was so eager to have those floors redone.

"Remember, you have to look at everything from a preservationist viewpoint. Refinished floors end up with an overly pristine appearance that's lost a lot of character."

Dawn's gaze swept the room. "But some planks are pretty worn."

"Worn, but not worn out," Kevin said. "It's good to retain that aged look."

Dawn rose to walk over to the fireplace. "Look at this one. It's sanded down. There's a dip."

Kevin joined her, examining the plank. Marnie noticed that Dawn had lost the stiff countenance she'd had when Kevin first arrived. In fact, she seemed to be fully engaged in the discussion.

"A little patchwork might be needed here and there." Kevin glanced over the rest of the floor. "The rest of it isn't bad. There's something called arrested decay. You stop it from decaying but avoid making it look brand new."

"I suppose this is worn down here"—Dawn pressed her toe against the plank in front of the fireplace—"because this is where some housewife stood for hours and hours, stirring the kettle."

"And *now* you're thinking the way the Historical Commission thinks." A slow grin tugged at the corners of Kevin's lips, and Dawn smiled back, before bashfully looking away . . . and Marnie saw it all.

She grabbed her purse. "Dawn, can you give Kevin the full tour? I'll be back in an hour."

"Where are you going?" Dawn's brow furrowed in suspicion.

"The cancer support group." It was the one errand Marnie knew Dawn couldn't object to. Last night Lincoln had told her he wouldn't stop asking until she stayed through one full meeting. Reluctantly, she agreed to attend, but when Kevin arrived at the door, she felt she had a solid-gold reason to skip it. Until now. Until she saw the look that passed between Kevin and Dawn. Instantly, she changed her morning plans.

As she was heading out the door, she overheard Kevin ask, "Your mom has *cancer*?"

Marnie popped her head back in. "*Had*. I had cancer. It's gone." Then she closed the door and went on her way to the community center. She couldn't help cracking a smile.

● ● ●

An awkward silence filled the Creamery after Mom left. Awkward for so many reasons—all of which Dawn wanted to blame on her mother. But she couldn't. She was equally at fault. She had left the filing of paperwork to her mother—big mistake. She'd had an inkling that her mother had been in communication with Kevin and yet she hadn't wanted to face it—another big mistake. And she was confused and frustrated and angry and humiliated and . . . yet a small part of her was pleased and grateful that Kevin had come to help them out of the embarrassing disaster they'd created for themselves.

"Dawn," Kevin said in a tender voice. "Is that the real reason why you left your job for the summer? Because your mother has cancer?"

Slowly, chin on her chest, she nodded.

"Why didn't you tell me?"

Oh no. She wasn't going there. She refused to go back to that terrible, horrible night when he broke off their engagement . . . and then the next morning she found out her mother had cancer. She squared her shoulders. "We have a lot to cover this morning."

"We sure do, don't we?"

His voice was low and sad, and she couldn't bear it. "It all started with a hole in the roof. Let's go outside."

She needed fresh air.

* * *

Marnie sat in the same metal folding chair she'd sat on before, the one closest to the door. She saw Lincoln on the other side of the Cancer Room deep in conversation with that young mom who had asked for help with burns she'd received from radiation.

Marnie glanced at the clock. Three minutes to nine. She took in a deep breath. She could do this, she told herself. She'd handled much tougher situations than this. She was determined to stay today for the whole hour. It was important that she stay. Lincoln would be pleased and his approval mattered to her. She didn't want to think too closely about how much his opinion meant to her—or why. Bottom line, he'd done so much for the Main Street Creamery and asked for little in return. Surely, she could give him this one hour.

Even better, it would give Dawn and Kevin just what they needed—time alone. She had a bone-deep feeling this hour could be pivotal for them. They had unfinished business to work through before either one of them could move on, that much Marnie was sure of. She glanced at the clock again. Two minutes before nine o'clock. Her hands grew sweaty, her toes startled jiggling. She put her hands between her knees, trying to figure out some way to settle her restless legs short of tying her shoelaces together.

She must stay. Stay, stay, stay, stay, stay.

A deluxe-sized woman came in and plopped down next to her. "I've seen you here before. Twice."

"Oh?"

"I'm Nancy Broom. Breast cancer survivor. Three years now."

"Marnie. Marnie Dixon." She couldn't say anything more.

Nancy Broom leaned closer. "The thing is, Marnie, a support group is a give-and-take experience."

Marnie's eyebrows lifted in a question.

"You have to talk as much as you listen." She grinned. "Or in my case, listen as much as you talk." She laughed as if it was the funniest thing she'd ever said.

At that moment, Lincoln clapped his hands together one time to start the meeting and smiled when his eyes rested on Marnie. She tried to smile back but felt it came out wrong. She glanced at the clock. Two minutes after nine. Stay, stay, stay, stay.

She jumped from her chair to bolt out the door.

Chapter
TWENTY-TWO

The last laugh, the last cup of coffee, the last sunset, the last time you run through a sprinkler, or eat an ice-cream cone, or stick your tongue out to catch a snowflake. You just don't know.

—Lauren Oliver, author

Saturday, May 10

First things first. Dawn dragged the metal ladder from the side yard and leaned it against the shingle siding. She climbed the ladder, chattering away of what she knew of the kitchen fire and how the firemen had to break through the roof to let the heat and smoke out. When she reached the roof, she turned to look down at Kevin and realized he wasn't nearby as she had thought. She saw him come around the corner and stop at a window, examining it closely.

Watching him, her mind wandered, pondering what it would have been like if they'd kept to the plan and stayed together. They would've been married almost a month by now, would've returned to their jobs in Boston. She guessed life would be pretty close to what it had been like before they would've married—a busy, demanding workweek, both exhausted on Saturday, they would start to recover on Sunday, then Monday arrived and the workweek started up again. And for what?

It was a startling realization.

She shook off those thoughts. They had work to do. Focus, she told herself. Get back to the job at hand. Back to the here and now. She climbed down the ladder and joined him. "We don't have the budget for it, but I sure would like to replace those windows with vinyl clad."

"Too modern," he said, shaking his head. "First rule of thumb with Historical Commissions—better to keep something rather than replace it."

"That's just the kind of outdated thinking that seems so illogical in this day and age. So not-green. Those old windows are drafty."

"Old houses aren't going to win any awards for energy efficiency, that's for sure." He ran a finger along the edge. "It's possible to weatherize wooden double-hung windows."

"How?"

"I was just reading of a trick that contractors use with old houses. They permanently fix the upper sash and remove the window weights. The weights can be added to the lower sash and insulation can be tucked into the upper sash."

They walked over to the ladder and she stepped aside to let him start up the rungs. He gave her a slight smile of thanks, which felt awkward. They were both acting overly polite and . . . awkward. Weird, like they had just met.

"I didn't know you were interested in historical houses."

He looked down at her. "I've always wanted to work on old houses. Surely you knew that."

Did she? "Then why are you working for a firm that only builds commercial buildings?"

"Because . . . they recruited me out of college with the best offer."

"But if you wanted something else, why didn't you—"

"Because I had a lot of college debt to pay off."

Which he'd done. All of it. She knew he'd done it. She was the one who'd set up the spreadsheet for him. She was the one who refused to talk about marriage until all debts were paid off. But if he'd paid off his college debt, and if he wanted to pursue something else, why hadn't he made a change? He had never once mentioned that he might want to switch firms or go out on his own. Or had he? Had she just not been listening? She had a nagging sense of having missed something important.

He came back down the ladder and went straight to another window, examining it. "It might help if the windows had new putty. We can do that easily."

We, he said. As if he had a stake in this upside-down Marnie Dixon ice cream shop venture. But he didn't. "Do you think we're in for a fight with the Historical Commission?"

Slowly, he turned in a circle. "Well, this location is fairly prominent. Right on Main Street, highly visible, so my guess is they're going to scrutinize everything carefully." Then he looked straight at her. "So yeah, I think we're in for a fight."

A reckoning was coming. She could sense it. So this was what Mom meant when she could feel something bone-deep.

* * *

Marnie couldn't go back to the Creamery and face Dawn and Kevin. Not yet. So as she left the cancer support group rather abruptly, she headed straight to the lighthouse, went around it, and onto the beach. Thoroughly unsettled, she wanted to try to get a handle on her feelings before she went home to face more problems.

The day had started out sunny, but now gray clouds were coming in to block the sun. The wind was picking up, whitecaps limned the tops of waves. Rain was coming, which meant the beach was fairly empty for a Saturday morning in mid-May. A couple of seals kept pace with her, just twenty yards or so out in the surf. She walked as far as she could, then turned back. The seals kept popping their heads up and down, but eventually they grew bored with her and moved on.

She heard a dog's familiar bark and spun around. Charging toward her was Mayor, Lincoln following in long, unhurried strides. She felt a thump in her abdomen, wondering what to say when he reached her. She bent down to give Mayor a pat, then the dog spotted a low-flying seagull and took off after it. Marnie straightened, and walked toward Linc. When they were about six feet apart, she stopped. "Hi," she said, keeping her distance, even though part of her didn't want to. She pulled in a deep, shaky breath and felt her stomach quiver. "Linc, I'm so sorry."

He shook his head. "I'm the one who should be apologizing. I've been putting pressure on you." He closed the six feet between them, although he didn't touch her. He shoved his hands into his jean pockets and drew in a breath. "Marnie, can't we talk about this?" His eyes appeared troubled. "What is it about the cancer support group that makes you so . . . uneasy?"

Uneasy? That was a generous excuse. Crazy was closer to the truth. "Cancer is behind me. I want it to stay there."

Linc didn't say anything for a long while, not until they started slowly walking back toward the lighthouse. "Here's what I don't understand. You have a deep faith. I know you do. I've seen it at work in how you go full force with the Creamery. How you bounce back after setbacks. How you keep Dawn from sinking toward pessimism. You don't let problems stop you from moving forward. Your faith, it seems to sustain you."

True. "It's gotten me through some terrible times."

"So don't you think God would want you to use your situation, your faith, to bless someone else?"

That was so far from the direction she thought he was headed that she stopped short, staring at him. His words made her angry, though she didn't completely understand why, and the tender tone of his voice only added to it. "I . . . but I . . . I just can't." Tears pricked her eyes and she started off again, walking faster this time.

"Marnie?"

"I can't, Lincoln." She wiped away the infuriating tears.

"Marnie"—spoken softer this time while he gripped her arm to stop her.

She turned to him, her chin dropped to her chest.

He tipped her chin up with one finger. "Why not?"

Why not? What made that cancer support group so difficult for her? What was it? She didn't know. She couldn't put a name to it. It just brought up a terrible dread, a darkness.

And suddenly she knew.

Chapter
TWENTY-THREE

Umpiring is best described as standing between two seven-year-olds with one ice cream cone.
—Ron Luciano, American Major League baseball umpire

Saturday, May 10

Marnie walked over to a log that had drifted onto the beach and sat on it. Lincoln called Mayor to his side, and the big dog galloped toward him from the water's edge, kicking sand in his wake, heading straight toward him. They joined Marnie at the log. Linc plopped down, patted his hand on the sand, and his dog sat beside him, panting hard.

Marnie watched Linc stroke the dog's thick fur, gliding his splayed fingers through his coat, until the dog settled and curled into a ball, resting peacefully. Lincoln had a calming effect on others, animals or human. She wondered if he'd always been that way, or if it resulted from that pivotal point in his life when he realized he was all alone. She wasn't quite sure if she would have liked the pre-cancer Lincoln, at least the way he had described himself. He seemed nothing like the post-cancer Lincoln, whom she liked quite a bit.

Lincoln simply gave Marnie the comfort of his silent strength. After a long while, he quietly said, "I won't ask you to go to the support group anymore. I never meant to upset you."

She shook her head. "You haven't. The problem isn't the support group. The problem is me." Tears clouding her vision, she stared at the open expanse of the ocean. She knew Linc was waiting patiently for her to continue. Finally, she let out a breath she hadn't realized she'd been holding. "Recurrence."

"Recurrence?"

"I'm terrified of it." Tears started spilling down her cheeks. Embarrassed, she wiped them away, but they kept coming.

Lincoln reached out to pull her against him, holding her tight, rocking back and forth gently. With her eyes closed, she listened to the wind, the pounding surf, the seagulls crying overhead, Lincoln's steady heartbeat. The lull of the ocean eventually calmed her. She breathed in the scent of the salt and sea, and soaked in a long dose of comfort. As peace began to steal over her, she pulled away from Lincoln.

"Thank you," she whispered.

"It's healthy to address that fear, head-on."

She let out a light laugh. "I didn't even know I had it."

"So going to the group brings up the fear of recurrence."

"I think so. I've just been in such a hurry to get it all behind me . . . and coming here, to Chatham, the ice cream shop—it seemed like a fresh start. A new beginning. But then . . . you came into our life. You've been such a godsend to us, a huge help in so many ways. Don't misunderstand—I'm thankful for you, Lincoln. But you've also brought the cancer support group along with you."

His eyes gentled with a smile.

"Isn't recurrence something you fear? Doesn't everyone at the support group fear recurrence?"

"Of course. I can't imagine anyone who's had cancer who doesn't fear its return. All the statistics in the world don't matter when you're the one waiting for results."

"What about you? Don't you think about it? Worry about it?"

Lincoln didn't answer for a long time, as if gathering his thoughts. "There's a verse in the book of Ecclesiastes that I circle back to quite often. It goes something like this." He lifted his eyes, as if reading the words in the sky. "Since no one knows the future, who can tell someone else what is to come? As no one has power over the wind to contain it, so no one has power over the time of their death." He dropped his chin and turned to Marnie. "A cancer diagnosis is a reminder that we're not going to live forever, but it doesn't have ultimate power over us. God determines the length of our lives, not cancer."

"But God may use cancer to end our life."

"Maybe."

"Don't you see, then? The fear of recurrence? I don't want to die from cancer. I don't want to die at all, of course, but especially not from cancer. Frankly, I don't want to know that I'm dying. Best-case scenario . . . die during my sleep." She sighed. "I guess I just don't want death to hurt."

He laughed. "That is a conversation worth having with God."

A seagull shrieked overhead and they watched it circle in the sky.

"Marnie, having a sense of passing time, that's not such a bad thing. In fact, it's a gift. It's the reason I sold my business and moved here. I don't want to waste time anymore."

"It's the reason I bought the ice cream shop."

"There. You see? You found a gift from cancer."

She rolled her eyes. "A gleaning. That much I'll grant you. I'm still not sure I'd call anything about cancer a gift."

"Living one day at a time brings a wonderful freedom. Most people live in the past or the future."

Philip came to mind, and then Dawn. They both spent an enormous amount of time planning for the future, making goals, plotting ways to achieve them. At times, it seemed almost an obsession, as if they enjoyed planning for something more than the actual . . . something. Dawn wanted to make partner, marry, buy a house, and have a child before the age of thirty. Philip wanted to retire at age sixty and run an ice cream shop. He died at fifty-nine. She wondered what he might have done differently had he realized his time on earth would be cut short. She wondered about Dawn.

"Looks like we're in for some rain," Linc said.

"That's not what I thought you were going to say."

"Well, those are some pretty dark clouds."

She smiled. "Not about rain. I meant about living with recurrence."

"What did you think I was going to say?"

"That there are no guarantees in life, so carpe diem."

He shook his head. "Nope. I am confident that my life will not be one minute shorter than God wants it to be, nor one minute longer. And when the time comes for me to take my final breath, I will enter into the presence of the Lord. That's my guarantee." He smiled. "And that is why I do not fear recurrence."

"Another leap of faith."

"The best kind."

The first sprinkles of rain fell on them. Lincoln rose to his feet, brushing sand from his backside. He offered a hand to Marnie to help her up. Impulsively, she wrapped her arms around him and gave him a big hug.

"What was that for?" he asked once she'd finished.

Despite herself, she laughed. "For being such a good friend, Lincoln."

He said nothing in return, but his eyes said much. As they made their way back to the Creamery, she thought she might just give the cancer support group one more try.

● ● ●

Heavy rain on Saturday afternoon kept people indoors. Kevin sat at a table by the window in the front room, wading through paperwork and filling out forms. Dawn worked on a new flavor of ice cream after Mom and Lincoln returned. Blackberry Chocolate Chunk. She remembered that Kevin had always liked berries and chocolate together. He came into the kitchen as she was scooping the ice cream into a container, alternating with blackberry mixture and chocolate chunks. She let him sample a spoonful and tried not to look overly pleased when he asked for a second spoonful, then a third.

He looked at her. "You're good at this."

She lifted one shoulder in a careless shrug. "It's . . . just cream and eggs and sugar, mixed together."

"No, it's more than just cream and eggs and sugar. You love it and it shows. It's outstanding, Dawn," he said, licking the spoon. "Beyond outstanding. Superb. Best I've ever had."

The unexpected compliment left her flustered, unsure of what to do or say next. She decided what he must really want was another spoonful. Kevin was a serious clean-your-plate man; he usually finished off anything she might've left on her plate. Never gained a pound, either, while she could gain weight just looking at food.

She had to reach around him to pull a bowl from an overhead cupboard. Despite her best efforts, she brushed against him. "Sorry," she said, avoiding his gaze, ignoring the tingle she felt where his arm had touched hers. "Small space." She turned away and scooped out a generous helping of ice cream into the bowl. He grinned, accepting it from her, and she grinned in return. For the longest moment, all they did was stare at each other. Ever so slightly, he leaned forward, as if he intended to kiss her, but he stopped and gave his head a slight shake, as if that thought must be cleared.

Mom popped her head around the doorjamb. "Lincoln went to the lumber store to see about some replacement planks for the hearth. I thought I might run over to a tag sale in Sandwich and check on some glass water jugs with spigots. Seems like just the thing to offer customers drinking water. Maybe infused with cucumber and mint. I'm hoping no one will be out in the rain." She grabbed her purse off the kitchen counter. "Kevin, stay for dinner."

He glanced at his watch. "Thanks, but I need to get on the road soon." He hesitated, then said, "I've picked up my violin again and started taking lessons with my old music teacher. He only had one time slot left and it happened to be Saturday evening." He shrugged. "But it's not so bad. I've been staying over at my folks' on Saturday night, so I get to hear Dad preach on Sunday mornings."

Dawn felt a sting. Whenever they'd visited his family on the weekend, she was the one who had insisted that they not stay the night. She had wanted to protect their leisurely Sunday mornings, their only quiet time in the week. Kevin didn't object, but now she realized she was the one who had swayed him from going to church on a regular basis. Maybe he felt more strongly about church attendance than she did. Maybe he felt more strongly about a lot of things.

He finished the last spoonful of ice cream and set the empty bowl in the sink. "Marnie, that reminds me. I hadn't realized you sold the Needham house until Mom mentioned it."

A sudden silence filled the room. Dawn felt her chest tighten. "Wait. Mom, you did . . . what?"

"Uh-oh." Kevin's eyes darted between the two women. He looked slightly uncomfortable.

"Mom, you *sold* the house?" Something cold and snakelike coiled in Dawn's belly.

Mom had been searching through her purse for something when Kevin broke this news. She froze for a moment, then went on with her hunt, riveting her attention to the purse. "That friend of your dad's, Ed Nelson, the real estate agent, he had always wanted to buy it. For his son, he said." Mom blustered on, carefully avoiding Dawn's eyes. "So I called him and asked if he was still interested and he said he was and we agreed on a fair price and . . . he drove to Hyannis with all the paperwork to sign. He took care of everything. Even brought a cash deposit."

Mom's emergency slush fund.

The truth struck Dawn like a slap. Unable to speak, she stood across the kitchen from her mother, watching, waiting, her mind spinning. Was it possible? Could Mom have done it again? Made a massive life-changing decision without consulting her, without even telling her.

"On Thursday, I met Ed in Hyannis to sign some papers. Afterwards, that's where I found the copper dry sink." Mom pointed over her shoulder to the front room, then returned to her task, eyes trained on her purse.

For a moment, Dawn closed her eyes, gulping, unable to swallow the lump of fear that clogged her throat. "You never mentioned a word."

Mom lifted the car keys out of the purse. But still, she wouldn't look at Dawn. "I was waiting for the right time."

Kevin cleared his throat. "I'm sorry about that."

"Don't be," Dawn said, giving in, tossing her hands in the air. "I'm not sure there would've ever been a right time." She told herself to stay calm. That everything was going to be fine. But it wasn't. "First you said the money for the Creamery would come only from Dad's life insurance policy. Then you said you had stocked away an emergency slush fund."

"Both are true. But things cost more than I had expected." Finally, she risked a glance at Dawn. "I didn't want to worry you. There was the pasteurizer, then we needed a new freezer, and then you thought we should get a smaller display case"— she lifted a hand before Dawn could object—"and it was the right call. It gave us room to add a frozen food display freezer. You've been working so hard on the ice cream and Linc was doing so much to help get the building into shape . . . selling the house seemed . . . like the right decision. The only decision."

"You didn't consider asking me for the money?"

"You? No, of course not. Your savings belongs to you."

"You didn't consider going to the bank for a loan?"

"I . . ." Mom looked puzzled. "No, I didn't even think of that as an option. Your dad was always so adamant about paying cash for things. It never occurred to me to seek a loan."

Dawn was so angry she could hardly breathe. "Excuse me," she murmured, striding to the back door to hurry outside. She took in great gulps of air, feeling a chill that ran from her toes to her head. She rubbed her arms to keep warm, but she knew the chill came from fear. Mom was going to lose everything Dad had worked for, all the financial security he had spent his entire life trying to create. *Everything.* All gone, in just a few months. How to stop this craziness!

The door opened and Kevin came outside. "I'm sorry. I really mucked things up."

"You didn't do anything wrong. You only said what you knew to be true." She sucked in a deep breath to calm herself. "My mother is living her life as recklessly as she always did. But now Dad's gone and I'm the one who has to clean up her mess."

He looked behind him at the Creamery. "It's not a mess. Sure, it's a little complicated, but it's not a mess. And I'm not so sure she's being reckless. She's creating a dream. In a way, by selling the Needham house, it's her way of saying to herself that there's no going back. She's all in."

"All in," Dawn echoed, then grew quiet. She wondered if that was a general observation or if he was aiming it specifically at her. Kevin had complained that she didn't open her heart to him, not completely. She wondered if this, too, was another reason he had broken things off. Unlike her mom, she wasn't *all in*.

"What's the worst thing that can happen?"

Wasn't that obvious? Lose it all.

He read her thoughts. "Maybe the Creamery won't be quite the success your mom is hoping it will be, but I doubt it'll be the complete flop you have in your mind." Frowning, he added, "Dawn, maybe you should ease up on your expectations."

Unfair, she thought. She was here, wasn't she?

"Your mom's trying to make a new life for herself. There's bound to be a few stumbles along the way. That's just life."

She let out a sigh. "I'm glad to hear you're playing your violin again."

His eyebrows lifted. "Are you?"

"Of course. Of course I am." Why wouldn't she be? Kevin was an accomplished musician. During one stretch of college, he'd even thought of making a career as a classical violinist, but job uncertainty and low pay put him off. Or was it her? Had she unknowingly discouraged him in that pursuit? She wondered. "It must feel good to play again."

"Not quite yet. I'm rusty. Really rusty. I'd forgotten how taut a violin's strings can get. I have to keep loosening them so they don't snap."

Dawn's anger at her mother's decision about the Needham house was starting to wane. "I suppose you'd better get on the road to get to your lesson on time. If I remember correctly, your Ukrainian teacher brooked no nonsense."

"Yeah, it's getting late." He pulled his car keys out of his pocket and glanced over at the Creamery. "You know, it's pretty impressive. What your mom is trying to do." He looked back at her. "Maybe it would help if you left a few things to God to take care of."

She tipped her head slightly. "Sounds like you've gone and got religion."

"If by that you mean going regularly to church, then yeah, I guess so. I've come to realize that having faith is a lot like drawing close to a fire. You back away from it and the coals grow cold. You have to tend the fire for faith to grow." When she didn't respond, he said, "I'll be off then."

She watched him get in his car and drive off, feeling almost numb.

You should ease up on your expectations.

Your mom's trying to make a new life for herself. She's all in.

There's bound to be a few stumbles along the way.

Leave a few things to God to take care of.

Six months ago, Kevin would never have thought those things, much less said them to her. They'd shared similar feelings about avoiding anything church related—after all, they'd both had more than enough of religion in their childhood. Someday, they told themselves, they'd get back to church. After Dawn's dad died, the spiritual dimension of her life shrank even further.

Having faith is a lot like drawing close to a fire.

You back away from it and the coals grow cold.

You have to tend the fire for faith to grow.

Dawn lifted her head to the sky. The rainstorm had blown through, leaving a smattering of gray clouds behind. She released a long sigh. "What is wrong with me? Why am I so afraid of making a mistake?" She'd always been overly careful and cautious, as long as she could remember. She didn't even let her dad remove training wheels from her bike until long after all the other kids her age were riding without any help. When she finally did ride solo, she didn't fall. At age six, she'd been proud of herself for that accomplishment.

Her dad bragged about it. But was skinning a knee such a bad thing?

She let out another sigh. Her shoulders lowered as the defiance left her. No answer from Above. She wished she'd gotten one. She wished there'd been bright lights and loud trumpets to announce an angel, swooping down from Heaven with a clear and concise message for her. But there was nothing.

●　●　●

Sunday, May 11

After church on Sunday, Marnie stood in line to get a cup of coffee for Dawn and Linc. She still felt shocked that Dawn had come down to breakfast this morning, dressed for church, as if out of habit. Ha! So, so far from a habit for her daughter. Marnie did her best to act nonchalant. Inside, she was squealing with joy. All during the sermon, she sat on her hands to stop them from fidgeting. She wouldn't allow herself to glance at Dawn, not a single time, to see if she found the sermon interesting or illuminating. She delivered an Oscar-winning performance of a cucumber-cool mom.

Marnie wondered if Dawn's willingness to come to church had to do with their conversation over breakfast about the Needham house. Over coffee, Marnie had apologized for not informing Dawn of the decision, for not even asking her about it. She did feel guilty. This was her daughter's childhood home, after all. Even though Dawn had moved her belongings to her Boston apartment, she would've fought tooth and nail to hang on to the house. And for what? Memories? That was no reason to cling to the past.

"Dawn, hear me out," she had said, while filling her mug with freshly brewed coffee. "It's looking like Maeve and Paul Grayson are getting pretty serious. My guess is that it won't be long before she moves to Three Sisters Island in Maine. Of course I'm happy for her, but with Maeve leaving Needham, there's just not much left for me. Your dad is gone, your life is in Boston, and while I do have other friends, Maeve was special. But I am sorry. I should've considered your feelings."

Dawn had only one question. "What are you going to do about emptying out the house?"

A fair question. Ed Nelson had been extremely accommodating to Marnie, but he did request for the house to be cleaned out by the Fourth of July weekend—the busiest time on the Cape. There was no way Marnie could give up the time needed to go through all the contents of the house. No way could she leave Dawn to run the Creamery on her own. So Marnie called in her reinforcements. "Maeve O'Shea. She's handling everything. She's ordered one of those storage pods for the furniture and everything. And she's organized the Bible study ladies to help."

Dawn's face scrunched up. "Mom, you've got a lot of . . ."

"I know, I know. A lot of stuff. I told Maeve to have a tag sale and sell it all, then take everyone out to a fancy dinner with the money."

"What about important papers? Photo albums? Tax records? Sentimental things."

"Maeve suggested going through those kinds of things over FaceTime."

"Seems like a lot," Dawn said, running a finger around the top of her coffee mug, "to ask of a friend."

"Well, this is Maeve. And she gets what widowhood is like. After your dad's funeral, she left a note on my pillow. 'A single arrow can be easily snapped in two, but a tight little bundle of arrows can withstand the strongest pressures.' That's the kind of friendship she offers."

"Still . . . cleaning out a whole house?"

Marnie agreed. It wasn't an easy phone call to make, but Maeve turned it around and made it easy. "She said it's her gift to me for the second half."

"The second half?"

"Of life."

For several long minutes Dawn said nothing. She was thinking, and Marnie wondered what all was running through her mind. Last night, she'd gone out the door so angry about the selling of the Needham house. Kevin had followed her out. Whatever had happened between them had shifted Dawn into a completely different state of mind. Twenty minutes later, she came in the door, went straight to the kitchen, and made another batch of Blackberry Chocolate Chunk. The Needham house wasn't brought up, not until Marnie mentioned it this morning.

Eyes still on her coffee mug, Dawn said, "Does Maeve happen to like ice cream?"

"She does." Marnie smiled. "Her favorite flavor is lemon."

"Lemon," Dawn echoed. "I've been meaning to try a new recipe for Meyer lemons. They're a little sweeter than your average lemon." She picked up her mug. "Last night, I read about a company that ships frozen foods using dry ice. They provide everything you need. Maybe . . . I'll call them. Send Maeve some ice cream as a thank-you."

"She would love that."

"Maeve"—Dawn looked up to meet Marnie's eyes—"is a very good friend to you."

Marnie nodded. "The best."

The church line for coffee moved along, and it was then that Marnie noticed a familiar cobwebby French twist hairstyle ahead of her in line. She opened her mouth to say hello, then snapped it shut. Nanette was standing next to Mrs. Nickerson-Eldredge. When she heard Nanette mention the Main Street Creamery, her ears went on high alert.

The two women stood shoulder to shoulder in the slow-moving line. Nanette was doing most of the talking. "It just seems as if you could be a little friendlier to someone who is trying to make a go of that dumpy old building."

"Friendlier?" Mrs. Nickerson-Eldredge practically spat the word. "I have no intention of bending the rules. Not for anyone."

"But do you need to scare her off like you did Bonnie?"

Marnie heard Mrs. Nickerson exhale impatiently. "If I *can* scare her off, then she deserves to be gone."

Marnie's shoulders sagged in defeat. She slipped out of line and returned to Dawn and Lincoln, offering a lame excuse that the coffee looked like weak tea and she'd rather treat them to the real stuff at Monomoy Coffee Shop.

All afternoon, Marnie couldn't shake a growing sense of dread about tomorrow's meeting with the Historical Commission. So Mrs. Nickerson-Eldredge had scared off Bonnie? She didn't seem like someone who would scare off easily. *Lord*, she prayed over and over, *you've brought us this far. We're so close, Lord. Help us see this through. For me, for Kevin, for Lincoln, for Dawn. Especially for Dawn.*

Please, please, please, please, please.

●　●　●

Monday, May 12

On Monday morning, Dawn dressed in her best clothes, which weren't really her best because those were in her closet back in Boston. But they were close to her best, dark and serious, and gave off a professional vibe. After all, she wanted the Historical Commission to take them seriously. When Mom emerged, Dawn glanced down at her tropical blue maxi dress and sandals and vetoed the entire outfit, insisting she wear a conservative navy blazer over a white T-shirt and khaki pants.

Mom looked in the mirror, straightening the collar of the blazer. "I look like a flight attendant."

"Nonsense. You look like someone who should be taken seriously." Dawn brushed off a stray hair. "You have to dress the way you want to feel inside."

A slow smile crept over Mom's face. "Sooner or later, we all quote our mothers."

Dawn gasped. "I did *not* just quote you!" She clasped her cheeks. "Oh . . . I did. I even remember you saying it." Hands still on her cheeks, she lifted her shoulders with an exaggerated shudder. "This whole experience is turning me into my mother."

Brushing her hair, Mom grinned at the mirror like a cat in the cream.

Dawn went downstairs to refill her coffee cup and heard a knock at the door. She opened it, expecting Nanette to come with the morning gossip.

"You!" Kevin. Caught off guard, she tried not to let her delight show. Of course, she'd known he was due to arrive in Chatham this morning—though not quite so early—but having him actually present made her feel better about everything.

"Yup. Me." Kevin walked right in, taking her coffee cup out of her hand. "Thanks. I skipped breakfast."

"I thought you said to meet at the community center."

"Even better," he said, sipping the coffee. "As I was driving back to Needham on Saturday afternoon, I was struck with a brilliant idea. I called the number given for the Historical Commission, and a woman picked right up, almost like she was just sitting by the phone, waiting for me to call. I explained the situation and asked if someone from the Historical Commission could meet us at the Creamery, so we could show the work that's been done, rather than just talk about it."

"Is that possible?"

"Well, you know how things work. It all depends on who you ask. And I think I happened to have asked *just* the right person. In fact, she couldn't have been more accommodating. I really think we'll stand a better chance with appeals by having someone coming here"—he winked at her—"especially if you serve up Blackberry Chocolate Chunk ice cream."

"Right. It just depends on who that someone is."

"The chairman would come, she said." He grinned, proud of himself. "How's *that* for clout?"

Dawn's chin dropped to her chest.

Chapter

TWENTY-FOUR

When everyone has let you down, you still have ice cream.

—Keegan Allen, actor

Monday, May 12

Mrs. Nickerson-Eldredge was the most frustrating person Dawn had ever met—male or female, bar none. She was both rude *and* cranky.

And yet no one, Dawn was sure, could have handled Mrs. Nickerson-Eldredge any better than Kevin Collins. He was gentlemanly, almost courtly, calm and capable and just a little bit sexy, presenting his case with clear and compelling evidence. The old biddy nearly purred like a cat when he quoted sections by heart from the code book for the Chatham Historical Commission.

How was he able to memorize it in less than forty-eight hours? Dawn was seeing Kevin in a new light and felt a little dazzled. She'd never seen him quite so . . . what was the word? Convicted. Single-minded. Resolute.

Weird. She'd always bragged to her friends about how easy-going Kevin was, how he didn't insist on his own way like so many of her friends' boyfriends did. But now she wondered if he might've had more opinions than she'd thought—things like which movie to see, or which new restaurant to try. Maybe he just didn't voice them.

Was it just like their wedding? He said nothing, and she assumed that meant complicity. But it didn't. It *really* didn't.

She watched him as he adroitly managed Mrs. Nickerson-Eldredge—listening carefully to her while remaining completely in control of the direction of the conversation. The Historical Commission did not have jurisdiction over the interior, he pointed out, yet his clients (Dawn and Marnie!) were fully compliant to the code. Uncovering the fireplace was just one example. Removing the carpet that covered the original floorboards. And the exterior improvements were justifiable—they were repairs and not additions or demolitions.

Whenever Mrs. Nickerson-Eldredge brought up an objection, Kevin listened carefully, nodding his head in all the right moments. Dawn thought of how impatient she'd been with the older woman, curt and crisp, assuming the worst of her. She was actually starting to soften toward her, starting to believe Mrs. Nickerson-Eldredge was just doing her job because she loved Chatham so much and not because she had a vendetta against them . . . when she rose to her orthopedic-clad feet and said, "There is still the matter of the mechanical support reinforcing the pier under the house."

"What about it?" Dawn said.

"It's not authentic to the nineteenth century, when the house was built."

"By Chatham's standards, that makes it practically new." As soon as the words came out of Dawn's mouth, she wished them back.

Kevin frowned, Mom elbowed her, and Mrs. Nickerson-Eldredge let out a huff.

Mom stepped in to redirect attention away from Dawn's big mouth. "The metal structure could be considered interior. After all, no one can see it from the street."

"Oh, but I can," Mrs. Nickerson-Eldredge said. "This discussion will have to be continued at the Board of Appeals for the Historical Commission."

"When," Mom asked, a look of concern pulling her eyebrows together, "would that be?"

"The Board of Appeals meets the fourth Tuesday of every month." She sniffed. "Common knowledge to all local residents."

"Hold on," Dawn said. "That means . . ."

"Correct." Mrs. Nickerson-Eldredge smiled that cold smile, the one that was not really a smile. "The next meeting will be held the Tuesday before Memorial Day."

Dawn started running through the last week of May in her mind. Wednesday was the final health and safety inspection. Thursday was the Creamery's soft opening, their run-through. Friday was the grand opening—advertising had already been paid for in the *Cape Cod Chronicle*. "And if our appeal is denied . . ."

"The Creamery can't open to the public until the situation has been rectified." With that, Mrs. Nickerson-Eldredge clasped her folder to her chest and left the Creamery in her brisk, no-nonsense way.

Dawn exchanged a look of panic with her mom. If that meeting went badly with the Board of Appeals, the Main Street Creamery would become a house of cards, all tumbling down.

Dawn hurried outside to speak privately to Mrs. Nickerson-Eldredge. "Wait!" When she reached her on the sidewalk, she leaned forward to whisper, "There's a lot riding on our success. More than you might imagine. I don't see why the Historical

Commission can't give us a little grace period." She might as well have been speaking in a foreign language. Mrs. Nickerson-Eldredge's face remained stonelike. Okay, then. It was time to pull out her trump card. "You see . . . my mother . . . she's a new widow and she's had cancer recently . . . and she's put nearly everything she has into buying this building. Everything she has, and I mean *everything*, is riding on its success. Please. We're not trying to do anything outrageous—we're just trying to open by Memorial Day."

Mrs. Nickerson-Eldredge looked over Dawn's shoulder toward the Creamery. Her prim mouth relaxed, and a troubled look filled her eyes. For the briefest of moments, Dawn thought the tough old bird might be softening . . . but then she opened her mouth. "All the more reason to do things the right way. Go through the proper channels and wait until you're given approval." And away she went, marching like a Hessian soldier.

Slowly Dawn turned to face the Creamery. What a contrast to her first impression of the building—neglected and dreary. The kind of shop that would make you pick up your pace to pass on by. No longer. It looked crisp, cared for, inviting. The exterior appearance alone would make tourists want to stop and head inside. She walked up the path and paused at the threshold. Each time she came through the door, the shop took her by surprise. The way the sunlight moved through the building, the warm tone of the now-exposed wooden floors. Even the air seemed fresher. Mom's hunch was right. Uncovering the fireplace had been spot-on—it drew you in. The tables and chairs she'd dragged home from all over the Cape were the perfect size—inviting customers to linger without causing a traffic jam at the counter.

There was still a lot to get done in the next few weeks, not to mention a lot of ice cream making, but she felt proud of what they'd accomplished so far. At the very least, Dawn consoled herself, if they couldn't get approval to open the Creamery, they could probably sell it without losing money. Maybe Mom's crazy endeavor wouldn't end up as a giant money pit, after all.

Kevin was over by the fireplace. "What's this?"

Mom joined him, running a hand over the newly installed mantel. "Linc found an old chunk of barn wood and spent all Sunday afternoon tweaking it to make it look like it's been there all this time." She took a few steps back. "What a difference it makes."

"It does. It looks fantastic. But I meant this." He reached for the metal box that sat on the edge of the mantel.

"That's something Linc found down in the cellar."

"In the ash dump," Dawn said. She walked over to the fireplace.

Kevin picked it up and gave it a gentle shake. "Have you opened it?"

"We meant to," Mom said, "but Linc needed a certain tool."

With that, Kevin went to his messenger bag and pulled out a tool. Since when did he carry tools in his bag? The Kevin whom Dawn had known used to call for roadside assistance when his windshield wipers needed changing. She watched him carefully bend the latch, working slowly so the metal didn't break off.

Gently, he maneuvered the latch open, and held the box out to Dawn to examine first. They were standing close. A little too close. Every inch of her body was aware of every inch of his. *Focus*, she told herself. *Focus, focus, focus.*

Head down, she sifted through the box and picked up a yellowed paper. "Looks like odds and ends. Buttons and coins and an arrowhead." Gingerly, she unfolded it. "An old receipt with the name Nickerson on it. For shoeing a horse."

Mom was at her side in a flash. "You're kidding."

"I'm not. Look." Dawn held out the paper to her. "Dated 1893."

Mom stared at that paper for the longest time. Then she snapped into action like a general issuing a battle plan. "Kevin, you work on the appeal. Dawn, you start building up our supply of ice cream for Memorial Day weekend. We're going to need it." She strode to the door, then spun on her heels and returned to take the metal box out of Kevin's hands, the receipt out of Dawn's, put it into the metal box, closed it up, tucked the box under her arm, and headed to the door.

"Mom, where are you going?"

She opened the door and pivoted, a pleased look on her face. "I'm off to go grease the wheel. To prime the pump. Say a prayer!"

●　●　●

Marnie knocked once, twice, three times. She knew Mrs. Nickerson-Eldredge was inside her house because she kept seeing the curtain move. She waited a moment, then knocked a fourth time, fifth time, and finally, the door opened. Mrs. Nickerson-Eldredge welcomed her with a frown.

"Why are you knocking my door down?"

"Because of this." She held up the metal box. "This was in the fireplace's ash dump. At the Creamery."

"So?"

"It's filled with curious old items. Buttons and coins. A few arrowheads."

"You can donate it to the local museum."

"There's also an old receipt with the name Nickerson on it."

For the first time, a spark of interest flicked through the woman's eyes.

Marnie held the box out to her. "I thought you should have it."

Mrs. Nickerson-Eldredge accepted it, holding it in her hands. "This doesn't change anything with the Historical Commission."

"Of course not." Marnie turned to go and went a few steps

down the path when she heard Mrs. Nickerson-Eldredge call her name. She spun around.

"Your daughter said you're a cancer survivor."

"Dawn told you that?"

"She did. It was yet another attempt to try and persuade me to bend the rules of the Historical Commission."

Marnie frowned. Dawn had no right telling her private business to people. As soon as she got home, she would let her know. "My apologies. She was out of line."

"Is it true?"

Marnie took a few steps back to the door. As she came closer to her, she could see that her question was laced with concern. "Yes. It's true."

"If you don't mind my asking . . . what kind of cancer?"

"I don't mind." And for the first time, she really didn't mind. "I had breast cancer." A troubled look came over Mrs. Nickerson-Eldredge's face and something inside Marnie snapped, and she understood. "Oh honey." She wrapped her arms around the older woman and held her close. "Oh honey. Don't you worry. You're going to get through this. And I'll be with you every step of the way." She pulled back and put her hands on her shoulders. "Let's go inside. I'll make coffee and we can talk."

Chapter

TWENTY-FIVE

Always serve too much hot fudge sauce on hot fudge sundaes. It makes people overjoyed, and puts them in your debt.

—Judith Olney, cookbook author

Tuesday, May 13

Over the next two weeks, Dawn and Mom worked and worked. From sunup to sundown, they worked. Lincoln kept coming around one o'clock each day, and stayed late to finish projects, like replacing the worn wood planks in front of the fireplace, then scrubbing and oiling the entire floor. Dawn made batch after batch of ice cream to fill the new freezers, the one in the kitchen and the one for take-home containers.

Mom kept popping out for errands—who knew where she went? When Dawn asked, she was evasive—but she did finish the projects she had started at the Creamery. Painting the rooms, ordering glass tops for the tables, installing new lighting with Linc's help, and just putting final touches on everything. She'd lugged huge clay pots from the nursery, and

Nanette helped fill them with blooming bright red geraniums. One was put by the front door and the others on the patio. Mom also bought periwinkle-blue Adirondack chairs to place around the Creamery in sets of two.

"For customers to linger," Mom told Dawn. She had style, that mother of hers.

Dawn ordered all the supplies they'd be needing for customers—to-go containers, labels, cups, wooden spoons, napkins with the Main Street Creamery logo. She'd taken on social media—starting an Instagram countdown to the grand opening blitz. She'd never done much marketing before, but she had fun showing off her latest flavors, posed deliciously in an ice cream cone or bowl, cleverly staged in front of the Main Street Creamery quarterboard. She hadn't considered how far-reaching Instagram posts could be until she received a text from Kevin in Boston:

> Dark chocolate with blueberry compote? Save a
> cone for me.

She smiled. That was a reference to today's post. So, Kevin must follow the Main Street Creamery. There were only fourteen followers, so this was a big deal. She took her time responding, thinking it through.

> Too bad. Already gone.

> Figures. On another note, could you take some
> pictures of the new floor planks around the
> fireplace? Needed for the appeal.

> Will do.

From that text on, there was something almost daily that Kevin needed from Dawn to help prepare the appeal. It made sense that he asked Dawn rather than Mom, because she was the one who had taken pictures, and she was the one who was quick to respond. His texts had a businesslike tone, but now and then, he'd ask her how things at the Creamery were progressing.

How's it looking for the grand opening?

Impossible. Nearly hopeless.

What would your mom say if I asked?

That everything is right on schedule.

Last night, just as she was heading to bed, she noticed he had sent another text.

How did your day go?

She climbed into bed and pulled the covers up.

Surprising.

What made it surprising?

Cowboy Leo asked me to go steady. I told him I would have to think it over.

A long pause. Then the bubbles started.

If you decide to turn him down, tell him I have a five-year-old niece I can introduce him to.

Will keep that in mind.

She set her phone on silent and turned out the light, smiling.

* * *

Monday, May 26

On the day before Tuesday's Board of Appeals meeting, Kevin drove down to Chatham to go over the appeal with Marnie and

Dawn and look for any possible holes in his case. There were none to be found, even by Dawn. They were both astounded by his thoroughness. Kevin had checked and double-checked everything like an OCD airplane mechanic.

When Lincoln heard that Kevin had planned to stay in a hotel for the night, he insisted he spend the night at his cottage. Dawn had brought home from the market an armful of fresh basil, so Marnie whipped up a pesto sauce to go with a big bowl of hot pasta, made a green salad with pears and blackberries and lightly toasted pecans tossed with a light vinaigrette, and completed the meal with garlic bread. Actually, the meal was truly completed after sampling Dawn's ice cream experimentation for the day: Fresh Pineapple infused with Basil.

"Extraordinary," Linc said, holding his dish out for more. "Sublime. Stupendous. Superb."

It really was, Marnie thought. A perfect palate cleanser after a very garlicky meal.

As Kevin accepted another scoop from Dawn, he asked, "How'd you come up with that combination?"

Dawn rubbed her nose and chuckled nervously. "Well, the basil had just come in at the market and it was near these beautiful ripe pineapples, and suddenly, it just seemed so obvious. Pineapple and basil."

A far cry from vanilla, Marnie realized. She'd never thought she'd see the day when Dawn took creative risks with her ice cream. With her life.

When Dawn put the lid back on top of the container, Marnie jumped up to take it to the new freezer—one that was upright and allowed for more space in the kitchen. It was hard to take in all the changes that were happening to them these last few weeks, and she paused for a moment to listen to the pleasing hum of conversation coming from the other room.

A slow, surprised smile played over Marnie's face. It seemed impossible, but they were acting like a family. She knew not to make any mention of it. Some things were fragile like that. Like a hummingbird hovering at the feeder, or a butterfly lighting on your hand. You couldn't call attention to it without scaring it off. If Dawn and Kevin became conscious of it, one or the other would get nervous and head for the hills.

Closing the freezer, Marnie lifted her eyes ceilingward. *Thank you, thank you, thank you, thank you.*

* * *

Later that night, Dawn lay on her back, squaring her head on the pillow, trying to get comfortable on the lumpy bed. She twined her fingers and looked down her chest at them. When was her last manicure? Way too long. She wiggled her bottom until she found the right spot. If she stayed past Labor Day, she was buying a new mattress.

She put her hands behind her head. Would she even want to stay past Labor Day? Think of all it would mean—she'd have to give up her job, her apartment with Brynn, her beloved nest egg of financial security.

A favorite hymn of her dad's popped through her mind. *Rock of Ages, cleft for me, let me hide myself in thee.*

Her eyes opened wide. Where did that come from? It wasn't an audible voice . . . and yet in a way, it was. Weird. It didn't come from *her.* It wasn't the path her thoughts were wandering along. Dad would sing it to her on stormy nights when she had trouble sleeping.

She sat up in bed. Was that the kind of message Mom was always claiming to get? Like she'd somehow tapped into a supernatural radio frequency? It unsettled her.

Dawn looked up at the ceiling. "So now you're talking and that's all you have to say? Well, okay, if that's what you want, then it only seems fair that I get a chance to talk too. Here goes." She took in a deep breath. "I am angry with you, so angry. You took my dad, you took Kevin, you nearly took my mom. And why? Why dole all this trauma out on me at once? What have I done to deserve all that? You've got some explaining to do." She paused, listening for a response. "If your point has been to make sure I know that God is the Rock of Ages, then I think it's a cruel lesson. You're too hard on me."

She lay back down. *Rock of Ages, cleft for me, let me hide myself in thee.* She wondered what that meant, or could mean. This last year, she'd certainly discovered how fragile life was, how combustible plans could be. In fact, nothing had gone as she had planned. Other than her precious nest egg, her world had been turned upside down.

Rock of Ages, cleft for me, let me hide myself in thee.

"Is that what you're trying to say, God? That when all else is gone, you're still there?"

She listened for a response. There was none. She supposed it could seem a little arrogant to demand a response from God, but she did wish he could be a little more direct in his communication. More to the point.

She vacillated for a long time between whether it was better to hide her feelings from God or to reveal more. No lightning bolt had struck, so the latter won out. "Here comes another honest prayer. I am asking you for help tomorrow. Actually, I'm begging. Please give Kevin the right words to say. And please protect my mom." She inhaled a deep breath, then exhaled. "If you can just do that for me, then I will start going back to church. Regularly. Amen."

Still no sign of lightning. Could she do that? Strike a bargain with God? For several seconds she concentrated on listening for an answer. She didn't get one, not the way she wanted nor the one she wanted, but she did feel something warm break free in her chest. She felt calmer, even a little sleepy. At the very least, she decided with a yawn, it was the first honest prayer she'd prayed in a long, long time.

Soon, she drifted off.

* * *

Tuesday, May 27

Marnie tossed and turned all night. When she saw the morning light creep around the edge of the window shutters, she got up and tiptoed downstairs to start the coffee. Not that she needed caffeine. She was as antsy as a hen in a crate off to market. She'd been spending a lot of time with Mrs. Nickerson-Eldredge, accompanying her to doctor appointments. Acting as a sounding board, mostly, because there were so many decisions to make, so quickly. Surgery was scheduled for the Tuesday after the Memorial Day weekend, and Marnie promised she would be there. She wasn't quite sure how she would manage both the Creamery and the caretaking of Mrs. Nickerson-Eldredge, but then again, she wasn't entirely sure the Creamery would be open by then. It was a strictly off-limits topic with Mrs. Nickerson-Eldredge, which Marnie knew because she had brought it up once and received a stern scolding. The Creamery's future wasn't the reason she was coming alongside Mrs. Nickerson-Eldredge. It wasn't the reason she was keeping everything a secret because that was what Mrs. Nickerson-Eldredge wanted. Marnie was doing it because of what Linc had suggested: to use her own experience with cancer to be a blessing to someone else.

Still, Marnie was nervous about today. If there was one thing she had learned about Mrs. Nickerson-Eldredge in the last two weeks—she was not a woman who adjusted for anyone. Her cantankerousness was both private and public. Even the surgeon seemed a little intimidated by her and moved his schedule around to suit her. Marnie knew better than to expect any leniency from her. Today's outcome was resting solely on Kevin's presentation to the Board of Appeals.

At seven o'clock sharp, Marnie heard a rap on the Creamery's back door and hurried to open it. Kevin! She wasn't sure what to expect, but she was surprised by his countenance. Calm, relaxed. Yet there was an eager light in his eyes, almost like a Thoroughbred preparing for a race. She hadn't seen that gleam in his eyes before. He'd always been laid-back, yet she wondered now if his amiability might have been masking a lack of passion, self-confidence. She smiled. No longer. The man who stood in front of her was a man with purpose.

"Morning. Ready?"

"Ready or not," she said. "How did you sleep?"

"Like a king." He hung his messenger bag on the hook by the door. "Lincoln's cottage is not exactly what I'd call a cottage."

Oh? She'd never seen it. Lincoln had never invited them to his home. They were always here, at the Creamery, working. "Bigger than he described?"

In an odd voice, Kevin whispered, "Beautiful."

"The cottage?" When he didn't answer, Marnie closed the door behind him and looked up. Kevin was staring at something. Marnie turned to see what had captured his attention. Dawn was at the bottom of the stairs in a pale green linen A-line dress with a crisp V-neck. She'd washed her hair, which Marnie knew because all the hot water had been used up this morning, but she didn't know Dawn had spent time blow-drying her tangle of hair until it was glass-straight. Her long red hair hung over one shoulder. She looked, in a word, stunning.

•　•　•

At eight o'clock, after arriving at the Annex building where the Board of Appeals meeting would be held, Kevin, Dawn, and her mom were sent to a small room with cold plastic chairs. Here they would wait for the board members to arrive at half past eight. They had come early for a reason. Kevin had created a PowerPoint presentation and had asked for tech help to set it all up.

Dawn and her mom sat quietly, watching it unfold. Little by little, the board members trickled in, chatting with each other, settling into their places behind the long table up front. Dawn assessed each one, trying to decide if they'd be agreeable or difficult. Two older men in pastel-colored polo shirts appeared pretty easygoing, yakking it up about golf. Good. Those two would rather be golfing than stuck in a cold office room. *They won't care about a little gadget that helps to hold up an old building. They'll keep things moving along,* she thought.

A thin, wiry man with thick eyebrows scowled at Dawn like his mind was made up on just about everything. There were three women whose foreheads were practically touching as they whispered feverishly to each other. One seat in the middle remained open.

At twenty-five minutes after eight, Nanette burst in the door. "Has it started? Am I late?" She spotted Mom and sat down next to her, patting her shoulder. "I came to represent the support of neighboring businesses, hon. We're all cheering you on." She leaned over Mom to whisper to Dawn. "Those of us on the other side of the street couldn't stand looking at the Creamery until you spruced it up so nice." She waved to the women seated at the board's table. "I have that recipe you wanted, Lorraine!" She dug around in her enormous purse for a little index card, pulled it out, and held it up like a trophy.

Lorraine smiled and gave a little five-finger princess wave in return.

Nanette's unexpected appearance worried Dawn. She had a tendency to be overly helpful . . . proven in the next moment. Out of Nanette's big purse emerged a cellophane bag of cookies. She lifted it in the air. "I brought my famous Spritz cookies, if anyone is getting hungry." She offered some to Dawn and Mom, who declined, and then set the bag on the panel's table. The polo shirt guys helped themselves.

"I brought them to keep everyone's blood sugar up," Nanette

said. "Whenever my Michael gets a little peckish, I just whip out these cookies and then he's as sweet as a lamb."

Dawn rolled her eyes. Mom gave her a slight jab with her elbow. "She's showing support." True. She half expected Leo the Cowboy to show up next, but hoped he was in kindergarten where he belonged.

At twenty-nine minutes after eight, in walked Mrs. Nickerson-Eldredge. She avoided any eye contact with Marnie and Dawn, heading directly to the open seat behind the table.

Dawn had to swallow a smile at the old woman's formality—you'd think she was the Chief Justice of the Supreme Court—and wished Lincoln were here to witness it. Mom said he had some commitment to keep with his volunteer work and would try to get done early and join them. But really, Mom reminded her, today was all up to Kevin.

As the meeting opened, Kevin was asked to introduce himself as the representative. He rose to his feet, introduced himself, Marnie as the property owner, and pointed to Dawn as her daughter. At the sound of their names being spoken aloud, Dawn shivered. It made everything so real. There was so much at stake today. On the walk to the Annex building this morning, she'd asked Kevin what chances the Creamery had of opening on Friday if today's outcome didn't go well.

"Not good," he said. "First, you'll have to submit an approval to the Historical Commission, then you'll have to line up a contractor. Hopefully, they won't require that you'll have to hire an architect. I don't think so. Still, realistically, I think you'll be lucky if you can open by the Fourth of July. Maybe later, if you have trouble finding a contractor with free time."

She grew quiet on the rest of the walk, and he noticed. At one point, he put his hand on her shoulder. "Hey, lighten up. There's a fifty-fifty chance that we'll win today."

Fifty-fifty had never seemed like great odds to her.

On the overhead, Kevin started the PowerPoint presentation with a slide that showed the Creamery's property on a site map of Chatham. "Obviously, this property falls in the main business district and thus is subject to the Historic Chatham Business District Commission. Our appeal is to prove that everything the owner did to the property was in compliance with the Historic District's requirements, that it actually fell under the category of hardship, and that she did not need to seek approval."

Last evening, Kevin rehearsed the planned questions with Mom. Afterward, so politely, he encouraged her to say less, to only provide answers to his questions. To stay tightly on topic. So, so hard for Mom.

Standing between the table of board members and the audience of three—Dawn and Mom and Nanette—Kevin asked Mom questions, like a lawyer with a defendant, which, in a way, they were. Dawn saw Mom's hands quiver slightly, clenched tightly together in her lap, a sure sign of her nervousness. Dawn felt nervous too. One of the things that worried her was that Kevin felt it would be best to present the full picture of repairs on the Creamery to the Board of Appeals, and not just stay focused on the metal support. "They need to see how you have conscientiously preserved the building in all areas." Revealing the original fireplace, he thought, would sway them. Dawn hoped he was right.

"When we first took possession of the property," Mom said, "there was a puddle of water on the kitchen floor. A hole in the roof made by a recent fire had to be dealt with immediately. We just had to dive in—there was no option."

Perched on the edge of her chair like a bird ready to take wing, Nanette chimed in, without being asked. "She's absolutely right. It was a dis-as-tah. Bonnie left in such a hurry, you know, because of her torrid love affair with her Alaskan boyfriend. She just wanted to cut and go—"

Kevin cleared his throat, Dawn gave Nanette the look, and she took the hint. She settled back in her chair as Kevin presented before and after pictures of the interior of the Creamery. "As you can see, these aren't renovations. They're repairs. Owner Marnie Dixon had to address the things that made the house unsafe to live in. But her purpose was also to preserve what was originally there." He advanced another few slides to reveal the fireplace.

Every single member of the board stared at it, charmed. They asked question after question, about the mantel, the safety of the fireplace, whether it would be able to be used (and it could—Linc had called in a favor from a chimney sweep), whether all the bricks were original.

Good call, Kevin. Dawn was impressed.

The small man with thick eyebrows broke the spell. He squinted at Kevin. "Those are all interior shots. What about the exterior? Isn't that why you're here today? About a foundation pier? That's what we're concerned about."

"Oh, for Pete's sake," Nanette said too loudly. "That's John Broom. I play mah-jongg with his wife Nancy. John is the pharmacist in town and he can be a little persnickety—"

Kevin cleared his throat. Dawn gave Nanette the look. She quieted.

"I'm getting to the exterior." Kevin lifted one finger in the air. "Just to be clear—it is not a foundation pier. It has nothing to do with the foundation skirt. It's merely an interior pier." He dropped his hand to his side. "First, though, I'd like you to see the improvements that the homeowner has done. No alterations. No new constructions. No additions. Simply basic upkeep and maintenance." Kevin clicked to another slide, showing the front of the building. Before, then after.

John Broom frowned. "Looks like the exterior trim has been recently painted."

"Sanded and repainted in the shade of white that the Historical

Commission had approved for all neighboring business owners." Kevin advanced through a few more slides, showing all
surrounding businesses. The Creamery matched them like a
glove. "As you can see," Kevin continued, "there was reasonable
repair and maintenance on the shingle siding as well as to the
hole in the roof." Next slide. "Putty was applied to the windows,
but there was no demolition involved."

Lorraine raised her hand. "How were the nails applied to
the roof and siding shingles?"

Kevin cleared his throat. "The owners had started with a nail
gun, but once they learned about the importance of hammering nails by hand, they returned the nail gun to the hardware
store and commenced with only handheld hammers."

Mom held up her hands. "See? Calluses."

Dawn lifted her palms. "Hard-earned ones."

The women board members asked quite a few questions,
intelligent ones, and Kevin was able to answer each one. He
seemed to not only have the correct lingo down, but he had
a clever way of connecting his answers to the heart of the
matter—preserving the historicity of the building.

The two men in pastel polo shirts, the golfers, the very ones
whom Dawn thought would be the easiest, proved opposite.
"The question that plagues me," one polo shirt said, "is whether
or not that metal support would fall under exterior or interior
jurisdiction. If considered interior, then we have no jurisdiction over it. If exterior, it means you'll have to remove the metal
support and replace it with a wooden support."

"Clearly, it is exterior," the other polo shirt said. "It's visible
to the public. I drove past the building this very morning and
noticed it. The glare from the sun practically blinded me."

Oh, for Pete's sake. Such an exaggeration! But polo shirt
wasn't entirely wrong. Dawn had hoped the metal support
wouldn't be quite so noticeable. It was an elevated foundation,
so the piers could be visible if someone were really looking for

them. Kevin had deliberately taken pictures of the foundation skirt late in the afternoon, while shaded.

"A building in that part of Chatham should look as if it's always belonged here," he continued. "And that metal support is a glaring indication that the building has been altered."

Silence fell. Mrs. Nickerson-Eldredge craned around at the board members. "Are there any other questions?"

So soon? Shoot. This was not ending on a good note. Dawn looked at Kevin to see if he felt the same way, but she couldn't read his expression. Mom seemed surprisingly calm. Dawn tucked a stray lock of hair behind one ear, wondering why she was the only one worried.

When no one responded, Mrs. Nickerson-Eldredge puffed out her chest and locked her wrists beneath it, and said in her usual magisterial tone, "Then, the time has come for a vote."

One by one, the board members cast their vote. Three denied the appeal, three approved it.

It was all coming down to Mrs. Nickerson-Eldredge. Dawn felt her stomach clench. No way. No way. They were going to lose everything. She glanced at Mom, wondering if she shared the same gut-wrenching fear of impending disaster. Her hands were clasped tightly in her lap. Praying or wringing them, Dawn didn't know.

"I suppose," Mrs. Nickerson-Eldredge said, her lips tightening in a straight line, her gaze sweeping the room before settling on Marnie, "I suppose that bushes could be planted in front of the foundation skirt. And then the public wouldn't be forced to encounter the metal support."

Mom clapped her hands. "Hydrangeas!"

A smile tugged at the corners of Mrs. Nickerson-Eldredge's mouth. "That's exactly what I would recommend. There's a specific varietal that is fast growing and easy to maintain." She picked up her gavel. "I believe we have resolved this situation. The improvements to the property known as the Main Street

Creamery were maintenance related and therefore not within the jurisdiction of the Historical Commission. This Board of Appeals meeting is adjourned. And"—she looked left to right at each board member, one by one—"we on the Board welcome you to Chatham and wish you well in your endeavor." With that, the gavel hit the tabletop with a thud.

Dawn looked at Mom, stunned. It was going to be okay. Everything was going to be okay. The Main Street Creamery would be able to open as planned. "How in the world did that just happen?"

"Kevin," Mom said. "All Kevin." She let out a happy sigh. "He's finally found his calling."

Chapter
TWENTY-SIX

My advice to you is not to inquire why or whither, but just enjoy your ice cream while it's on your plate.
—Thornton Wilder, playwright

Tuesday, May 27

Dawn felt different. Lighter. She was back at the Creamery, burden of her worries washing off her skin as easily as the warm water running over her hands in the kitchen sink. The Historical Commission had handed Mom some paperwork to close out the appeal process, and Kevin's eyes had widened in alarm—knowing full well Marnie Dixon would find some excuse to delay it—so he volunteered to sit down with her right then and there and finish it up.

Dawn decided to return to the Creamery to make up another custard base for Thursday's soft opening. In the middle of the Board of Appeals meeting, she suddenly had an inspiration for a new flavor: Sweet & Salty Chocolate with Potato Sticks. Crazy, but in an odd way, it represented the Creamery building to her. Sweet and salty—her favorite combination. And the potato sticks were, well, the pier foundation.

While the ice cream base was cooling, she thought she might do something to celebrate. Something extraordinary. After all, Mom's impulsive purchase of a tired old ice cream shop was going to turn out all right.

Mom had made a good decision, even though she needed a lot of help to make it happen. And Kevin Collins, of all people, had been the game changer, providing invaluable expertise. Dawn felt elated, astounded, grateful.

She checked the temperature of the base and decided she had time for a run on the beach. She pulled the apron over her head, draped it on a chair, and hurried up the stairs to change out of her professional clothing and into her favorite Chatham clothing. A baggy Cape Cod T-shirt given to her by Nanette and black yoga pants. She gathered her hair and tied it with an elastic, then slathered her face and arms and legs with sunscreen.

Five minutes later, as Dawn walked through town, she waved cheerfully to the shop owners out on the street—washing windows or planting flowers in the boxes. She noticed things she'd missed—blooming lilac bushes and snapping flags. There was something special in the air and she was pretty sure it wasn't just her imagination. And it wasn't just her good mood. There was a simmering excitement about the upcoming summer season, shared by all.

She wondered if this happened each year in Chatham and if she would notice it sooner next year and then she stopped abruptly, surprised by her own thoughts. She found she wasn't quite so eager to return to the intensity of the city. She liked it here. The pace of life, the nosy neighbors, the proximity to the ocean. In just a few months she would be back in Boston, back at the accounting firm, and the thought depressed her.

* * *

Marnie intended to sit with Kevin in the Annex building and finish things up. That was her intention . . . until she came to the box that asked for today's date and had to look it up on her phone. As soon as she realized it was May 27, she made a lame excuse and abruptly left Kevin with the paperwork, promising to return soon.

Outside, standing in the middle of the sidewalk with people passing by her, Marnie remained frozen. Tightness enveloped her chest, making it difficult to breathe.

She had lost track of the days. She had completely forgotten the anniversary of Philip's death. There was no excuse for that.

"Marnie?"

The voice came from behind her. She didn't have to turn around to know Linc was calling her name.

"Are you all right? Did the Appeals Board turn you down?"

She turned to face him, trying to fake a smile. "They . . . approved us."

He came closer, studying her face, looking at her with a combination of warmth and serious intensity. "Then why do you look like someone died?"

With that, she covered her mouth with one hand in a useless effort to hold back the sobs.

He put an arm around her to shield her from curious stares of onlookers and led her to his car. He opened the passenger side and helped her in, then went around to the driver's side. He handed her a box of tissues and started the car, setting the air conditioner on low. She turned away, embarrassed, and then felt Lincoln wrap his arms around her. He didn't say anything—not any word at all, even a well-meaning one—and she was so grateful. Somehow, he understood things that didn't come with words.

Her shoulders shook as she gave in to renewed grief, to her shame at forgetting Philip on this day. Soon, she was hiccupping and struggling to breathe, soaking tissue after tissue. It took several minutes to regain control of herself. Lincoln just let her cry until it all stopped, and she rested for a moment against his shoulder.

Finally, she pulled away, recovering her composure enough to explain what had caused this emotional breakdown. "Today was—" she started, stopped, then started again. "I just realized that a year ago today, Philip died. Today is the first anniversary. I'd . . . completely forgotten."

He handed her another tissue to wipe her cheeks. "I've always thought," he said in a quiet voice, "that it was better to remember someone's birthday than the day they died. The beginning, rather than the end."

"I suppose you're right. But you'd think I would remember a day like that one."

He shifted in his seat to face her. "What was it like?"

She lifted her shoulders in a slight shrug. "It started as just an ordinary day. Philip went off to a job like any other day. But something went wrong." She struggled to keep her voice even. "He had climbed a telephone pole to repair a wire to a house, and somehow he touched a live wire."

A moment of stunned silence followed. "That's how he died?"

"Instantly," she said. "Philip was always so careful. It was just . . . an accident."

"I'm so sorry, Marnie." His voice was deep with caring.

"It was a terrible day." Fresh tears ran down her cheeks. "I think the worst part of the day was telling Dawn that her dad had died. All I could think was that it should have been me. I should have been the one that died. Dawn and Philip were so close. She and I, we've never had that kind of relationship. They were so alike, compatible. Philip and Dawn, they always remained on a totally defined path. Never veering from their plans. But me, I've always sort of wandered off the path to see what I might be missing." She wiped her cheeks. "I didn't think I'd ever, ever forget May twenty-seventh."

"Did Dawn remember?"

Marnie shook her head. "I don't think so. We've been so focused on all the things that are in place this week—the Board of Appeals meeting, tomorrow's health and safety inspection, the soft opening on Thursday, then the grand opening on Friday . . . there just hasn't been time to think of anything else."

"So how would Philip want you to think about May twenty-seventh?"

She took another tissue from the box and wiped her tears, then let out a sigh. "He'd probably be glad I forgot." He would say that she shouldn't be thinking of sad moments when they'd had so many happy ones. A slight smile tugged at the corners of her mouth. "And I'm very confident that Philip wouldn't like to be remembered for a mistake."

Again, Lincoln had nothing to say. But Marnie did. She handed him back the box of tissues, nearly empty. She searched for a way to express the fullness in her heart. But there was no way. No way to express what the last fifteen minutes had meant to her. "You have an amazing knack for showing up at just the right time. How can I ever thank you for being such a good friend to me?"

Lincoln's eyes gentled with fondness. "You," he said, "just keep being you."

* * *

Dawn had rarely been to the beach midday, and it surprised her to see so many people here, on a Tuesday, though it was a beautiful day, a hint of summer's coming. Even the water was glass-smooth, reflecting light that seemed to shimmer. She glanced up and down the beach. On a day like this, did most people just stop what they were doing and head to the beach? Is this the kind of thing she'd been missing because she was so focused on her work?

She passed families on large blankets who were picnicking, women reading paperback novels under umbrellas, and a middle-aged guy who'd fallen asleep, his forehead roasted bright red by the sun.

Two little girls screamed like banshees, running down the beach to build up steam, then doing cartwheels in the sand, just for the sheer joy of being alive. Dawn had to stop short to avoid running into them and took a moment to watch them. If Mom were here, she would join them, Dawn felt sure.

Dawn Dixon was twenty-seven years old, and yet she couldn't remember if she'd ever done a cartwheel on the beach. She was so buttoned up. So tightly wound. So rule conscious. She shook her head, disgusted with her inability to let go and express such lighthearted frivolity. Something Kevin had told her about his violin circled through her mind. *I'd forgotten how taut a violin's strings can get. I have to keep loosening them so they don't snap.*

She grinned. She would do it. Feeling wildly adventurous, and after just a little more hesitation—she was her father's daughter, after all—she ran behind the two little girls, planting first her left palm and then her right palm in the sand. She flung her legs up, up and over her head, and it wasn't until that moment, with her world turned upside down, that she remembered she'd never been any good at cartwheels.

But it was too late. Her arms collapsed in on themselves, her legs overshot, and she fell flat on her back, so hard the wind was knocked out of her. As she lay sprawled out on the sand, feeling more than a little silly, she heard the little girls ask each other if she was dead. She opened one eye to see them peering down at her. "I'm . . . just fine," she mumbled, and they ran off. She closed her eyes again to recover—both to catch her breath and to get over her embarrassment.

"Are you really okay?"

Her eyes popped open. Kevin! He stood over her, a concerned look on his face. His feet were bare, his tie was gone, his button-down shirt was open at the collar. Despite her humiliation at the cartwheel gone awry, she felt the same flutter in her stomach that had always accompanied the unexpected sight of him. She pushed herself up onto her elbows.

He flashed her a grin. "Were you doing what I think you were doing? Or trying to?"

"Yes. A cartwheel." She wiped sand off her mouth with the back of her hand. "It didn't work out the way I planned."

As she sat up, Kevin plopped down on the sand beside her. "So like life."

And wasn't that the truth? "Except for the Board of Appeals meeting. Kevin, you gave a . . . stellar performance."

A slow grin started. "It went pretty well, didn't it?"

She gave him a gentle jab with her elbow. "It was like being in a movie! You just seemed to understand the way the board thought, like you had answers prepared for every question they might have had. And the way you handled Mrs. Nickerson-Eldredge . . . masterful!"

"She's not so bad. She kind of reminds me of my grandmother."

"Well, I'm truly in awe."

He looked pleased. "Thank you."

"Did you already finish up the paperwork with Mom?"

"No. Something came up and she left suddenly. I followed her out, then I saw she and Lincoln were in a car, talking, and, well, it seemed like a good time to take a break. And then I saw you running like a gazelle toward the beach."

She coughed a laugh. Hardly a gazelle! But it was a nice thing to say.

He crossed one ankle over the other. "Do you think there's something going on between Lincoln and your mom?"

"What? No! Of course not." A ridiculous thought. Wasn't

it? No. Mom would never be interested in another man. Dad was the love of her life.

As if he knew what she was thinking, he said, "She's young, Dawn. Both in age and in the way she thinks about life. It would be nice if she found a companion. I think your dad would've wanted her to move on with her life."

She stared at him. "I'm not, um, ready for this conversation."

"Well, there's another conversation that needs to happen."

Oh no. Those happy feelings she'd had as she headed to the beach had evaporated. She looked down at the tops of her sneakers. She had known this moment was coming. Kevin was leaving. He'd come to say goodbye, and this time it would be for good. The midday sun was burning a hole in the top of her head. She should've worn a cap. "So you're leaving?" she said. Even mentioning it caused her pain.

He didn't answer her question. "I've decided to go back to school to get a master's degree."

She straightened her back. "You are? In what?"

"In historic preservation. Part-time for now. But I'm quitting the Boston firm. I've already given notice." He gave her a sideways glance. "I've got it all worked out. I found a grad school where I can take classes online. I'm going to move to a place where there's a lot of history still to preserve. I'll support myself with drafting jobs while I'm in grad school. Hopefully I can connect with an architect who does historical architecture, so I can get experience. Eventually, I'd like to hang up my own shingle. Be my own boss."

He was moving? She looked at him in confusion. "Where are you going?"

His gaze remained on the ocean. "Here. To Cape Cod. To Chatham."

Here? Kevin wanted to move *here*?

He hesitated a moment as if to gather his thoughts before shifting on the sand to meet her eyes. "If you don't want me to move here, I'll respect that. I'm sorry I hurt you the way I did, I really am. Looking back, it wasn't just our relationship that was making me panic. I wasn't happy doing the work I was doing and I felt as if I couldn't make a change. I felt . . . trapped. And the only option seemed to be to cancel our wedding." He scraped his chin with one hand. "And since then . . . I've been watching you do something so daring and brave . . ."

"Making ice cream? That's daring and brave?"

"Yes, that. More than ice cream. You stepped away from the tight, fixed corporate path you were on to come live in a beach town and make ice cream with your mom. You lost your chance at becoming partner."

Had she lost it? Probably. The funny thing, she didn't really care anymore. She bent her knees and wrapped her arms around them.

"As I watched you, I realized that I wanted to get to know you, to really know you. Not the girl I thought I knew, but the woman you're becoming."

She felt as if she were hearing him in a time delay, like everything he was saying was so completely unexpected that it took a few extra seconds to grasp. "You're talking about us . . . starting over?" she said, then waited for him to back away. To jump to his feet and run off.

"Yes," he said simply. "I don't want us to be over. I still care about you. I love you, Dawn."

For a second, she was genuinely confused. "I, uh—" She thought about how shattered she had felt when he broke their engagement. Hurt, humiliated, devastated at the loss. But as brutally painful as it was, it was the right decision. They weren't heading down a healthy path. Within a few years, they'd probably end up divorced, hating each other, blaming each other.

She had needed a wake-up call. About work, about life, about faith.

When she didn't respond, he said, "Dawn, I need to know if

moving here, being here, if you're okay with it." He turned all the way around to face her. His expression was stark, honest, intense. "I need to know if you're willing to try." His words were low, ragged, and filled with intent.

Her gaze traveled over his familiar features with a sense of disbelief, of wonder. Kevin still loved her. She could see it in his eyes. He *loved* her! "You're really moving to Cape Cod?" Then, "For me?"

He leaned forward and reached out a hand to gently stroke her cheek. "For you. For me. For both of us."

She nodded, trying not to act too excited. "When?"

"Is Friday too soon? I thought, maybe I could help out with the grand opening. And I thought"—he glanced at her—"I hoped . . . you might make more of that Blackberry Chocolate Chunk ice cream."

"Friday," she said shyly, "would be good. The Chatham Village Market manager said he would save blackberries for me."

Tears filled her eyes, but they were the happy kind. The best kind. Everything about this felt good and right. She didn't think she could hide her happiness if she tried. She flung her arms around him and hung on as if she would never let go, because that was her plan.

Chapter

TWENTY-SEVEN

I guess ice cream is one of those things that are beyond imagination.

—L. M. Montgomery, author of *Anne of Green Gables*

Friday, May 30

A smooth event was all about prep work. At a time when so much seemed like a dream, the joy of yesterday's soft opening had been wonderfully real. Marnie and Dawn had opened the Main Street Creamery for only four hours because they didn't want to run out of ice cream for today's grand opening, and they ended up having to turn people away. Marnie promised them a free scoop tomorrow if they'd come back . . . and two if they'd bring friends.

Dawn had panicked when she heard about the promise of free scoops. The ice cream machine hummed until after midnight, long after Marnie went to bed.

Valuable things had been learned, which was the whole point of a soft opening. Things like, the tables needed to be farther away from the door because of the winding line of customers. And which ice cream flavors were the most popular. And most people preferred a cone over a paper cup. As they talked over their findings at dinner last night, Dawn decided she should try to make cones from scratch. Not now, Marnie finally persuaded her. Maybe down the road. For now, she was happy with the cone supplier she'd found.

All in all, it had been a great day. Today, Marnie had a hunch, would be even better.

Dawn hurried into the front room to where Marnie sat at a table. "I made an extra batch of vanilla this morning. You know, just in case." She gave her a smug smile. A well-deserved smugness. Yesterday, twice as much vanilla ice cream was sold over any other flavor. "While the machine is churning, what else needs to be done? You've got my full attention for seven minutes."

Marnie loved Dawn's energy and drive and attention to detail. It was contagious. "I think we're ready to go."

Dawn scanned the room. "Are you sure? Everything's ready? Have we forgotten anything?"

Marnie pressed her clipboard and tablet against her chest and ticked off her fingers. "Ice cream and supplies replenished from yesterday. Floor swept and mopped. Water dispensers filled with freshly cut cucumber and mint." She dropped her hand. "Look around and see if we've missed anything." She waved to the tables with their custom cut-glass tops gleaming, to the frozen food display freezer, where pints of ice cream were lined up for takeaway sales, to the ice cream cabinet, where Dawn's creations waited for customers: vanilla, chocolate, Chatham Bars, Lighthouse Lemon, and her latest one—Nickerson Nut Crumble. Its vanilla base was swirled with a raspberry compote, with add-ins of dark chocolate–covered hazelnuts and homemade granola. To the chalkboard hanging from the ceiling, with its daily offerings. "I think we're as ready as we'll ever be."

Dawn visibly relaxed. She turned and went back to the kitchen. Marnie heard the back door squeak open and Dawn greet someone. Around the kitchen door came Linc, a big smile on his face. He produced a bouquet of red roses, which he'd been hiding behind his back. "For you, Marnie." He bowed ever so slightly.

They locked eyes as Marnie breathed in the fresh flower scent. His eyes revealed more than words could express. She broke the spell by deliberately pulling her eyes away from him. In all her life, she had never had a man look at her the way he did. Not even Philip. Maybe it had something to do with age, with growing older, with knowing that life was short. Unpredictable.

It appalled her that the idea of a romance with Lincoln had even crossed her mind. But it had crossed her mind, and more than once. For now, it was too soon. But maybe . . . someday. "Thank you, Linc. We couldn't have done this without you."

"She's right," Dawn said, taking the roses out of her hands to put into a vase. "You made such a difference."

"Well, that's the whole point of life, isn't it?" He looked at his watch. "I hope you're ready. Because your customers are lining up. I didn't even try to come in through the front."

"A line? We don't open for another half hour." Marnie hurried to the window. A line had formed, all the way to the sidewalk, with more people coming. Patiently waiting, they were chatting with each other, chuckling over one thing or another. Why, it was just the way she'd imagined it when she'd made that illegal entry to slip into the Creamery, just the way she'd seen it in her mind.

She wished Philip were here. This was originally his dream, finally coming to fruition. But she had to be honest with herself that if he *were* here, the Main Street Creamery would be a very different ice cream shop. Philip had insisted on doing everything himself, almost as if he assumed Marnie couldn't do it. But she was finding out she could!

*   *   *

Dawn peered over Mom's shoulder to see the line that snaked down the path and onto the sidewalk. She saw people of all ages coming up and down the street, moving into formation behind the line. A mom bent over a stroller to put a pacifier into her unhappy toddler's mouth. An elderly couple held hands as they waited. A clump of teenagers took up the full width of the sidewalk. Leo the Cowboy stood in front of the teenagers, watching them in his solemn way. And then, across the street, peering into Nanette's T-shirt shop, she spotted Brynn! Around her were a handful of their Boston friends. She'd told Dawn that they were coming down today, but she hadn't expected them so early.

Dawn had been worried about how to get customers in the door. Suddenly, her worry changed to how she could keep up with the demand.

Even more than the long line, what surprised Dawn was how many people she recognized. Nanette and her husband Michael, the pastor from church, the two polo shirts from the Board of Appeals, the Chatham Village Market store manager whom she'd driven crazy with the pursuit of perfect milk and cream . . . and then she saw Kevin's car pull up and park, and she couldn't hold back a squeal of happiness if she had tried. He hopped out of his car and went around to the passenger side to help someone out. Mrs. Nickerson-Eldredge, of all people. She tucked her hand around his elbow, and they crossed the road to come toward the Main Street Creamery. She waved her cane and people immediately parted, like Moses and the Red Sea, allowing her to cut to the front of the line.

Mom saw it too. "Those two are getting thick as thieves." A girlish giggle burst out of her. "Life is just full of surprises."

Dawn glanced at her mom. These last few months, she'd seen things in her mother she had never seen before. For most of her life, she'd focused so much on the wrong things that she'd missed all the right things. Such as how her mom didn't write people like Mrs. Nickerson-Eldredge off the way Dawn did. How she found a way to make others feel special, important. How she trusted that God would take care of her future, even when the situation seemed bleak. And how brave she was. All in. Marnie Dixon was "all in" to everything.

Mrs. Nickerson-Eldredge marched right up to the door and rapped on it with her cane. Kevin saw them through the window and lifted a hand in a wave, laughing. "It appears," Mom said, "that our newest chapter in life is about to begin."

Watching her as she unlocked the door, Dawn wondered if it was too late to turn out like her mother. She hoped not.

Questions for Discussion

1. The relationship between mothers and daughters can be complicated. What is (or was) your relationship like with your mother? With your daughter?

2. Did you find yourself resonating with Marnie? Or with Dawn? Alternating points of views between mother and daughter allowed readers to see how a character felt and thought, why they did what they did. Depending on which character you felt more drawn to, did your perspective change as the points of view changed?

3. There was something about the Main Street Creamery building, something that called to Marnie. Like it was just longing for another chance, a fresh start. Like it wasn't done with living yet . . . there was more it had to offer this world. So much more. Was Marnie talking about the building or about herself?

4. How did you feel about Marnie's impulsive purchase of the Main Street Creamery? Did it make you cringe? Or did you cheer her on?

5. Knowing Marnie was a recent widow, and that she'd had a bout of breast cancer, did you agree with Dawn's assessment—that her mom was stuck in denial? How did your thoughts change about Marnie's purchase of the Main Street Creamery as you finished the book?

6. In the first half of the book, Dawn was fixated on the making of perfect vanilla ice cream. She wasn't wrong. Getting that one flavor right is a critical step to any ice cream maker, because the taste of vanilla is so pure, anything that's wrong with it will be obvious. Stronger flavors, like chocolate or coffee, can mask impurities or delicate tones. Not vanilla. In Dawn's case, vanilla ice cream became a metaphor. How would you describe its importance to her?

7. As Dawn finally tried some new flavor combinations, what do you think was happening to her emotional/spiritual journey?

8. Marnie told Dawn that God wanted honest, unfiltered prayers. So that's exactly what Dawn did—she told God she was angry, so angry. He had doled out too many traumas at once. He was too hard on her, she pointed out. What did that prayer reveal about Dawn's dormant faith?

9. How did Dawn's shallow faith grow or change? Compare her faith journey with Marnie's, Lincoln's, and Kevin's.

10. In what way was Dawn's prayer a start in the right direction, and in what way was her bottled-up anger a result of flawed theology?

11. Walking the beach became the scene for most of the deeper, more intimate conversations held between characters. It's where Dawn let herself break down over her broken engagement. It's where Marnie told Lincoln the real reason she couldn't handle the cancer support group. It's where Dawn and Kevin revealed their feelings to each other. What is it about a vast ocean that can spur on intimacy?

12. Lincoln Hayes is a secondary character in this story. He becomes a great friend to Marnie, helping her with the Creamery, encouraging her to face the very thing she doesn't want to face. Yet there's a bit of mystery to him. A slice of his backstory is revealed, but not too much. All readers know is that his cancer diagnosis became a wake-up call, and that he's trying to make up for lost time, lost years. When have you, or someone you love, experienced some kind of a wake-up call? What kind of change did it bring about?

13. Readers are first introduced to Dawn and Kevin's long relationship at its bitter end. How and when did your opinion of Kevin change? Looking back, why was the broken engagement the best thing for them—both of them? How did that painful experience end up saving their relationship?

14. The plot in this book revolves around preserving the past while moving forward in life. The rehabilitation of the Main Street Creamery building is one example. Dawn and Kevin's relationship is another. It might've been easier to knock down the old building and start fresh. It might've been less complicated for Dawn and Kevin to part ways, to start over with someone new.

But what made it worth the trouble? For the Creamery? And for Dawn and Kevin?

15. Is there something you've always wanted to do, like Marnie's purchase of an ice cream shop, but felt as if you couldn't or shouldn't? Why or why not?

16. There's a Bible verse that kept circling as I wrote this novel. It seemed the kind of message that each main character in this story needed to hear, and deeply absorb, and act on. Maybe I was the one who needed it! But I have a hunch that most of us have a tendency to keep looking in the rearview mirror and miss what the Lord is doing right in front of us. Here it is (worth memorizing):

> Forget about what's happened;
>> don't keep going over old history.
> Be alert, be present. I'm about to do something brand-new.
>> It's bursting out! Don't you see it? (Isa. 43:18–19 MSG)

Author's Note

Not long ago, while playing tennis, I was startled to realize that three out of four players on my court were survivors of breast cancer. The statistics are staggering—it's the most common cancer diagnosed in women, excluding skin cancers. One out of eight women will be diagnosed with invasive breast cancer over the course of her life. That means the average woman's breast cancer risk is 12 to 13 percent. And as women get older, the risk increases. Pretty scary odds.

Hold on. There's a bright side. Such a common cancer has the attention of the medical world. Strides are being made in treatment, with breakthroughs occurring frequently. A diagnosis does not mean the cure will be worse than the disease. Nor does a diagnosis mean a death sentence. In 2014, the American Cancer Society reported that deaths from breast cancer have declined 38 percent since 1990.

Even better than improving treatment's effects on cancer is its prevention. There's work in progress toward a breast cancer vaccine currently in clinical trials at the Sylvester Comprehensive Cancer Clinic at the University of Miami and at the Mayo Clinic in Jacksonville, Florida.

Until then, the best thing women can do for themselves is to keep up with annual screening appointments and regular self-exams. Hopefully, prayerfully, breast cancer will never be part of your life story. But if it might, to quote my friend Charlotte, whose own mother had died of breast cancer at a much-too-young age: "Catch it quick. Catch it early." Early detection is a game changer.

And then, be like Marnie Dixon, and use your experience to be a blessing to others.

●　●　●

To learn more, visit these resources:

American Cancer Society—cancer.org

Breast Cancer Research Foundation—https://www.bcrf.org/breast
-cancer-research-breakthroughs

Forbes magazine—https://www.forbes.com/sites/robinseatonjefferson
/2019/10/11/mayo-breast-cancer-vaccine-could-be-available-in-less
-than-a-decade/?sh=13b9f4c327c7

Miami Herald—https://www.miamiherald.com/news/health-care
/article250974549.html

Can't Get Enough of This
SWEET STORY?

Turn the Page for a SNEAK PEEK
of Book 2 in the
CAPE COD CREAMERY Series!

Coming Soon

Chapter ONE

Ice cream brings people together.

—Doug Ducey

Penn State Ice Cream School, State College, Pennsylvania
Friday, January 28

Ah, the irony. Two months ago, Callie Dixon had been the executive chef at one of the largest convention hotels in Boston, a hotel so highly esteemed that the Food Safety Conference chose to hold their annual meeting there. Today, she was serving up bowls of ice cream to amateurs who had hopes of becoming the next Ben & Jerry's. She wore a shapeless smock and a hairnet that made her look like a cafeteria lady, and her salary had dropped from six figures to minimum wage.

Even worse, she was lucky to have the job. A temporary job that would be over after Penn State's Ice Cream School ended. From that point on, she had no idea what she would do. Her sterling reputation in the culinary world was ruined.

And it wasn't her fault! Well, mostly it was. But not entirely. During the conference, the hotel's event planner had kept circling through the kitchen, clapping her hands and telling the staff to step it up because attendees complained of waiting too long for their meals. Flustered, Callie had neglected to put a sauce for the next day's chicken entrée in the refrigerator. It stayed on the counter overnight, warming to room temperature, bacteria dividing and multiplying. Sauces could be tricky like that.

The next day, a meal contaminated with C. perfringens had been served . . . resulting in food poisoning. And the rest of the conference was ruined for over two hundred attendees.

While her boss informed her that he was sorry to have to let her go (Oh, just say it. *Fired!*), he was sure she realized someone had to take responsibility for this. It was no small mistake. It was catastrophic. Then he added, "Callie, you do seem extremely distracted lately."

No, she wasn't extremely distracted lately. But yes, she did understand that someone's head had to roll, and she was that someone. What irked her was how pleased the event planner looked as Callie had bid goodbye to the staff. This woman—who'd been at the hotel for ages and ages—had never been a fan of Callie's. They'd had numerous run-ins from vastly different opinions about menu options. Quite simply, she did not like Callie. (That in itself was absurd! Who didn't like Callie! During high school she was president of the student body, homecoming queen, and—her favorite—voted most likely to become a benevolent dictator. Now and then she volunteered at an animal shelter. Once a month she fed the homeless. Everyone liked Callie! Except for the event planner.) The unfortunate sauce incident became the golden opportunity to have her fired.

And just like that, Callie's meteoric rise in the culinary world was DOA. Who would ever hire a chef responsible for poisoning the entire Food Safety Conference?

That's how she ended up at Penn State's Ice Cream School.

When Jesse, her friend who helped run the school, heard what had happened at the Food Safety Conference, he insisted she come to Penn State during January. "No one's hiring in the winter months, anyway," he'd said.

True, but timing wasn't going to be the problem in finding a new job. It was her name—it was mud. She was no better than the dirt beneath people's feet.

So she packed up her bags and she drove to State College. Penn State's Ice Cream Short Course had been held every January since 1892. Past participants read like a Who's Who in the world of ice cream: Baskin-Robbins, Ben & Jerry's, Dreyer's, Dairy Queen, on and on. There was also a three-day Ice Cream 101 workshop held later in the month for serious ice cream lovers and small business owners.

Today was day one for the workshop. The class had been listening to the principle instructor give an overview of ice cream making and was about to taste samples made with different grades of milk.

Callie carried a tray full of ice cream cups to the table in the back and set a cup in front of a woman.

"Callie? Is that you?"

Callie looked up to see who had recognized her. The woman, middle-aged-ish, pretty features, blue eyes, her strawberry-blond hair held back in a ponytail.

"Aunt Marnie?"

Marnie Dixon had been married to her dad's eldest brother, Philip, and Callie hadn't seen her in years. She'd been unable to attend Uncle Philip's memorial service. There simply wasn't time.

Marnie was peering at her with a puzzled look. "Are you okay?"

"I'm fine!" But Callie was hardly anything close to being fine. *Change the subject*, she thought. *Quick.* "What in the world are you doing here?"

Marnie lifted the ice cream cup. "This."

The man sitting next to Marnie cleared his throat to remind Callie of the others waiting for ice cream. She handed a cup to the man and worked her way down the line, but her attention stayed on her aunt.

"But . . . why?" she asked as she circled back toward her aunt.

"Didn't you hear our news? No? Dawn and I moved to Cape Cod and bought an ice cream shop."

"GET OUT!"

Chairs clattered as everyone spun to look at Callie.

She looked around the room at the confused group. "I didn't mean get out, like 'go,'" she explained to everyone. "I meant, like 'you've *got* to be kidding me!'"

"Perhaps," the instructor said, "you could save this conversation for after class."

"Right," Callie said. She emptied her tray of ice cream cups, then bent low as she swept past her aunt. "You and me. During the break. I want to hear all about this."

Marnie grinned and gave her a thumbs-up.

Wow. Aunt Marnie had left Needham and bought an ice cream shop on the Cape. Gutsy! Bold! Brave! Callie tried to remember the last updates she'd heard about her cousin Dawn. She was rocking it as a CPA and engaged to her high school sweetheart, and . . . hmmm . . . whatever happened to that wedding, anyway?

Callie went back to the kitchen to get more ice cream cups from Jesse. He looked up from scooping when he realized she was standing right in front of him. "What's that big smile for?"

"Because I just saw someone special!"

He grinned. "Aw, shucks. Thanks."

"Funny." She rolled her eyes. "My aunt is attending the workshop. My favorite aunt of all. The world's best aunt."

"Yeah? What makes her the world's best?" He began reloading her tray.

"Aunt Marnie's the type who always remembers to send cards. Cards for birthdays, cards for graduations, cards for Valentine's Day, for Easter. Sometimes cards to just say she was thinking of me. She's just . . . wonderful."

"What's she doing here?"

"She said she and her daughter Dawn are running an ice cream shop on Cape Cod." She turned the tray around so he could add more cups on the other side.

"I didn't know you had a cousin."

"Lots of them. But Dawn and I are closest in age. Close in everything. More like sisters than cousins. We adore each other."

"Yeah? I've never even heard you talk about her."

"You know, life gets"—she shrugged—"busy."

"Well, you've got some spare time now."

She snorted. True. In fact, she had a surfeit of spare time. A frightening abundance of it. Callie had never done well with downtime. She avoided it.

"Maybe it's no accident that you're here now and so is your aunt."

"What do you mean?"

"Why don't you go visit your best-aunt and sister-cousin on Cape Cod?"

"Not happening." She shook her head. "I've got my next best job to find."

He paused. "Callie, have you ever thought that there's a reason you got fired?"

She froze. "Uh, because the sauce that smothered the chicken should've spent the night in the refrigerator instead of on the counter."

He rubbed his chin. "Well, that's one way of looking at it. Maybe this . . . pause . . . could give you a little time for personal reflection."

"Personal *what*?" Her eyebrows shot up.

"Never mind. All I'm saying is that a little breather right now could do you some good." He paused again. "Callie, you gotta do something."

She took all that in. Then she let out a long sigh.

He added the last few cups on her tray. "Everybody needs a little help sometimes."

"Tell me about it." Callie nodded, as if she knew exactly what Jesse meant. She certainly knew what it was like when someone needed help. She just wasn't clear on how to ask for it.

● ● ●

Marnie
Dawn! Guess who's at Penn State's Ice Cream School?

Dawn
Who?

Your cousin Callie! She says she's in between jobs.

Mom—do NOT invite Callie to Cape Cod.

I didn't invite her.

Good.

She invited herself.

Chapter
TWO

An ice cream a day keeps the tension away.

—Unknown

Marnie was shocked. She'd barely recognized her niece Callie, not until she heard her unmistakable sandpapery voice. She hadn't seen her in years, but the girl she remembered had *presence*. Callie would burst into a room and spray exuberance over everyone like a can of whipped cream. A tad overwhelming, even Marnie had to admit, but she was happy, upbeat, confident. Over-the-top positive.

It was only in that one split second, when Callie yelled "Get out!" that Marnie had seen the old Callie. This young woman in a hairnet and big floppy smock and a defeated countenance was a stranger.

No, not entirely a stranger. Marnie had seen this side of Callie once before.

It was the summer Callie's dad had remarried. Marnie had had a hunch that her brother-in-law might've been ready to move on sooner than his daughter was ready for such a change, so she invited Callie to come stay with them in Needham. Callie and Dawn were about the same age, and both were only children. Marnie thought it would be an ideal opportunity for the two cousins to get to know each other.

Such a bad idea.

Callie made everything a contest, and Dawn, daughter of Philip Dixon, couldn't resist competition. The two girls competed over the most ridiculous things, from how quickly they brushed their teeth to playing the piano to side-by-side lemonade stands—and Callie always won. Always.

The summer ended with Dawn discouraged and frustrated. Callie left their home transformed into a happy little girl again. The best summer of her life, she'd said. A magical summer. She asked to come back the next summer, but Dawn threw a fit, and Philip, of course, supported her. He didn't like seeing his daughter come in second, even to his own niece. Summers after that were planned by Philip. Dawn attended every camp for gifted children that he could find. When Richard heard about those camps, he signed Callie up for the very same ones. The relentless competition between brother and brother, cousin and cousin, continued.

Marnie had wondered if part of Philip's obsession for Dawn to be successful had a lot to do with how he felt about his brother, who was always on his heels of achievement. Just like Callie and Dawn, the two brothers, Philip and Richard, had competed over everything. And Philip had always come in second, just like Dawn. And just like Callie, Richard had seemed oblivious to how others felt when they constantly came out as the loser.

What Philip and Dawn could never see was that Richard and Callie made them better, pushed them farther than they might have pushed themselves, inspired them to stretch and reach and grasp. Because of Callie and Richard's can-do attitude, Dawn and Philip were influenced to try things they might never have tried. Learning how to play musical instruments, running for class offices at school, trying out for sports teams.

And then there was ice cream.

As a teenager, Callie had made pints of homemade ice cream to sell to neighbors and friends. She'd made quite a name for herself—the local paper had sent a reporter and photographer to do a piece on her, and she'd become a bit of a phenomenon. Boy oh boy, did Richard make sure Philip knew about that. Philip and Dawn's interest in ice cream making skyrocketed after that news, so much so that they attended Penn State's Ice Cream School. Look where that hobby had taken Dawn—she was making ice cream in her own shop on Cape Cod! And loving it.

The last few years had been so tumultuous that Marnie hadn't kept up with extended family like she usually had. She wasn't exactly sure what had been happening in Callie's life, but something was clearly wrong. She had a bone-deep feeling that Callie needed them, much the way she had during that summer when she was ten years old. In a strange way, Marnie could see past the competent young woman standing in front of her to the hurting little girl inside.

What if this had been Dawn? What if Marnie had ended up like Callie's mom?

But the clincher had come with Callie's last remark during the class break. "Aunt Marnie?"

"Yes?"

"All those cards. Thank you for sending them."

So! So they had made a difference, after all. Marnie had never been sure if it was worth the effort. She'd sent cards off to Callie with regularity—birthdays, graduations, holidays—but she'd never heard anything back. Philip had said she was wasting her time, that it was like mailing something into a galactic black hole. But Marnie hadn't stopped until the last few years, after Philip died and life had turned upside down. She supposed she'd sent those cards because she felt some kind of responsibility to her sister-in-law, to try to provide some kind of "mothering" to Callie the way her mom would have, had things been different.

So when Callie asked if she could come visit them in Cape Cod, Marnie said yes. How could she not? She was glad she was here and Dawn was there.

She felt her phone vibrate in her pocket, thankful she'd remembered to leave it on silent. Not thirty seconds later, it vibrated again, and she pulled it out to see the text that had come in.

Dawn
Mom, pick up! We need to talk about Callie's visit.

Can't talk. In class. Instructor discussing prepackaged bases.

Avoidance strategy! Not fair.

No kidding. Marnie smiled and tucked her phone back in her pocket.

* * *

Chatham, Massachusetts

Dawn had been in the middle of experimenting with a new ice cream flavor this afternoon when her mom texted her about the coming of Callie. Since then, she'd been marinating in resentment.

What was Mom thinking? A visit without an end date. In their tiny house!

Callie's personality would fill up the house like a balloon. All personal space would be gone, pushed to the edges. And the *kitchen.* She shuddered. *Don't even get me started on that.* The kitchen belonged to Dawn. It was her personal terrain. Mom knew that, Kevin knew that, Mom's very good friend Lincoln knew that. Leo the Cowboy knew that. Even Nanette, the nosy T-shirt retailer across the street who respected no boundaries whatsoever—she knew that.

But Callie, being Callie, would be blind to that reality. Dawn had it all pictured in her mind, just like a movie: she'd done it at Dawn's first apartment in Boston. Who could forget that exasperating event?

Mom had been gently nagging Dawn to invite Callie for dinner sometime, so she finally did. Callie had sat on the kitchen stool and watched Dawn cut an onion. It wasn't a minute before she hopped off the stool and took the knife out of Dawn's hand. "I just want to show you a better way," she said. She started chopping the onion with her fancy chefy techniques, then picked up the green pepper and sliced it expertly, then diced the tomatoes. Dawn finally sat on the stool and watched Callie finish the entire meal. Most irritating was that it ended up tasting far, far better than Dawn's version. As Kevin had said, you can't ask a chef to dinner. It just doesn't work.

Her thoughts slid toward Kevin. He had proposed to Dawn on New Year's Day—symbolic, he had said, of their new beginning together. Dawn and Kevin hadn't made many plans for the wedding, not even setting a firm date, but they had sent Mom off to Ice Cream School so she could get up to speed to make ice cream properly while they were away on a long honeymoon. That was the only decision that was firmly in place—the "take two" honeymoon. This time, Kevin and Dawn were going on an African safari. Dawn wasn't going to shortchange Kevin from the kind of honeymoon he really wanted. Not this time. But once Callie got wind of a wedding in need of plans, she'd take it over just like she took over everything.

The steady hum of the ice cream machine reminded Dawn of the task at hand. She grabbed a bowl to check the results of this Kevin-inspired flavor. He was studying for his master's degree in preservation architecture and had been working on some renovation projects in nearby towns. Last summer, when the Main Street Creamery opened, they'd made quite a splash with locally inspired ice cream flavors. Since then, Kevin kept encouraging Dawn to branch out to other towns. "I challenge you to come up with something delicious for Mashpee," he'd said just last evening. Mashpee was a small town on Upper Cape, a place where the first Cape Codders—the Wampanoags—had a reserve.

Dawn could never resist a challenge.

This afternoon, she'd set to work on a flavor that celebrated the town of Mashpee. To the cooled base, she had stirred in mashed green peas, green matcha, curry, and mint, poured the mixture into the machine, closed the gate, turned the switch on, turned the refrigeration button on . . . and waited. She listened to the sloshing sound as the dasher started to whirl and set the timer for seven minutes. When it was done, she opened the gate and let a small amount ooze into her bowl to sample flavor and consistency. Sweet. Creamy. Cold on the tongue. A curiously savory taste. But way too soft. She set the timer for another minute. Then she added white chocolate chips and let it mix one more minute. She set the bowl beneath the barrel again and opened the gate, allowing a dollop to slide out. She heard the front door open and a rush of cold air swept into the shop. She closed the gate and popped her head around the corner to see Kevin. "Hi! You look cold."

He smiled when he saw her. "I look cold because I *am* cold. The wind cuts right through my clothes." He unzipped his coat and hung it over a chair, then slid off his scarf. He looked around the shop. "No customers?"

"Not many this afternoon. Hold on, I have something for

you." She grabbed two spoons and went to meet him with the bowl. "Are you too cold to try a new flavor?"

"It's never too cold for ice cream."

She held out a spoonful for him. "It's still a little soft."

Kevin took the spoon and tasted the sample. "Great flavor, but an odd color."

Dawn looked into the container. "I was mixing in curry to the base when Mom texted with bad news. I think I got distracted and added too much. The turmeric in the curry turns everything bright yellow. I thought the green peas and matcha might tone it down, but it turned everything kind of . . . brown." And not a luscious chocolatey brown. A disgusting shade of brown. But the taste—that was surprisingly good. She'd have to keep fiddling with it.

"What bad news could your mom possibly have from Ice Cream School?"

She dropped her shoulders in an exaggerated sigh. "My cousin Callie is coming for an open-ended visit."

"Callie, as in, the cousin who outdid you in everything?"

Dawn frowned. "She didn't always outdo me." She sighed. "Well, yes. She did."

Kevin took another spoonful of ice cream. "This flavor is strangely addictive."

"I know, right?" Dawn dug in her spoon to try another taste. Creamy, sweet, yet slightly savory.

"Is Callie still working as a chef at that fancy downtown hotel?"

"Not just any old chef. *The* chef." She frowned. "She was only twenty-five when she was promoted to executive chef. Uncle Richard made sure everyone knew what a big deal that was." And it *was* a big deal.

"Callie's always been a real slacker." He grinned at her.

Kevin wasn't taking her seriously. "It's just that . . ."

"You're jealous of her."

"Insanely jealous."

He grinned again and tugged at her hand to pull her close to him. "You know, don't you, that you have no reason to be jealous of Callie."

She resisted his tug. "Don't think I don't remember how you and your goofy friends used to drool around her."

"That was back when we were idiots. We've matured since then. Me, especially."

"Yeah? Let's wait till you see Callie."

"I don't have to." He leaned forward to kiss the tip of her nose. "You're the only one I'm looking at."

She smiled. "Good answer," she said, and kissed him. The bowl nearly slipped from her hand, and she remembered there was ice cream waiting to be scooped out and popped into the freezer.

With her hand on the gate, she froze. *This machine!* Her gleaming 6-quart Emery Thompson ice cream maker! If Callie dared to try out Dawn's precious ice cream maker, her beloved baby, Dawn would send her packing—no matter what guilt trip Mom laid on her.

She heard a text come in on her phone and glanced over at the counter, cringing when she saw it was from Callie.

Hello to my favorite cousin! Did your mom tell you that we bumped into each other? Did she tell you I'm coming for a visit? Don't worry about finding a spare bed for me. I'll bring my air mattress. It'll be just like old times!

That. That was exactly what worried Dawn.

Acknowledgments

Cape Cod holds a special place in my heart. My dad was raised in nearby Bourne on a farm bordered by Great Herring Pond, a short distance from the Cape Cod Canal. One of his brothers had a dental practice in Chatham, the other was up north in Cohasset. My cousin Carleton Woods had once been a tennis pro at the Chatham Bars Inn. A special thanks to my aunt Nancy Woods, who provided a lot of helpful insider information about special details that are unique to Chatham. Like, church bells are heard only on Sundays. Or that the historical part of Main Street is called Chatham center or Chatham downtown. Or that the Squire is the best place in town to get a casual meal. After all, it's one thing to visit someplace, it's another thing entirely to live there, year-round, when the weather changes and the buzz of a tourist destination settles down to a quiet hum.

As for the Historical Commission—most of those details came from studying Chatham's permit requirements plus those of nearby historical villages. I tried to remain true to their intent of preserving Chatham's history while allowing for progress, but I'm sure the processes—permits, applications, violations, Board of Appeals—would be unique to each case. Any and all blunders are mine.

Another thank-you to the team at Revell, who work so diligently to help a book become the best it can be. Lindsey Ross, who attended the Penn State Ice Cream School and happens to be an outstanding maker of ice cream, read through the draftiest first draft to provide insights and suggestions. She's heaven-sent.

My heart is always full of gratitude to the Lord, for giving me the opportunity to write—something I love so dearly—and for providing the spark of imagination. And a thank-you to my wonderful, faithful readers, who make this author gig such a pleasure. Dear readers, if you haven't gone to Cape Cod, I hope you'll put it on your bucket list. Go to Chatham and stroll its iconic Main Street. Walk through the beautiful lobby and sitting room of the Chatham Bars Inn. Wander around the lighthouse, and head down to the beach. Before you leave town, be sure to make a stop at the Main Street Creamery, to try out whatever flavor of the day Dawn's come up with. And maybe add a scoop of vanilla too.

Suzanne Woods Fisher is an award-winning, bestselling author of more than thirty books, including *The Moonlight School* and the Three Sisters Island, Nantucket Legacy, Amish Beginnings, The Bishop's Family, The Deacon's Family, and The Inn at Eagle Hill series. She is also the author of several nonfiction books about the Amish, including *Amish Peace* and *Amish Proverbs*. She lives in California. Learn more at www .suzannewoodsfisher.com and follow Suzanne on Facebook @SuzanneWoodsFisherAuthor and Twitter @suzannewfisher.

"Memorable characters, gorgeous Maine scenery, and plenty of family drama. I can't wait to visit Three Sisters Island again!"

—IRENE HANNON,
bestselling author of the beloved Hope Harbor series

Following the lives of three sisters, this contemporary romance series from Suzanne Woods Fisher is sure to delight her fans and draw new ones.

"An unforgettable story about love and the transforming power of words and community. Deeply moving and uplifting!"

—LAURA FRANTZ,
Christy Award–winning author of *Tidewater Bride*

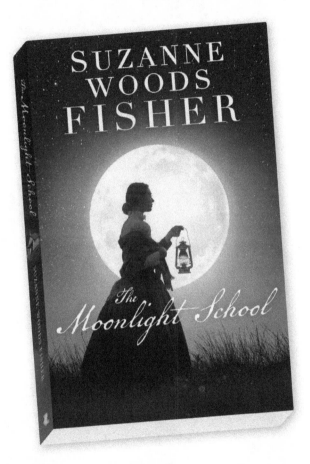

Based on true events, a young woman used to the finer things in life arrives in a small Appalachian town in 1911 to help her formidable cousin combat adult illiteracy by opening moonlight schools.

ℛ Revell
a division of Baker Publishing Group
www.RevellBooks.com

Available wherever books and ebooks are sold.

"There's just something unique and fresh about every Suzanne Woods Fisher book. Whatever the reason, I'm a fan."

—SHELLEY SHEPHARD GRAY,
New York Times and *USA Today* bestselling author

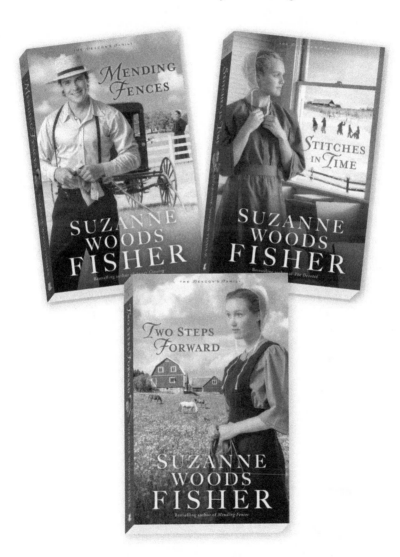

Don't Miss Any of
The Bishop's Family

"Suzanne is an authority on the Plain folks. . . .
She always delivers a fantastic story with
interesting characters, all in a tightly woven plot."

—**Beth Wiseman,** bestselling author
of the Daughters of the Promise and the Land of Canaan series

Connect with SUZANNE

www.SuzanneWoodsFisher.com

Printed in the USA
CPSIA information can be obtained
at www.ICGtesting.com
LVHW101753060823
754480LV00004B/101